TELL ME EVERYTHING

Tell Me Everything

...

A NOVEL

ELIZABETH STROUT

RANDOM HOUSE

NEW YORK

Published in the United States by Random House, an imprint and division of Penguin Random House LLC, New York.

RANDOM HOUSE and the HOUSE colophon are registered trademarks of Penguin Random House LLC.

LIBRARY OF CONGRESS CATALOGING-IN-PUBLICATION DATA
NAMES: Strout, Elizabeth, author.
TITLE: Tell me everything: a novel / Elizabeth Strout.
DESCRIPTION: First edition. | New York: Random House, 2024.
IDENTIFIERS: LCCN 2023058179 (print) | LCCN 2023058180 (ebook) |
ISBN 9780593446096 (Hardback) | ISBN 9780593446102 (Ebook)
SUBJECTS: LCGFT: Novels.
CLASSIFICATION: LCC PS3569.T736 T45 2024 (print) |
LCC PS3569.T736 (ebook) | DDC 813/.54—dc23/eng/20240116
LC record available at https://lccn.loc.gov/2023058179
LC ebook record available at https://lccn.loc.gov/2023058180

Canada trade paper ISBN 978-0-593-97746-0

Printed in the United States of America on acid-free paper

randomhousebooks.com

1st Printing

FIRST EDITION

Book design by Barbara M. Bachman

To my dearest friend and first reader of forty years, Kathy Chamberlain, whose sensibilities have enabled me to be the writer I am—and whose advice was responsible for the very voice of this book—

And to my husband, Jim Tierney, who allows me the freedom to write—

And also to Jim Howaneic, premier defense attorney of Maine and a generous source of information—

Book One

...

I

THIS IS THE story of Bob Burgess, a tall, heavyset man who lives in the town of Crosby, Maine, and he is sixty-five years old at the time that we are speaking of him. Bob has a big heart, but he does not know that about himself; like many of us, he does not know himself as well as he assumes to, and he would never believe he had anything worthy in his life to document. But he does; we all do.

*

AUTUMN COMES EARLY to Maine.

By the second or third week in August a person driving in a car might glance up and see in the distance the top of a tree that has become red. In Crosby, Maine, this year it happened first with the large maple tree by the church, and yet it was not even midway through the month of August. But the tree began to change color on its side facing east. This was curious to those who had lived there for years, they could not remember that being the first tree to change color. By the end of August, the entire tree was not red but a slightly orange yellowy thing, to be seen as you turned the corner onto Main Street. And then September followed, the summer people went back to where they had come from, and the streets of Crosby often had only a few people walking down them. The leaves did not seem vibrant, overall, and people speculated that this was because of the lack of rainfall that August—and September—had endured.

A FEW YEARS EARLIER, people entering the town of Crosby from the turnpike's exit would drive past a car dealership and a donut shop and a diner, and also by large run-down wooden houses whose porches held things like bicycle tires and plastic toys and coat hangers and air conditioning units that had not been used in years, and in one of these houses a middle-aged man named Ricky Davis lived. He was a large man and frequently drunk and could often be seen leaning over the rail of his side porch with his pants halfway down showing his huge bottom, crack and all, to the folks driving by, and those who had not seen this before would turn their heads to watch with a sense of wonderment. But then the town council had voted to put in the new police station at that spot, and so Ricky Davis and the house he had lived in were now gone; it was rumored that he was living out near the old fairgrounds in a Hatfield Housing unit.

WHEN YOU GOT into the middle of the town you could see a large brick house that stood a little off Main Street. After the clocks were set back in November, making it dark earlier, the few folks driving by, and those who might be strolling on the sidewalk across the street, could see into the windows of this house, yellow from the lamps turned on inside, and Bob Burgess and his wife, Margaret Estaver, might be observed cooking together in their kitchen until they tugged their curtains closed. People knew who they were, and in a way not fully conscious there was a sense of safety that came from this couple living right here in the middle of town: Margaret was the Unitarian minister, and she had her following. Bob had been a lawyer in New York City for many years in his younger days, but nobody held this against him, probably because he had grown up in Shirley Falls, forty-five minutes away; he had returned to Maine almost fifteen years ago when he married Margaret. He still took occasional criminal cases in Shirley Falls and was known to keep an office there, though he had mostly retired by now. And also—people spoke of this quietly—Bob had suffered a tragedy in childhood: He had been playing with the gearshift of the family car and it had rolled down the hill of the Burgesses' driveway; people in town understood that the car—and therefore Bob—had killed Bob's father, who was checking on their mailbox there.

OLIVE KITTERIDGE, who was ninety years old and living in the retirement community called the Maple Tree Apartments, knew this about Bob Burgess and she had always liked him, she thought he had a quiet sadness to him, most likely from this early misfortune. Olive did not particularly care for Bob's wife, Margaret. This was because Margaret was a minister and Olive did not like ministers—except for Cookie, who had married her to her first husband, Henry. Wonderful man, Reverend Daniel Cooke. And wonderful man, Henry Kitteridge.

The pandemic had been hard for Olive Kitteridge—hard for everyone, really—but Olive had endured it, day after day in her little apartment in this retirement community, yet when they stopped allowing people to eat in the dining room and started bringing their food to them instead, she thought she would go absolutely batty. By the end of that first year, though, with her vaccinations and then later a booster, she was able to get out a bit more, someone might drive her into town or take her down by the water. But the real problem was that during the pandemic, Olive's best friend, Isabelle Goodrow, who lived two doors down from her, had taken a bad fall and—of all the awful things that could have happened—had been moved "over the bridge" to the nursing home part of the place. Now Olive went to visit Isabelle every day, reading her the newspaper from front to back. But it had been hard, and it still was.

OUT ON THE end of the point of Crosby, high up on a cliff that looked over the (mostly) roiling waters of the Atlantic Ocean, lived a woman named Lucy Barton, who had arrived with her ex-husband, William, two years before, escaping New York City during the pandemic, and they had ended up staying in town. There were mixed feelings about this: The natural reticence toward New Yorkers was part of it, but also housing prices in Crosby had gone through the roof exactly because of folks like this Lucy Barton, who had decided to stay in town, and anyone from Maine who had been hoping to move into a nicer house now found that they could not afford one. Lucy Barton had grown up in a small town in Illinois and had lived in New York City her whole adult life; she had never even been a summer person in Maine before arriving here with her ex-husband. Also, Lucy Barton was a fiction writer, and that made people have different feelings; mostly they would have preferred her to go back to New York, but nobody seemed to have anything bad to say about her; and except for her walks along the river with her friend Bob Burgess she was rarely seen. Although she was sometimes observed going through the back door that led up to the little office space she rented above the bookstore.

ON MAIN STREET THERE were HELP WANTED signs or HIRING NOW signs in most of the store windows, and along the coastline a few restaurants had to close because there were not enough people to work in them. What had gone wrong? There were different theories, but it would be fair to say that most inhabitants of Crosby did not know. They only knew that the world was not what it had once been. And most of these people in the town of Crosby were old, or almost old, because this is the way the population of Maine had been for years. Some said that this was the problem, that there were no young folks to take these jobs. Others argued that the unemployment situation was happening not just in Maine but all across the country; some speculated that it was the opioid crisis, that people weren't able to pass their drug test in order to work. And then others claimed that the younger generation was at fault; Malcolm Moody's sixteen-year-old grandson, for example, had come to visit for three days and was playing videogames on his iPhone constantly. What could you do?

Nothing.

AND THEN IN October the foliage exploded, shattering the world with a goldenness. The sun shone down, and yellow leaves fluttered everywhere; it was a thing of beauty. The days were cold and at night it rained, but in the morning there was the sun again, and all the glory of the natural world twinkled and nestled itself around the town of Crosby. The clouds that were low in the sky would suddenly block out the sun, and then just as quickly the clouds would part and it was as though a bright light had been turned on and the sky was blue and bright again with the yellow and orange leaves floating quietly to the ground.

*

A THOUGHT HAD taken hold of Olive Kitteridge on one of these days in October, and she pondered it for almost a week before she called Bob Burgess. "I have a story to tell that writer Lucy Barton. I wish you would have her come visit me."

The story was one that Olive had been reflecting on with more and more frequency, and she thought—as people often do—that if her story could be told to a writer, maybe it could be used in a book one day. Olive did not know if Lucy was a famous writer or not quite a famous writer, but she decided it did not matter. The library always had a long wait list for Lucy's books, so Olive had ordered them from the bookstore instead, and she read through them, and something made her think that this Lucy might like—or could possibly use—the story Olive had to tell.

SO ON THIS particular autumn day, the yellow leaves of the tree seen through Olive's large windowed back doorway were quivering to the ground as she waited for Lucy Barton to show up. Olive, sitting in her wingback chair, saw two chickadees and a titmouse at her feeder. She leaned forward and spotted a squirrel. Olive rapped her knuckles against the window, hard, and the squirrel scurried away. "Hah," said Olive, sitting back. She hated squirrels. They ate her flowers, and they were always bothering her birds.

Olive found her glasses on the small table next to her and picked up her big cordless phone, which was also on the table, and pressed some numbers on it.

"Isabelle," said Olive. "I can't come visit you this morning, I'm having a visitor. I'll tell you about it when I come see you this afternoon. Bye now." Olive clicked the phone off and looked around her small apartment.

She tried to imagine the place through the writer's eyes, and Olive decided it was all right. It was neat, and not cluttered with hideous knickknacks the way so many old people had in their homes, tabletops crowded with photographs of their grandchildren, such foolishness. Olive had four grandchildren, but she only had a photograph of one of them in her bedroom, a small photo of Little Henry, who was not so little anymore. And in the living room on her hutch she kept a large photograph of her first husband, Henry, and that was enough. She looked at it now and said, "Well, Henry, we'll see if she's responsive."

AT FIVE MINUTES before ten there was a light knock on her door that faced the hallway, and Olive yelled out, "Come in!"

In stepped a small woman who looked meek and mousy. Olive could not stand meek-and-mousy-looking people. The woman said, "I'm sorry I'm early. I'm always early, I can't seem to help it."

"That's fine. I hate people who are late. Sit down," Olive

said, and she nodded toward the small couch against the wall across from her. Lucy Barton came in and sat down. She was wearing a blue and black plaid coat that went to her knees and jeans that Olive thought were too tight for a woman her age; Lucy was sixty-six, Olive had looked it up.

The sofa was a stiff one, Olive knew this, but the woman somehow—the way she sat on it—made it appear even stiffer. And she had the strangest things on her feet, boots with long big silver zippers right up the front of them. Olive could see the small ankles and the tight pants that were tucked into them.

"Take your coat off," Olive said.

"No thank you. I get cold easily."

Olive rolled her eyes. "I would hardly say it's cold in here."

Olive was disappointed in this creature. A silence fell into the room and Olive let it sit there. Finally, Lucy Barton said, "Well, it's nice to meet you."

"Ay-yuh" was all Olive said, swinging one foot back and forth. There was something odd about this woman: She wore no glasses, and her eyes were not small, but she had a slightly stunned look on her face. "What are those things you've got on your feet?" Olive asked.

The woman looked down at them, sticking her toes straight up. "Oh, they're boots. We went to Rockland last summer and I found these in a store."

Rockland. Money. Of course, Olive thought. She said, "There's no snow on the ground, don't know why you need boots."

The woman closed her eyes for a long moment, and when she opened them she did not look at Olive.

"So, I hear you're with us in town to stay," Olive said.

"Who told you that?" The woman asked this as though

really curious to know the answer, and she continued to look slightly bewildered.

"Bob Burgess."

And then the woman's face changed; it became gentle, relaxed, for a moment. "Right," she said.

OLIVE TOOK A breath and said, "Well, Lucy. How are you liking our little town of Crosby?"

"It's quite a change," Lucy Barton said.

"Well, it's not New York, if that's what you mean."

Lucy looked around the room and then said, "I guess that is what I mean."

Olive continued to watch her. For a few moments there was only the ticking of the grandfather clock and the slight whirring sound of the refrigerator in the alcove kitchen. "You told Bob that you had a story to tell me?" Lucy asked. She slipped off her coat then, letting it stay on her back, and Olive saw a black turtleneck. Skinny. The creature was skinny. But her eyes were watching Olive now with a keenness.

Olive swung an arm lightly toward the stack of books on the bottom shelf of the small table beside her. "I've read all your books."

Lucy Barton did not seem to have any response to this, though her eyes briefly dropped down to the books on the shelf.

Olive said, "I thought your memoirs were a little self-pitying, myself. You're not the only person to come from poverty."

Lucy Barton again seemed to have no response to this.

Olive said, "And how does your ex-husband William feel, being written about? I'm curious to know."

Lucy gave a small shrug. "He's okay with it. He knows I'm a writer."

"I see. Ay-yuh." Olive added, "And now you're back with him. Together again. But not married."

"That's right."

"In Crosby, Maine."

"That's right."

AGAIN, THERE WAS a silence. Then Olive said, "You don't look a bit like your photograph on your books."

"I know." Lucy said it simply and gave a shrug.

"Why is that?" Olive said.

"Because some professional photographer took it. And also my hair isn't really blond anymore. That photo was taken years ago." Lucy put her hand through her hair, which was chin-length and pale brown.

"Well, it was too blond in the photo," Olive said.

A sudden slant of sunlight came through the window and fell across the wooden floor. The grandfather clock in the corner kept on with its ticking. Lucy reached behind her and took her coat and placed it on the couch next to her. "That's my husband," said Olive, pointing to the large photograph on the hutch. "My first husband, Henry. Wonderful man."

"He looks nice," Lucy said. "Tell me the story. Bob said you had a story you wanted me to hear." She said this kindly. "I'd like to hear it, I really would."

"Bob Burgess is a good fellow. I've always liked him," Olive said.

Lucy's face got pink—this is what Olive thought she saw. "Bob is the best friend I have in this town. He's maybe the best friend I've had ever." Her eyes dropped to the floor as she said this. But then she looked up at Olive and said, "Please—tell me the story."

Something in Olive relaxed. She said, "Okay, but now I don't know if it's worth telling."

"Well, tell me anyway," Lucy said.

*

THE STORY WAS THIS: Olive's mother had been the daughter of a farmer in a little town in Maine called West Annett, about an hour away from Crosby. And oh, by the way, Olive did not like her mother. But that was probably irrelevant.

"Why didn't you like her?" Lucy asked, and Olive thought about it and said, "I suppose because she didn't like me." Lucy nodded. "I was five years old by the time my little sister was born, and I have a memory—who knows if it's true—of having asked my mother why I didn't have any brothers or sisters, and she had looked at me and said, 'After you? We wouldn't dare have another child after you.' But then they did."

"Why would she say that? What was so wrong with you as a little kid?" Lucy asked.

"Well. For one thing, I didn't like to cuddle and, oh, Mother just *loved* Isa, who would cuddle with her. Mother loved to cuddle, and apparently I did not."

"Isa? Your sister. Great name, okay, go on." Lucy picked something off her jeans.

So, Olive's mother—"What was her name?" Lucy interrupted, looking over at Olive—and Olive said that her mother's name was Sara. "With an 'h'?" Lucy asked, and Olive shook her head. No "h." Sara had one brother, Sara remained

devoted to him throughout her life, even though he was completely nutty. "I think his testicles never dropped," Olive said.
"He never had a beard, and he had a high voice, and he was a
very peculiar person, oh, he got married to a woman named
Ardele, she was a nut too, and they never had kids, but anyway,
Mother remained devoted to her brother, she even died at Ardele's house."

So, Sara was raised on this small farm in the town of West
Annett. She was very short, and a cheerful person—and pretty.
"I have never been pretty," Olive added. Lucy just sat watching
her, and Olive had to look out the window. "Go on," Lucy said
quietly.

Olive glanced down at her belly, which stuck out like a basketball, she tugged the side of her jacket over it and continued.
"Mother wanted to become a schoolteacher, so she went to
Gorham Normal School. Normal school was what it was called
to train teachers back then." Olive added, "This would have
been around the second half of the 1920s."

At the end of the first year Olive's mother had taken a job
waitressing at a resort farther down the coast; she had lived at
the resort while working there. And she had fallen in love with
the son of the woman who owned the resort.

"Are you listening?" Olive asked.

Lucy said that she was.

"Money. His mother had money, came from money. Don't
know what had happened to the father—dead, I think." But the
point was that Olive's mother, Sara, had really fallen in love
with this fellow, his name was Stephen Turner. And as far as
Olive knew, this fellow loved her back.

Stephen's mother also owned a resort in Florida, so although
Olive's mother went back to Gorham Normal School, she sud-

denly quit at the end of that first semester and went down to
Florida to work in this woman's—this Mrs. Turner's—resort.

"Your mother told you this?" Lucy asked.

"She did."

"Go on."

"And by the time she came back to Maine—"

"Was the fellow there in Florida?" Lucy asked, and Olive
said, Oh yes, Stephen was there. But by the time Sara came
back, she and Stephen were no longer a couple. Mrs. Turner
had decided that Sara was not sophisticated enough for her son,
so she had broken them up in Florida. Stephen was going to be
a doctor, which meant that Sara was simply not good enough
for him, having come from just a poor, small farm.

"Wait. You heard all this from your mother?" Lucy asked;
she was leaning slightly forward.

"Well, yes. Mother told me all this when I was a young girl,
twelve or so, I don't know, but Mother told me. Only one time,
though. I don't remember her ever mentioning it again."

"Go on," Lucy said.

Sara went back to normal school in Maine, and three months
later she met Olive's father at a barn dance.

"He was sitting on the end of a bench because he couldn't
socialize, so he stuck himself on the end of the bench and
Mother started talking to him, and two months after that they
got married." Olive's mother became a teacher—her first job
was in a one-room schoolhouse—and Olive's father, who had
never finished high school, went to work in a canning factory.
He lost his job during the Depression, and he could not pay for
groceries.

Olive remembered going with her father to the little grocery store, and the grocer refused to give them food on credit.

She remembered that her father had tears in his eyes as he walked out of the store.

Olive paused and looked out the window again. Finally she turned back and said, "Now this part is not so much the story I wanted to tell, but I do want to tell you: My father was an exceptional man."

"In what way?" Lucy asked.

"In every way," Olive said.

"All right," said Lucy.

Olive turned back to the window. "He was a man of very few words. He came from a dreadful background. His father beat him, and his father would try and beat the smaller children, but Father always intervened and took the beatings for those younger kids."

Lucy said nothing. She was just sitting and watching Olive, her coat still next to her on the couch, her hands in her lap.

"When my father was fifty-seven, he took a rifle and shot himself." Olive said this glancing at Lucy.

"Where?" Lucy asked quietly. "Where did he do this?"

"In the kitchen. He was in the kitchen when Mother got home from teaching. Brain stuff splattered all over the ceiling."

"Whoa," Lucy said, very quietly.

"But that's not part of the story."

"Go on with the story," Lucy said. "We don't know if that's part of the story or not."

Olive felt surprised by that, but she continued. "So, when my mother died, three years after my father did—"

"What did she die of?" Lucy asked.

"Brain tumor." Olive squinted across the room and said musingly, "It's interesting, sort of, I think, because her doctor told me that she may have had that brain tumor for years but the distress of my father's death—the suicide—may have set it off, growing. I always thought that was interesting."

"It is interesting," Lucy said. She settled herself against the back of the couch. "You know, I knew a woman who had two of the most adorable kids you ever saw, they were small, and she had a husband who became a famous writer, and he went to some university for a semester and ran off rather quickly with a different woman, and his wife got a brain tumor and within a year she had died. I always wondered if it was related."

Olive said, "Godfrey. What happened to the husband?"

"He ended up alone and not famous at all after a while."

"Well, *good*," Olive said, and Lucy shook her head slowly and said, "No, it was really sad."

Olive rolled her eyes.

Lucy said, "Go back to your story. So your mother died. At Ardele's house," she added, and that pleased Olive, that Lucy Barton had remembered that detail.

"Yes, she died at Ardele's house, and in her handbag—" Olive shifted slightly in her chair and leaned forward. "In her handbag, when I went through it, I found a tattered old clipping. It was not in her wallet but slipped into a little pocket on the inside of her handbag that zipped shut. A newspaper clipping. Now, back then, at that time, when someone of so-called importance came to town there would be a silly little newspaper article about it. And this clipping was dated from back when Mother would have been married about seven years and already had her two daughters. And the clipping was this."

A small newspaper article in the *Shirley Falls Journal*—with a photograph—saying that Dr. Stephen Turner—son of Blah-blah and the late Blah-blah Mr. Turner—and his wife, Ruth, had come to town with their daughters. Stephen Turner was a doctor in Boston, his wife, Ruth, was the daughter of some hoity-toity in the Boston area, and they also had two very small girls who were also in the photograph.

THE GIRLS' NAMES were Olive and Isa.

OLIVE WAITED.

Then Lucy said, "Oh my God." And Olive nodded her head. Lucy began tapping her knees together, and she looked around the room, her hands on the sofa. "Oh my God," she repeated, looking at Olive now, and again Olive gave a small nod.

"Ay-yuh," Olive said.

"So your mother kept that clipping her whole life."

"She did."

"And his kids had the same names as you and your sister."

"That's right."

Lucy shook her head slowly. "So your mother and Stephen Turner must have spoken of the names they wanted to call their kids."

"Well, I did wonder about that," Olive said.

"You *should* wonder about that." Lucy sat forward. "It couldn't possibly be a coincidence, the names are too unique." One of Lucy's hands moved as she said slowly, with a sense of wonder, "They talked with each other about what to name their kids. And of course Ruth, the man's wife, never knew that. No woman would name her kids the same names that her husband had planned to name his children with a previous girlfriend."

"Well, this is what I thought—"

But Lucy continued. "So for the rest of their married lives they were never in touch, your mother and Dr. Stephen Turner?"

"Oh no, I don't think so. No, no, I don't think that was ever part of the story."

Lucy nodded. "Probably not."

Lucy sat back and looked straight in front of her, and then she looked down at her hands, and finally when she looked back at Olive her eyes were very red. And then tears came out of her eyes. Tears!

"I thought you never cried. Isn't that what you wrote in your memoir?" Olive said.

"I think I wrote that it was hard for me to cry." Lucy was looking through her coat pocket. "Right there," Olive said, pointing to the table at the other end of the couch, and Lucy got up and took a tissue and sat back down.

"Now, why is this making you cry?" Olive really wanted to know.

"Because it's such a sad story!"

"Well, it's an interesting story. At least to me."

"Mrs. Kitteridge, this is a *sad* story."

Olive looked out the window again. "Yes, I guess it is."

"It's sad because your mother and this Stephen fellow—they were really in love. They were young and deeply in love—talking about what to name their kids—and his mother breaks them up and they never forget each other. So the whole time your mother is married to your father, every time he does something she doesn't like, she thinks of Stephen and how wonderful he would have been in that situation. And Stephen's wife, this Ruth woman—the same thing, probably. Every time she disappointed him, he would think of his pretty, cheerful

Sara and what a life together they might have had. So both these couples lived their entire lives with these ghosts in the room. And *that* is sad. Sad for everybody, but especially for your father and Ruth, who didn't even *know* they were living with these ghosts."

Lucy was no longer crying. But she wiped her nose with the tissue.

Olive said, "My parents did not have a happy marriage. Father would try and please her, but she was not to be pleased. He would go and get her every week during the Depression, she taught three towns away, and he was the one to take care of us when we were little, and he would go and get Mother in his old beat-up truck that was always breaking down, every Friday afternoon, and one time he stopped and picked her a bouquet of mayflowers. And I don't think she even cared."

Lucy was sitting far back on the uncomfortable couch, her skinny legs stretched out in front of her. And then she sat back up.

"What are mayflowers?" she asked.

"Oh—" Olive looked around the room and then she said, "They're a wildflower that you find in the darker parts of the pine forests, and Father had stopped by the side of the road and gone into the woods and picked her a little bouquet of them."

"How do you know your mother didn't care? Did your father tell you that?"

Olive considered this. "In my memory Mother told me, and she said it—oh, not exactly disrespectfully—but as though she didn't care. As though he would think it might help them, but what were mayflowers going to do? That's how I always understood it."

Lucy tapped her hand against her mouth. Finally she said, "So do you blame your father's suicide on your mother?"

Olive felt a small stinging in her chest. She looked straight ahead and said nothing for a long time, and then she said, "Yes, privately I have."

When she finally looked over at Lucy, Lucy was watching her. Olive said, "What? What is it you're thinking?"

"I'm thinking his father was probably more responsible for it than your mother."

Olive thought about this, and then she said, "Well, two of his brothers died the same way."

"They *did*? Then your mother couldn't have been responsible." Lucy let out a huge sigh and said, "But it's a sad story. Carrying that clipping with her all her life." She shook her head and said, "Jesus Christ. All these unrecorded lives, and people just *live* them." Then she looked at Olive and said, "Sorry for swearing."

"Phooey, swear all you want." Olive added, "Well, that's the story. I always wanted to tell someone. But for whatever reasons I never did."

Lucy said, contemplatively, "I wonder how many people in long marriages live with ghosts beside them."

"Henry and I never did." Though as Olive said that she had a quick memory of Henry liking that foolish girl who worked with him for a while in the pharmacy, and she herself had been attracted to a man she taught with. But weren't those tiny drops of oil in a fry pan? Not like the story she had just told.

So she looked at Lucy and told her about the nitwit girl that Henry had liked briefly, and the man she had been drawn to briefly.

And Lucy listened and said, "Yeah, that's not the same thing. I mean, how long did those last?"

"Oh, not even a full year," Olive said.

Lucy waved her hand. "Little infatuations, unacted-on crushes, they're not like living with a ghost." Then Lucy's phone pinged, and she took it out of the pocket of her coat. She had to really squint at it, and she held it close to her eyes. "'Scuse me for just one minute. It's Bob. He wants to know if we're through. He picked me up at my studio to bring me here, and he's going to pick me up now."

"Well, I guess we're through," Olive said, though she was disappointed. She would have liked to talk to this Lucy Barton longer.

"Hold on, let me tell him." Lucy squinted hard and punched her phone with her fingers and then slipped it back into the pocket of her coat, looking over at Olive then.

"Awful glad to talk with you," Olive said, and Lucy said, "Yeah, it was great." She smiled, and what a difference that made to her face! Why, she was almost a pretty little thing! "Really great," Lucy repeated.

Olive said, "Glad you have Bob as a friend. A good friend makes all the difference. I have a friend, Isabelle Goodrow—"

But Lucy's face had grown pink again. She said, "His wife, Margaret, she's a good person too."

"Never took to her myself. There's nothing wrong with her. Except that she's a minister."

Lucy said, "No, she's a really good person." Then she said, "You know, Bob is the main reason I—" She stopped herself. "The reason I got to meet you."

But when the knock came on the door and Bob Burgess walked in, Olive saw something. She saw Bob's face, how he looked at Lucy. He was in love with her, and when Lucy looked up at him from the couch, her face changed so radically, it became so soft and happy-looking, and she said, "Hi, Bob."

"How'd it go?" Bob asked, looking at Olive, then back at Lucy.

"Success," Olive said.

2

BUT—OLIVE KITTERIDGE WAS wrong about Bob and Lucy. They were friends, and that was all. They were old enough to be grateful for this friendship that had arrived in their later years, and both Margaret and William were glad for the friendship of these two as well; it made their lives even more comfortable to have their partners have a friend to really talk with.

It felt to both Bob and Lucy that they had known each other far longer than they actually had.

Here is an example of their friendship: Bob had become a (secret) smoker again. After having smoked for much of his life, he had quit when he met Margaret, now almost fifteen years ago, but during the pandemic he started to smoke (secretly) one cigarette a day, and then it went to two. Lucy knew this about him, Margaret did not. That's all. It was innocent, because both Bob and Lucy were—in a strange, indefinable way—innocent people.

IT MAY BE helpful at this point to speak briefly of Bob's background, and of Lucy's. Bob had grown up a Congregationalist; he was the product of a long line of Mainers, going back on his father's side to the Puritans who had left England for Massachusetts because their religious practices were so extreme. These original Puritans were against almost everything—it seemed to Bob—except hard work. They were against music and theater because those excited the senses; even a celebration of Christmas was frowned upon. Bob had had an ancestor who was hanged as a witch, and he recoiled at most of these circumstances from which he had come. Also—and this is important to understand about Bob—the Puritans were *very* much against calling attention to oneself in any way. Generations of genes had not made much progress in taking away this particular aspect of Bob. His ancestry had shaped Bob, as these things do.

Lucy came from a similar cultural background; she had gone to the Congregational church in her Midwestern town for Thanksgivings. Her childhood had been especially difficult: She had come from such extreme poverty—and strangeness— that her family had been completely ostracized by their town. Her mother never touched her children except in violence, and her father had an anxiety left from World War II that manifested itself in frequent sexual urges, although he never approached his children in this manner. And yet Lucy had loved both her parents in an achingly poignant way. But her childhood had been challenging.

The real point here is—if we consider these things, and we should—that Lucy's ancestors had been similar to Bob's. They had come ashore in Provincetown, Massachusetts, and then traveled to the Midwest, as—as her mother once told her— "the brave ones did."

Margaret Estaver had been raised a Catholic before becoming the Unitarian minister that she now was, and William had been raised a Lutheran, as his father had come over from Germany after the war. We like to think that our lives are within our control, but they may not be completely so. We are necessarily influenced by those who have come before us.

*

LUCY, WITH HER hands in the pockets of her blue and black plaid coat, went with Bob to his car after her visit to Olive, and she said, "Oh, let's take a walk!" So she and Bob drove down to the river, which was beautiful because of all the yellow leaves and blasting sunshine. When they got out of the car and started to walk, Bob asked if Olive had been unpleasant to Lucy, and Lucy said, "Yeah, at first. But I understood she was just frightened, and then she got over it."

"Olive frightened?" Bob asked, and Lucy looked at him and said, "Yes, frightened, Bob. She's a bully, and bullies are always frightened. I liked her, though, and she ended up liking me." Lucy told Bob the story that Olive had told her. "Heartbreaking, right?" Lucy asked, looking over at Bob, and Bob said, Yeah, it really was.

"It made me cry," Lucy said.

"It *did*?" Bob turned to look at her.

"Yeah, it did. These four people, whose lives have never been recorded, living through such a—oh, I don't know—such a true situation. Both couples living with a ghost in their marriage. That's *sad*, Bob."

Bob nodded, and then after a moment he asked, "How is Chrissy doing? And little Aiden?" Lucy's daughter Chrissy had recently given birth to a baby boy, but Chrissy had been suffering from postpartum depression and Lucy had been worried about her.

"Much better, I think. And Aiden's fine."

Then Lucy said how her other daughter, Becka, who had recently finalized her divorce from her poet husband, Trey—Bob knew that part already—had decided that Trey was a narcissist. Becka had been talking a lot about this to Lucy: the traits of a narcissist. "So I've read the stuff she sent me, and I have to agree with her. I think she's trying, as they say, to process the whole thing." Lucy shrugged and said with a sigh, "Oh, who knows."

But here was something funny: Bob felt an uneasiness, and he remembered then how when he had first met Margaret, a disturbed parishioner of hers, a man, had said to Bob, "She's such a narcissist." It was a terrible thing for this person to say to Bob, and he thought he had forgotten about it, but it came back to him now as Lucy listed some of the characteristics of a narcissist.

> They could be charming.
> They cared only about themselves.
> They only helped other people to make
>   themselves look good.
> If you criticize them, they will gaslight you.
> And so forth . . .

So Bob told Lucy about the parishioner who had said that years ago about Margaret. And Lucy stopped walking and said, "He *said* that to you?"

"Yeah," Bob said.

"Jesus." They kept walking then, and after a moment Lucy said, "Well, anyway. I hope it helps Becka figure Trey out."

"Don't think about it," Bob said to Lucy, and she nodded. It was a small joke, the don't-think-about-it line between them, because they both felt like they thought about things too much. "Okay," Lucy said.

And then, as they walked the pathway, strewn with yellow leaves and sunshine, Lucy took a quick step and turned to Bob and said, "Bob, I wish I could still do cartwheels!"

"You did *cartwheels?*" Bob thought of Lucy's childhood as being so dismal that she never would have done a cartwheel. But then he remembered in a memoir Lucy had written about William, that William had told her he married her because she was filled with joy, and how could she have been filled with joy coming from the wretched background she had come from?

"Yes! My brother and sister never did, but I did, I just loved it. The body. Oh, the body weighs us down."

"I've never done a cartwheel in my life," Bob said.

They reached the granite bench where Bob smoked his cigarettes and they sat down, and he said, "Thanks, Lucy," he meant for her not caring about his cigarette, and she said, "Of course, Bob." They said this each time. Because of the way the wind was today, Bob could sit while he smoked, the smoke blew away from them. If the wind was different, or if there was no wind, Bob would get up and move around while he smoked, because, as he had told Lucy, he had learned this about surreptitious cigarette smoking: Keep moving, and the smell won't get on your clothes so much.

"Oh Bob! I meant to tell you this." Lucy turned to him. "Little Annie has been dropping her leaves—and I finally realized she needs to be transplanted."

Bob said, "Is that so hard to do?" He knew that she was speaking of her plant. Lucy had two plants: One had come from

New York and reached almost to the ceiling of her house—Bob had seen this when he and Margaret had gone to Lucy and William's home for dinner a few times—and the other plant, the same kind of plant, Lucy had bought about a year ago. She had bought it at the local pharmacy, and she loved it; Bob was surprised by Lucy's ability to love certain things, and he had looked at the two plants in their living room one night and said, "Hey, your plant has a little sister."

"Exactly! Her name is Little Annie." And Lucy had touched the leaves of it lightly.

"What's the big one named?" Bob asked, and Lucy just shook her head and said, "Doesn't have a name."

William had said, from the couch, running a hand through his white hair, which made it stand up, "She talks to her plants, you know. And I have to say, she's convinced me. I mean, I don't think it's crazy." He added, "You guys know I think Lucy is a spirit. She's different from the rest of us." He had tugged on his full white mustache after he spoke.

Now Lucy said with a sigh, "It seems too hard for me to do, transplanting her." She added, "So many things these days seem hard for me to do. I don't know why, I just feel a little scrambled in my head or something. Something about Chrissy finally having her baby and then getting postpartum, and . . . I don't know, Bob. The girls don't *need* me like they used to."

"I hear you," Bob said. She had told him this before.

They sat in silence for a while longer. When Bob had first started to take walks with Lucy during the pandemic, she had spoken frequently of her second husband, David. He had been a cellist with the Philharmonic, and he had died two years before the pandemic. She had clearly cherished David and had been cherished by him. But she hadn't spoken of him for a while now; Bob had noticed this and did not feel comfortable bringing him up.

Bob said, squinting at Lucy, "You know what I figured out recently? The reason I used to drink too much is because I'm terrified. I'm always terrified. But now I only have my one glass every night. But that's why I have my glass of wine. Terror." He inhaled and said, "That's why I smoke these too. Terror."

He watched her while he exhaled. Lucy looked straight at him, he felt he saw her receive this. "Oh, I get it," she said.

"I know you do," Bob said.

3

THERE ARE MANY back roads in Maine. Meaning narrow tarred roads with trees reaching overhead from both sides, and the roads themselves are often filled with bumps from the long winters of freezing and then thawing. These roads wind around from one small town to another, and if you are not familiar with them it is easy enough to get lost. But most of the people who are on these curving back roads know exactly where they are going, and in November there can be a stark beauty as you drive along these places because the trees are bare and the trunks and the branches of these trees stand out against the sky, and if the sun is out it can sink with a sharp display of yellow on the deep blue horizon. It might be fair to say that people who have lived there for years take this beauty internally; it enters them without their fully knowing it. But it is there; it is part of the landscape of their lives.

*

TWO WEEKS AFTER Lucy visited with Olive Kitteridge, this happened:

ON ONE OF these back roads a man named Matthew Beach lived with his mother; this was in the town of Shirley Falls.

Matthew Beach's mother, Gloria Beach, was eighty-six years old and she had been living with her son for ten years; they lived far down a narrow road with no other houses in sight; this was the house that Matthew had grown up in and had lived in his whole life.

One Friday evening Matthew drove to the grocery store, and when he got back, Gloria Beach had disappeared from their home. This was toward the beginning of November and a small bit of the foliage was still clinging to the trees, but mostly that golden shattering of color was gone.

MATT HAD CALLED the police right away, and there had been a search with the state troopers and their very bright flashlights. The woods of mostly pine trees and cedars around the house had been examined in a five-mile radius, and there was no sight or sign of her. Naturally, this was in the newspapers. Bob Burgess and his twin sister, Susan Olson, who still lived in the town of Shirley Falls, had spoken to each other about it on the telephone. "Bitch Ball disappearing!" Susan said. "I didn't even know she was still alive!"

Gloria Beach and her family had lived in Shirley Falls for years, and the middle child, a girl named Diana, had been in Bob and Susan's class at school.

The newspaper said that Walter Beach, Gloria's husband, had divorced her many years before—and he had been deceased for many years as well. Also, in the newspaper—for reasons no one quite understood—were three current photographs of the children, all grown up now: Thomas, Diana, and Matthew. Thomas was a psychiatrist in Oregon. His photograph showed a sturdy face and kind eyes (yet sort of cold, if you really looked). And Diana lived in Connecticut and had been a high school guidance counselor her whole adult life. In the—apparently current—photograph she looked beautiful. People did comment on that. She had been a pretty girl, but now that she was older, she still looked attractive! How had that happened? One woman in town suggested that she had had plastic surgery, and Susan Olson, peering at the photograph, realized that was probably it. The photograph of Matt, who had been living with his mother, was disturbing. He looked frightened and unkempt, and his hair was half over his eyes, which were covered by huge black-framed glasses.

"If he killed her, I don't *blame* him," Susan said to Bob. Bitch Ball had worked in the school cafeteria. Everyone had been terrified of her. Everyone.

Anyway, the case soon went cold.

BUT TWO HOURS SOUTH, in the town of Saco, around the same time Gloria Beach had gone missing, a car had been rented and not returned. The missing car had apparently been rented by one Ashley Munroe from Shirley Falls, but when she was investigated for auto theft after the car was not brought back, she said that she had never rented a car, that her driver's license and credit card had been stolen. In addition, Ashley Munroe had alibis all over the place. She had just given birth to a baby and was in Shirley Falls the entire time the car had been rented so far away and then gone missing. Ashley Munroe was not charged with theft, the car was not found, and nobody thought any more about it. Meaning, nobody put the two incidents together at that time.

———

BUT SUSAN OLSON remembered this:

As a third grader in Shirley Falls, Diana Beach was taller than her classmates, and she would often stand on the playground at recess time and tell stories to the other girls. The stories were always about horrific things that had happened to various women. Diana would have these small groups of girls—there would be three or four of them at a time, almost all a head shorter than she was—walk with her over by the basketball area, and in the springtime, bees would be flying around the garbage bins there. And then, looking around with her eyes almost closed, Diana spoke to the girls about men taking these women and doing certain things to them.

HERE IS AN EXAMPLE: A man would drive a woman to a spot in the woods and make her take off all her clothes. "Then she had to drink her pee-pee," Diana would say. She spoke with great authority and believability, and the girls watched her with terrified eyes. Very specific detail was given. A young woman's dress would be described, a striped dress that had a wraparound waistband—and the man got the young woman into his car by saying that her mother had been in an accident and he was going to take her to her mother. Diana told of the kinds of back roads these women were driven on until they were taken far into the woods and then forced to get out of the car.

"But what if she just said no?" a wary child asked, and Diana turned to her and said quietly, "Then he would kill her."

———

ANOTHER MAN TOOK OFF one of the spiky high heels that the woman had been wearing and stabbed her in her stomach with it, pushing it right down while the woman screamed and screamed.

Diana told of feces that were smeared on women, only she did not use that word, she did not know that word yet, so Diana said, "When she had a movement the man smeared it over her face."

The little girls she spoke to were terribly frightened, and then Diana would abruptly turn and walk away.

"STRANGE TO THINK of it now," Susan said. She was sitting on the large glassed-in front porch of the house of Gerry O'Hare, who years earlier had been the police chief in Shirley Falls. Gerry's bald head had red freckles sprinkled over it, and he frequently wore a blue cap, which he was wearing now. He had developed quite a paunch over the last few years—this aspect of himself he was not as aware of as he was his bald head. Gerry's wife had died a year ago, and he and Susan had fallen into the habit of having coffee on his porch two or three mornings a week. She had just told him her memories of Diana Beach. Gerry had gone to school with Susan and also Diana Beach, but he did not remember Diana very well. "Just a vague memory of her. Never especially knew her. But, yeah, what you just said— sounds really strange, telling those stories to kids on the playground." Gerry stretched out his legs; on his feet were white socks and moccasins with the backs folded down.

"There's the oldest kid," Susan continued. "He left town and lives in Oregon now, and he's a psychiatrist." Gerry nodded. "I don't really remember him, do you?" And Gerry said that he did not. Susan said, "But I remember Matt. You know, when he got cancer and his mother quit working and took care of him, remember that?" She shook her head and said, "Holy mackerel. And that's when she lost so much weight."

Gerry leaned forward slightly and said to her quietly, "Back when I was police chief . . ." He hesitated and sat back.

Susan said, "What? Come on, tell me."

He leaned forward again and said, "Back when I was police chief there was talk about Matt being a pervert. I mean it was kind of known around town that he was a perv."

"In what way?" Susan frowned slightly. "What do you mean, exactly? A pervert in what way?" She asked this with both hands holding her coffee cup.

Gerry sat back, took his cap off, and ran a hand over his head before putting his cap back on. "He used to ask pregnant women if he could paint their picture naked."

Susan didn't say anything. But she raised her eyebrows. Then she said softly, "But to *kill* his mother?" She added, "She *was* a bitch, though. Do you remember her?"

"Of course. Bitch Ball. Working in the line in the cafeteria. She scared me to death."

"I think she scared everyone to death," Susan said.

Gerry opened his hand, palm upward, shrugged, and said nothing.

Susan said, "Listen." She crossed her legs and leaned forward and said, "So this morning, before I came here to meet you, I was talking to Gail Young—do you remember Gail?— I thought you would—well, anyway, she called me up and she had been *friends* with Diana Beach when they were small, and she said that Diana would come over and spend the night at her house—Gail's house—and that she would boss around Gail's little sister, but I mean *really* boss her. Penny—Gail's sister—had just reminded her of this. Diana used to make Penny be her prisoner."

Susan sat back.

"Her *prisoner*?" Gerry asked.

"Yeah. Diana would tell Penny, You are my prisoner and you have to do everything I tell you to do."

"And what would Diana tell Penny to do?"

"Like walk into a room and sit on the bed and not move until Diana said she could go."

"And would Penny do this?" Gerry asked.

"Of course."

"Where was their mother?"

And Susan said, "Who knows."

GERRY HAD GROWN to be quite dependent on these mornings on his porch with Susan. She was comfortable to him in a way he would not have imagined. They had dated briefly in high school, and then he had broken up with her—they never talked about that. He thought about her a great deal, adding up in his mind the things he wanted to tell her when he saw her. He felt that they had an easy intimacy, and so why could it not go further? He did not know why. But it did not.

Now Gerry wanted to tell her about an incident last night at the grocery store where he had seen a woman fall, she was old, and she had pissed herself as she was lying on the floor.

But Susan said, "Gail told me she went to the Beaches' house just once, and the kid, Matt, looked perfectly dreadful, all dark around his eyes, so sick. She said the house had been clean, though. Gail's mother had wanted to know if the house was clean."

And then Gerry told Susan about the woman who had fallen in the grocery store and how she had peed herself, how you could see the urine creeping over her really old yellowish pants.

"Oh God. Oh dear God. Oh that's awful." Susan shook her head.

ANYWAY, AS WE have said, the Gloria Beach case had gone cold.

4

AND SO WINTER was here once again in Maine, the short days. Darker and darker it got, and even if the sun shone— many days it did not—the sun still did not climb high in the sky, and there was sometimes a sense of compression for Bob Burgess, of being squeezed. It was cold when you woke up in the morning, even colder when you stepped outside. In these past fifteen years Bob had gotten used again to the Maine winters after moving back from New York City and marrying Margaret. But he felt his heart flicker at times with a kind of anxiety now, and he thought it was the aftereffect of the pandemic—which was not entirely over—and also the state of the world.

Bob had been a criminal defense lawyer, as we have said, and every now and then he did still take a case in Shirley Falls, where he had grown up, forty-five minutes away from Crosby, and he did still like sitting in his office there, then going to the jail to speak to his defendants who needed him, although he found a disquiet to the heroin addicts who were facing prison instead of getting the help they needed. When Bob thought about the state of the country these days, he sometimes had the image of a huge tractor trailer rumbling down the highway and the wheels, one by one, falling off.

———

ONE DAY AS Bob sat in his office—the old radiator in the corner was making knocking sounds—he received a phone call from Olive Kitteridge. "I just thought you should know, in case you take that case, that I knew a person who knew that family back when I was square dancing."

"What family? What case?" Bob asked.

"That Matthew Beach case. If he did it, and I'm sure he did, I don't know that I entirely blame him."

Bob sat back in his chair. "I'm not taking the case. There is no case, as far as I know. But my sister Susan said the same thing, that she wouldn't blame him. Why do you say that?"

"Crazy, crazy, crazy things in that family. But if there's no case, fine. Bye now." And Olive Kitteridge hung up.

Bob looked out the window at the street below. There was very little sun today, and the street had only the slight flickering of snow that had come the night before. Bob saw a man, also a lawyer, walking out of the courthouse. And then Bob leaned back in his chair and called his older brother, Jim, in New York City. Jim had been a very successful criminal defense attorney, had once been known all around the country. This was way back in the day. "Oh, Matthew's guilty," Jim said now, after Bob mentioned the situation, and Bob said, "I know, I know. I honestly don't even care."

"You don't *care*? When did little Bobby Burgess ever not care?" Jim asked.

Bob closed his eyes briefly; he understood that nothing would change this attitude of Jim's that Jim had tossed upon him all their lives, and Bob accepted that.

"What's the motive, though?" Bob asked, sitting up straight. Only on some tiny conscious level did Bob understand that he was talking about a child killing a parent, what he had always thought he had done. Although Jim, years ago now, had confessed that he, Jim, had been the one who had played with the gearshift and caused the car to roll down the hill and over their father. But they had never spoken of it since; they were both from Maine, and all their years of living in New York City would not change that; people from Maine did not always like to talk of these things.

"Because he was driven crazy by her? Batshit crazy? She was awful," Jim said.

"Oh, I know." Bob looked out his window again. He was on the eighth floor of this building in Shirley Falls, and he saw a couple walking by; they appeared to be drunk. "But what exactly was so awful about her? I know she scared us to death, but how *exactly*? I've tried and I can't remember." Bob turned his chair away from the window.

Jim said, "Just the nastiest woman in the world. When I was in elementary school, we called her Beach Ball because she was round, and then in junior high school she became Bitch Ball because she was so mean. But don't you remember how she'd be standing there in the cafeteria, slopping out those mashed potatoes onto those pale green plastic plates, and she would just *glare* at some kid who was sort of recalcitrant about taking them and she'd say, 'You just be goddamn glad you have this food!' One time she asked that girl, I can't remember her name, 'Where'd you get that *pig* face of yours?'"

Bob said, "Oh yeah. I just remembered when she stopped the whole line because some guy wouldn't say thank you to her. Everyone had to wait, and she looked so furious at this kid, she held out this huge spoon like she was going to smack him with it, and she said, almost spitting, 'Say thank you,' and the kid wouldn't, and God it got really scary. Finally the kid murmured thank you, and she threw a spoonful of hot broccoli at him."

Jim said, "Tommy—remember the older brother, Tommy?"

"No," said Bob.

"Well, he was in my class, and he was really a prick. Very, very serious, and a prick."

"He's a psychiatrist now," Bob said, and Jim said he knew that, he had seen it in the paper, and Bob said, "You're still reading the *Shirley Falls Journal*?"

"Oh sure, online, every day," Jim said, and for Bob—well, a real sense of warmth moved through him, that his brother, who lived so differently in New York City, was still reading the daily paper from their hometown.

"Diana was always kind of touching to me," Jim said. And Bob said, "How did you know her? She was in Susie's and my class."

And Jim said, "Yeah, I know. But sometimes I'd see her walking home and there was always something sort of sweetly sad about her. Look, I have to run. Come down here and see us soon, we miss you. Helen misses you."

And oh, that made Bob so happy, he just adored his older brother; this had been true Bob's whole life no matter the things Jim said to him. And he loved his sister-in-law, Helen.

Bob said, "I'll come in two weeks when Lucy Barton goes to New York. She's taken a little studio apartment there in the city and she visits her daughters in New Haven, she has that little grandson now."

"You're going to stay with Lucy Barton?" Jim asked, and Bob said, "No, knucklehead, I'm going to stay with you guys." "Great," Jim said. "We'll be glad to see you." So Bob had that to look forward to.

BUT IN A WAY, these days were (sometimes) still a little bit hard for Bob. He could read books—and he did. But he did not read with the enthusiasm he had read with before the pandemic, and sometimes he wondered if his mind was going. He noticed that he did not shower as often as he used to. But his wife said nothing about that, she did not seem to notice. Margaret had many things going on with her church now that the pandemic— Well, it was not over, but it was maybe as over as it was ever going to be.

Margaret often went to her study at the church first thing in the morning and did not come home until five o'clock. Or she might go to Shirley Falls to help with the immigrant community there, which is what she had been doing when she first met Bob. But Bob, except for his walks with Lucy Barton, was (sometimes) just a little bit struggling. Although there were people in Crosby he did chores for, and he volunteered at the food pantry in town two afternoons a week and was also on the board of the Hatfield Homeless Shelter, though that did not require as much time as the food pantry did.

And then Jim called a week later and asked Bob not to come to New York after all. When Bob asked why, his brother paused and said, "Helen and I are going on a trip. Not sure where."

Bob felt his insides drop in a way that was familiar to him. "Why?" he asked again.

Jim said, "Why? Because we are. That's why."

5

CHRISTMAS BEGAN EVEN before Thanksgiving, the stores were suddenly filled with carols playing, large plastic Santa Clauses appeared on the front lawns of many houses, the town itself lit the big spruce tree in the middle of the park, and there were lights strung along Main Street from one lamppost to another, although there had been only sprinklings of snow. But the week before Christmas there was a huge snowstorm, and the plows went out all through the night and school was canceled and people seemed happy to have the mounds of clean white puffy snow everywhere. But the season was still hard on certain folks: those who had no family, those who had family they did not like and had to see, those with very little money and then the stress of running around at the last minute making sure there were enough things under the tree.

Bob Burgess had a quiet reaction to the holiday season: It made him sad. And this, he had come to (privately) realize, was because as a young boy he had said to his mother one day, with innocence, "I don't really like Christmas," and his mother had looked at him with abrupt anger, and then she had started to cry. The child-Bob was puzzled by this, and worried, and he had walked away. But he never forgot it, and as he got older he realized that Christmases, quite naturally, would have been hard for his mother: She had very little money and also her hus-

band was gone. That Bob had spoken those words to her remained a thumbprint pressed deeply into his soul of real sorrow
and regret.

He had told this story to Margaret when they first met, he
had also told his first wife, Pam Carlson, and they were both
kind about it, but it was one of Bob's adult understandings:
People did not care, except for maybe one minute. It was not
their fault, most just could not *really* care past their own experiences.

BUT MARGARET ENJOYED CHRISTMAS: She had her various
services, and people were glad to come to them in person after
so many months of Zoom services, though even now a few
showed up with masks. Margaret wore a mask except when she
took it off to give the homily. Bob sat in the third-row pew and
his stomach grumbled. Lucy Barton and her ex-husband, William, showed up at the Christmas Eve service and they came
back to Bob and Margaret's house afterward for a late drink.

Margaret's sermon had been on charity. "Never in the history of Crosby, Maine, have so many people lined up at the
food pantry for food. And never in the history of Crosby have
we had so many people without homes," she had said.

William said to Margaret, as he raised his glass, "Great job
tonight, Margaret. Really, really great job."

And Bob saw how pleased Margaret was, and so he echoed
it, as did Lucy, and Margaret said, "Well, one never knows how
it goes over, but I always try." And all three of them said that
she had succeeded, and she seemed to settle down after that,
and she asked William how his parasites were going: William
was a parasitologist who was working with potato farmers in

Aroostook County, trying to help develop a new potato breed, one that was able to withstand climate change. William answered her at great length (Lucy rolled her eyes at Bob), but they all listened; there was a comfortableness to their friendships with one another.

Then Margaret said, "And how is Chrissy doing?"

William leaned back in his chair and said, "Why that name? *Aiden.* I still can't figure it out." He ran a hand through his white hair, making it stand up on his head.

Lucy said, "She's fine, thanks, Margaret. She's doing much better with her postpartum stuff, I just saw her a few weeks ago, and they're getting into the swing of it."

"But why that *name?*" William asked again, one of his long legs crossed over the other. He tugged on his big white mustache, then sipped from his wineglass.

"I think it's a great name," said Bob, and Margaret agreed.

"But there's not a drop of Irish in either of them," William persisted, and Lucy reached over and tapped William's knee and said, "Enough with the name, William." She said it pleasantly.

On one of their walks Lucy had told Bob that she thought William had secretly been hoping the baby would be named after him. William said now, "He's a cute guy. Imagine a boy in the family, so great."

"So great," Margaret said, and then she mentioned that the locksmith in town was a heroin addict, and that mental health was the biggest crisis in the nation right now. Lucy—Bob noticed this—was drinking more than she usually did, and her face got pink. But it was all perfectly agreeable, they chatted about any number of things.

William said, "I figure I have two jobs: Lucy, and the parasites." He added, "Lucy comes first, though."

And yet here was something strange: When they got up to leave, Bob saw that Lucy had tears in her eyes. And her mouth trembled downward briefly. "Bye-bye," she said, and she went down the stairs carefully, touching the wall, followed by William.

"Lovely night," Margaret said, and Bob agreed that it had been.

BUT BOB THOUGHT about this, and he said to Margaret as they got into bed, "I think Lucy got upset tonight toward the end. I don't really like how William infantilizes her."

"I know, you've said that before." Margaret pulled back the covers and got under them, wearing her long flannel nightgown. "But I told you I think he just feels guilt about all his previous—"—she put her fingers in quotes—"—misdeeds." Margaret shifted herself so that she was looking at Bob with a hand beneath her head. "I think that's what it's about. It makes him feel important to take care of her. It's their role thing."

Bob said, "It's *his* role thing. She's not a child."

Margaret appeared to think about this. "No, but she is childlike." Margaret added, turning onto her back, "She's an artist, that's how they are."

BUT MARGARET CONTINUED to lie in the dark and she thought about Lucy and William, she was really fond of both of them. Lucy, this came to Margaret as a crack of light opening on a horizon, Lucy had a loneliness to her that she usually covered well, but it *was* a loneliness—and this was the crack widening on the horizon—that Margaret now understood about herself, that Margaret had devoted her life to the service of others because she desired—deeply, almost without knowing until right now—to connect with another person. She pondered this; it was one of the reasons she liked Lucy, because she could feel connected to her. Margaret did not always feel connected to her congregation—their earnest faces, or their bored faces, or the old man, Avery Mason, who always fell asleep in his front pew—this came to her then—and she thought, Oh, of course I feel connected to them. And she turned over in bed and within minutes she was lightly snoring.

*

AS WE MENTIONED EARLIER, housing prices in Crosby, Maine, had been going through the roof since the pandemic. And there were new condos and apartment buildings going up everywhere. Out by the old airfield you could see the construction of building after building—and they were not cheap, these new places. In the town itself, an old brick mill was being turned into condos, and these were even more expensive. The former police station was being turned into condos as well. Where were all these people coming from? Where was all the money coming from? No one seemed to know. But people agreed: It was going to change the town forever.

There was a woman named Charlene Bibber, who was fifty-five years old, and she had lived in Crosby all her life. She cleaned apartments at the Maple Tree Apartments retirement community three mornings a week, and she found herself now in possible financial trouble. Her property taxes, like everyone else's, had gone way up. Her husband had died many years before, and—sadly for them both—they had been unable to have children. So Charlene had recently sold the small house she had lived in with her husband, although it broke her heart to do so, and while it made her feel flush for a few days, she began to understand as she did the math that if she lived for another twenty-five years she could easily end up on the street. Because even with the sale of her small house she could not afford the rent of these newer places. After selling the house, she moved into one of the big old wooden houses that had cheap apartments, not unlike the one Ricky Davis—with his huge rear end—had lived in, until a few years earlier, when you first entered town. These old houses were very much in the town, tucked away a block or two over from the center of Crosby. And yet—oddly—it would be fair to say that the more affluent people of town, especially of course the newcomers, did not even see them. Partly this was location: You had to go down side streets you might not normally go down, but even if these well-off people happened to drive by these places, they still did not *see* them in a certain way.

CHARLENE UNDERSTOOD THIS. Weariness moved through her all the time.

SHE TOOK AN extra job as a checkout clerk at the big grocery store, but standing on her legs all day was very painful for her back, and she had to give it up after three months. And yet she was back working at the food pantry once a week. Charlene had not had enough food as a child, and this still stung her, so she stood there every week and packed bags of groceries for those families waiting outside in their cars for the food.

It had been at the food pantry—more than two years ago now—that she had first met Lucy Barton, who was filling in for Margaret Estaver one day. Charlene had found herself talking and talking to this Lucy woman. Charlene had found her to be different, quietly accessible as a listener, and later Charlene was embarrassed at how much she had talked to her, she felt that her loneliness had been leaking all over her, but later, when she saw Lucy in the park one day, Lucy said, "Oh Charlene! Come walk with me by the river!"

AND SINCE THEN, every few weeks, Charlene met Lucy by the river, and they mostly sat on one of the large granite benches near the start of their walk because Charlene had trouble walking too far. The day after Christmas, Lucy called her, and they were now sitting on one of these benches, bundled up against the cold. Lucy asked Charlene how her Christmas had been.

"I spent it alone," Charlene said, and Lucy placed her mittened hand on Charlene's knee. "I didn't have to," Charlene explained. "My cousins up in the county asked me there, but that's a three-hour trip each way and that's a lot of *gas*."

"I know it is."

"But the day wasn't so bad, really. I mean, Jerry and Louise came down—"—this was a couple who lived upstairs from Charlene that Lucy knew about—"—and they're nice. Jerry's having a terrible time because of his treatments. But he managed to sit there for a while with us. And then there's Boober." Boober was Charlene's dog, a rescue collie. Oh, Charlene

loved him! "He's kind of saved my life," she said now. She had
told this to Lucy before, and Lucy nodded. And then Charlene
said: "So on Christmas night I sat and had myself a really long
think with myself. And this is what I thought: People are
shits."

Lucy watched her.

"When I sold my house, that horrible realtor came to me
and said, Charlene, sell that house right now, someone wants to
buy it. And so I did. And then at the closing, that same realtor
said to me as we were leaving, 'Should have held on to this
place longer, Charlene, we could have gotten twice the money
for it.' He *said* that, Lucy! But he was just so anxious to get
whatever money he could, he took that first offer. Piece of
crap."

Lucy let out a big sigh and said, "Oh, that's awful."

"Life is just *hard*."

Lucy looked at her and then gazed out at the river. "I know,"
she said.

"How's your sister? She liking you any better?" Charlene
asked.

"No." The two women looked at each other and laughed.
Lucy said, "No. Vicky's life is hard too. Like I've told you."

"I know. That's why I was asking about her. Lucy! I forgot
to tell you. Olive Kitteridge gave me your first memoir to read.
Last week when I cleaned for her. She said as I was going out
the door, she said, Wait, you know Lucy Barton, right? Well,
take her book. So she gave it to me."

Charlene saw Lucy's face turn pink, and Lucy said, "Charlene, you don't have to read that."

"I want to. You know, Olive Kitteridge is the only person I
clean for who is nice to me."

"I know. You've said." Lucy pulled her coat tighter, squeezing herself with her arms.

"So there's a new couple now I clean for. From Connecticut. She's such a bitch. She doesn't even *see* me, Lucy. I mean, I'm just the cleaning lady, what does she care. Except she keeps telling me I'm doing the bathroom wrong. She wants me to clean the toilet by hand and not with the toilet brush." Charlene pulled her hat down closer onto her head. It was a red knit hat and not as warm as she always expected it to be. "No Christmas tip from her, either. They're just awful people. Olive agrees with me. One of the rules of working there is to never discuss other clientele with people who live there, but Olive lets me rest, and sometimes we just sit there and talk. She hates those people too."

"I'm so sorry," Lucy said, looking at Charlene.

"Yeah. Well. As long as I don't talk politics with Olive, we're good."

"You and I don't talk politics either," Lucy reminded her, and Charlene laughed and said, "I know that. That's fine."

"I used to clean house when I was in college. For a chemistry professor, I remember. She was nice. I guess." Lucy was shivering as she said this. "She had an au pair, and in the mornings the au pair, she was from England, would say, Would you like a coffee? And so I would sit with her in the kitchen and she scared me, even though I think she was perfectly nice, I just didn't know what to say to her."

"What's an au pair?" Charlene asked.

"Oh, it's a person to just watch the kids."

"This professor had you to clean and another person to watch the kids?" Charlene squinted at Lucy as she asked this.

"Yeah. I remember the au pair would say to me, Do you want milk and sugar?, but I was too shy, so I would just say no and sit there and drink black coffee." Lucy shook her head. "I must have been very strange." Lucy gazed at the river. "One day the woman asked me to clean the top shelf of her husband's closet, and there was all this pornography. Like, weird Victorian stuff. All these old black-and-white drawings."

"What did you do?" Charlene asked.

Lucy said, "I dusted it off and straightened them up, and left them right there."

Charlene liked being with Lucy more than she thought Lucy knew. Almost as much as she liked being with Olive Kitteridge. But Lucy was shivering now, Charlene could see this, and so she stood up and said, "Well, let's get going."

LATER THAT NIGHT, after watching the news on her favorite television channel, the only news show she ever watched, Charlene got into bed and started to read Lucy's memoir, but within a few pages she put it down. It took place in New York City and mentioned Lucy's kids when they were very young, and it made Charlene sad about her own childless state. She did not want to read about that. And she did not care about New York City. She put the book by the side of her bed, where it stayed unread.

*

WHEN BOB SAW Lucy for their walk the week after Christmas he asked her about the evening at his house with Margaret, if she had been all right. And Lucy took a deep breath and said, "I don't know, Bob. Sometimes these days, I just—out of the blue—get so *despondent*."

"It's almost like Chrissy's postpartum depression has become yours," he said, walking along beside her. And she stopped and looked at him. "You're so smart, Bob. That's exactly what it is. That new baby—oh, I mean thank *God* she had him—but sometimes I am just *stabbed* with this sudden grief. And it is exactly like that, like I took on her postpartum stuff." As they continued to walk she said quietly, "You know, Chrissy and Michael and Becka didn't even ask us there for Christmas, and that's *fine*, but somehow I thought it was going to be different, we asked them here, of course, but they have things they're doing, and honestly, Bob, that's *fine*, it really is, I just thought I would always have Christmas with them. Chrissy seems different with me, both girls do. Like I've become inconsequential to their lives. Oh, never mind. And Bridget—"—Bridget was the daughter that William had had with his third wife—"—I thought maybe she'd come up here for Christmas, and she didn't. But she's a teenager now and why would she want to hang out with old people?" Lucy let out a big sigh. "It's just funny about life."

"You mean how it doesn't work the way you think it will?" Bob asked, and Lucy said, "Exactly." Then Lucy said, "You know, when Chrissy was born, I got depressed. It felt to me that William and I had broken up, that's exactly what form it took for me, as though we were no longer a couple."

They kept on walking.

Bob said, glancing over at Lucy with a slight smile, "Don't think about it"—their private joke—and Lucy said, "You're right." And then she said, "Oh Bob! I finally transplanted Little Annie and now I'm *really* worried about her."

He listened while she described how she had put Little Annie in a bigger pot, but the soil had been from last year and it was very dry, and so she had googled it and found out you should never use old dried-out soil, and so she had pulled Little Annie out of her new pot and put in new, rich soil, but now Little Annie was in trouble, she was not soaking up the water, and Lucy was really worried about her. "I shouldn't have transplanted her this time of year," she said. And then she said, "Sorry to go on about her. I just love those plants so much."

And Bob said, "Go on about anything you want to."

"Nah, I'm done." She gave him a smile.

They sat down on the granite bench while he had his cigarette. The day was a sunny one, and across the river the bare trees could be seen reflecting in the blue water, so it looked like they were twice as tall as they were. Lucy said, "Look at that," pointing to the strip of trees. And Bob said, "I know, I was just thinking that. They're something." He smoked his cigarette, and when he was done with it he put the butt back into the pack, which is what he always did.

"Thanks, Lucy," he said, and she said, "Of course."

ON THEIR WAY back to the car Lucy said, "I think this country could be headed toward a civil war," and Bob said, "Me too." They had said this to each other before. And now Bob said, "It's not just this country, though. The whole world seems to be going crazy. Russia invading Ukraine."

"I know, I know, I know." Lucy swept her hand through the air. "I saw Charlene the other day."

"How is she?" Bob asked.

Lucy said, "Very lonely, I think. She spent Christmas alone, except the couple upstairs from her came down for a while. She hates the people she cleans for at the Maple Tree Apartments. She says they don't see her, and I know she's right."

Bob said, "Oh, I suspect she is right."

"Oh! So, I called my sister again, you know I call Vicky every week—"—Bob nodded—"—and she said she had to get going to help her son Donny pack for his trip, and I said, Where is he going? And she said he was going with some other fellows to a cabin in Belmont, Illinois, which is way out in the middle of nowhere, and I couldn't help it, it just popped out of my mouth, Bob, I *never* should have said this, but I said, Vicky, is this some kind of *militia* thing? And *God*, she got mad. She said, Lucy, you make me very, very tired. And then we hung up." Lucy turned to Bob and added, "I already know he has guns, she told me that before."

"Man, Lucy. Well— Who knows? But Jesus. A lot of people have guns, though."

"I know! I know."

They walked along for a few minutes and then Lucy said, "I've been thinking about my mother a lot for some reason, I don't know why. But I remembered this: One day when I was about eight years old, I asked her, Why does Row, row, row your boat end with the phrase Life is but a dream, what does that *mean*?, I asked her. And it was funny because she said, quietly, It means life isn't real. And I said, how can it not be real? And what I remember is that she stopped doing the dishes and stared out the tiny window above the sink, and she said—again, quietly— It means that it isn't real. And I always remembered that. It was as though she believed that, believed that life wasn't real. And why wouldn't she? Her life was so hard." After another moment Lucy said, "I love to talk. And I think my mother loved to talk. And I just didn't know it, Bob, I was too young, I didn't really get it."

"No one gets anything when they're young," Bob said.

He told her then about how when he was little he had spoken to his mother about not liking Christmas and how she had become angry and started to cry and he had walked away. "I think of that a lot, Lucy, and it just kills me every time. But I was a kid. I didn't really get how hard her life was."

Lucy stopped walking and looked at him. "Oh Bob," she said softly. And then Bob understood. She had heard him. She had absorbed this from him in a way that neither one of his wives ever could.

6

BY FEBRUARY THE days were starting to get longer, but it was still very cold. And yet when the sun shone, as it did only on certain days, you could see that the days really *were* lengthening. Bob Burgess had noticed this for years, and people in Maine generally understood these lengthening days, even unconsciously, and with that came a rising of hope. But for Bob right now life was a strain. When he spoke to his brother, Jim was terse, and this reopened the wound for Bob that had always been there. Margaret continued to be busy with her church. She came home one Friday and said, "Avery Mason is getting himself on the board of the church. Because Ted Wiley died and there's been that opening— Well, it turns out Avery Mason has been angling for the position and he's going to get it." Bob barely gave this a thought—it did not seem to him that Margaret thought about it much either. "You mean the guy who sleeps through every service?" Bob asked, and Margaret shrugged and said, "The very one."

But Avery Mason, without Bob or Margaret knowing it yet, was getting ready to threaten Margaret's job.

Lucy went back to New York for a couple of weeks, and then she and William were going from there to Florida for one more week. When she was in New York she sent Bob a picture of the view from her New York studio window of the skyline of Manhattan. Something about that view almost brought Bob to his knees. How he missed New York! But with his brother being so unpleasant to him (Bob still did not know where Jim and Helen had gone on their trip) he did not feel he could go to New York, and so he stayed where he was in Crosby, Maine. And he also missed Pam, his first wife, who still lived in New York; Bob had not seen her since before the pandemic. They had remained friendly since their divorce more than twenty-five years earlier.

BUT THEN, of all things, on one of these days—it was overcast, the clouds low and gray—in the morning, as he was heading out the door to go to the post office, Bob received a telephone call from Pam. She said that she was coming to Crosby to see him. "I need to see you. And you don't seem to come to New York anymore."

"When are you coming?" Bob asked; he had stopped on the stairway. And she said she was flying in tomorrow and would rent a car and stay at the hotel right there in town. "Are you *okay*?" he asked, and she said, "I don't know, Bob. I just do not know."

*

HERE IS WHAT had been happening to Pam:

During March of the first days of the pandemic, Pam and her second husband, Ted, had left their apartment in New York City and moved to their house in East Hampton, where they thought they would be safer from the disease. The house was big: Pam and her husband were very rich, and their house represented this wealth. It had a large central staircase and five bedrooms, all with long drapes that Pam had designed to blow in the summer breeze, but of course there were no summer breezes in March.

Anyway. This is the setting in which Pam emerged as a monstrous alcoholic. She became quite impressive in the secretiveness and ingenuity with which she carried this off.

Pam was sixty-four years old by then and was not yet a grandmother, which worried her, and her two sons were no longer living in New York, which made her sad. And also her favorite son, the younger one, who lived in San Francisco, was causing her distress of a different kind. Her husband, Ted, had been (honestly) tiresome to her for many years. She still thought of herself as young but understood that she was not. She had a number of friends, many in East Hampton as well, and yet— this had felt rather sudden to her—she could barely stand them. They had become unbelievably insipid. Lydia Robbins was the one Pam considered to be her best friend. Lydia was ten years younger than Pam and had an energy that Pam enjoyed. As they took their walks, Lydia's full glossy dark hair would fall across her face frequently as she turned to look at Pam, nodding at something Pam had said. But after they shared their confidences, Pam felt she couldn't bear Lydia.

Didn't anyone ever have anything *interesting* to say? They talked of movies they were all watching, of series on Netflix, they spoke about their children, but always carefully and in terms meant to hide their private disappointments, and they talked about one another. Of course.

——

IN HER DRESSING ROOM—Pam's private dressing room off the master bedroom, windowless but the size of a small bedroom—Pam hid vodka and wine bottles with screw tops. At five o'clock each evening she went into her dressing room, and from beneath her many hanging gowns she lifted the huge bath towel with which she had covered these bottles, and she drank from one of them steadily. If it was a wine bottle she would drink half of it, standing there wiping her arm across her mouth, and she always had gum to mask the smell, a certain kind that seemed sharper in flavor, and that was the start of her night. If it was a vodka bottle, she would drink three or four swallows. Then she would go downstairs and join her husband in the parlor for their pre-dinner martini, which he always made and handed to her, saying, "Here you are, my darling," as though they were living in a British country house a century before. "Thank you," she always said. She always said it politely.

Oh poor Pam!

Seriously, you should feel sorry for her.

AND THEN THEY were vaccinated, and another summer came around, and there had been parties to go to once more. Pam returned to New York City occasionally, but her life had become the one in the Hamptons.

And yet as fall arrived again, Pam understood: Life, as she had known it, had ended. As the pandemic continued and boosters were needed, and new mutations kept arriving, Pam understood: Her life had taken some strange and horrible turn. She began to drink with even more of a vengeance, she could feel it, every night she was drinking with a vengeance, these were the words she thought of as she tipped the wine bottle to her mouth in her dressing room. *Drinking with a vengeance.*

It was a terrible secret. And it *was* a secret: There was nobody she could tell this to, and what did that say about the kind of friends she had? Were they all drinking secretly too? She had no idea. Secret means nobody knows.

OF COURSE, THERE was the problem of what to do with the empty bottles.

WHEN A FEW of them piled up, Pam put them into a plastic bag and shoved them into the bottom of her huge leather bag. And then she would drive, either to the grocery store or to the next town, Southampton, or even sometimes to Amagansett, and throw the bottles into a public trash bin. It came to her one day that everything was captured on camera now, and so she worried that she would be caught on some tape, a middle-aged (older than that, really) woman slipping these bags into public garbage bins. Sometimes she stopped to put just ten dollars' worth of gas into her car so that while she waited by the pump she could nonchalantly dump her garbage bag into the trash bin the gas station had right there.

And, of course, she had to keep her supply up. She had cases of wine delivered to the house when she knew her husband would not be home, but this took work, and often she found herself in liquor stores all over Long Island; there were endless villages or towns to do this in. She bought vodka and the screw-top bottles of wine, talking gaily to the men behind the counter about "entertaining" a few people—"All vaccinated," she would say brightly, though she understood that they did not care. She thought of these different men—because it seemed only men that were selling liquor—she thought of them as drug dealers.

PAM HAD MARRIED her money. Having come from western Massachusetts, an only child raised by older parents, she had gone to college at the University of Maine, where she'd met her first husband, Bob Burgess. She and Bob moved to New York as soon as they graduated, and what a blast they had those first years! They lived in a tiny apartment in the Village, and Pam had worked at a lab at Albert Einstein College, she was a scientist, she worked with parasitologists there (this was where she met William Gerhardt for the first time, Lucy's now ex-husband; Pam had had an affair with him eventually), and Bob, after he finished law school, had worked for Legal Aid, and they made just enough money to get by.

When she met her second husband, Ted, he was already wealthy, a top executive at a pharmaceutical company. And then with the pandemic that company produced one of the vaccines and it was like a slot machine at a gambling joint, money just poured in. In her youth, Pam had not thought about money. It was not until she met Ted that she discovered this entirely different world in New York City, and she loved it. Or she became addicted to it. Which was another way she thought about it. She could not go back. Parties and receptions and tables at the opera and so many different clothes! And with Ted she had her two boys.

Bob had not been able to have children, his sperm count was not high enough, and Pam often thought that if he had been able to have kids, she would have stayed married to him; she thought she would not have had the affairs that she did.

SO THERE PAM was, drinking with a vengeance night after night.

THEN THIS HAPPENED, and it was ridiculous: Pam was in her dressing room one afternoon, it was in February, when one more variant of the virus had come and gone in New York— she had known people who got sick, Lydia Robbins had gotten sick two months before, but Pam had not. That afternoon she was in her dressing room, it was earlier than she usually started her drinking, this was around four o'clock, and she heard her husband come into the bedroom. She closed the door of the dressing room quietly and waited, even as she heard him call her name: "Pam?"

And then she heard him say, "It's safe, she's not here." And Lydia Robbins said, "Oh goody, goody, let's hurry," and Pam listened as Lydia performed on Ted a sexual act that Pam had long ago stopped performing on him. It was astonishing. She heard him almost yelping, "Lydia, Lydia, *Lydia!*" And then it was over, and she heard them both laughing, she heard him zipping up his pants, and they went into the bathroom briefly— she thought Lydia was brushing her teeth (!)—and they left the bedroom.

———

PAM SAT ON the floor, drinking from a vodka bottle, and when she went down that evening, her husband, looking the very same as always, said, "May I present you with the perfect martini, my dear?"

"Thank you," she said.

AND AFTER THAT MARTINI (and the wine that followed at dinner), Pam did not drink again.

For a week she felt unbelievably awful. She did not sleep, her left hand shook sometimes, and once she briefly thought she saw a person who was not there. She told Ted that she had some kind of bug, but he tested her for Covid.

After ten days of this—she was feeling better—she told Ted that she was going back to the city, and he said, "Would you mind if I stayed here?" And she said Absolutely not, she was simply tired of being in the Hamptons, this is what she said, and he was pleasant about it, and so she went to New York.

When she was back in New York—they lived on East Seventieth Street, very close to Central Park—she walked through their apartment, and she thought: I hate it all. I just hate it all. It was quite a moment for her. Even the sight of her sons' bedrooms did not move her.

After a few nights of being back in the city stone cold sober, she called Bob. "I'm going to fly up to Maine and see you," she said. She had not seen Bob in more than two years; he would visit her occasionally when he came to New York to see his brother, but of course he had not come to New York during the pandemic.

"When?" Bob asked.

"Tomorrow. If that's all right," Pam said.

*

WHEN BOB TOLD Margaret about this, she simply raised an eyebrow and said, "Lucky you."

And of course Bob did not sleep well that night. He lay awake in the dark and heard Margaret's tiny snores beside him and he thought about Pam, and he thought about their early days in New York, and yet he could not find a sense of these memories being *real,* and this disturbed him. It wasn't until he remembered Pam living with him and Susan and also their mother one summer in Maine after their junior year in college, living together in Bob's small childhood home in Shirley Falls—it was not until he remembered this that Pam became herself to him again. Her long brown hair that she and Susan had ironed one day on the ironing board, the way she would laugh with his mother . . . He remembered one summer night sitting in the living room with the three of them, and his mother mentioned something about birds that had once fallen down the chimney, adding, "Boy, I bet that toasted their tail feathers," and Pam said, "I'd say it boiled their eggs."

PAM.

He had loved her, oh he had. The *energy* of her!

*

PAM WAS DRIVING quickly and well from the airport. The car held its own on the highway, and she turned up the radio and sang along. It was an hour's drive, and she passed by many trees and also huge slabs of rock with muscular-looking ice attached to them. When she pulled off the highway to enter the town of Crosby, Maine, she was disconcerted by the sight of it. There was dirty snow on the ground, and it was cloudy, and when she checked into the hotel she was taken aback by how rudimentary it was.

Never mind.

She turned up the heat and sat on the queen-size bed—the place was clean, at least. And then she called Bob. "Room 202," she said. She put her mask back on. Pam was very germophobic.

*

WHAT BOB AND PAM each experienced at the same moment was a sense of shock at the sight of the other one. It was not just that each looked older to the other; there was another difference at work here. Pam, to Bob's eyes, looked rich. Her clothes were rich clothes is all he could think. Slacks that were gray, and a fitted top of dark blue. Her hair—thinner than he had remembered—was cut below her chin. But her eyes smiled at him with a familiarity.

Pam, for her part, could have died at the sight of this man, Bob Burgess, her first husband. It wasn't just that he looked old: He looked schlumpy. His jeans were baggy, and his jacket was so old that the collar was somewhat shredded. This thought went through her mind: He could be working at a gas station.

And the very moment she thought that, she understood that she had become a terrific snob, what was wrong with working at a gas station? His hair was badly cut and fell across the top of his eyes. Bob! She put her arms out and they hugged lightly, turning their heads with their masks on. Then Pam went and sat on the bed, and Bob slowly lowered himself into the armchair in the corner of the room.

"You look good," Pam said.

"You do too," Bob said.

AND THEN SHE began to talk. As she talked, Bob became the old Bob to her, the one who was so familiar, and she talked for a long while without stopping. "I was a drunk," she said, "a full-blown drunk," and she described how she would drink in her dressing room, and Bob never stopped looking at her once. She told him about her friends, how dull they were, how they only spoke of certain things and always made their families out to be better than she knew they were. When she paused, Bob said, "How are the boys?" He removed his mask and put it onto the small table beside him.

Pam took a deep breath and said, "Oh, the boys. Bob. They've left me."

Bob said, "That's what kids do, I think."

And Pam said, "Yes. Especially boys." She told him that Paul was in finance in San Diego, and Eric was living in San Francisco. Pam paused for quite a long time and then she said, "Eric wears women's clothes."

Bob said, "*Really?* Is he, you know, transitioning?"

"He says no, he just likes to wear women's clothes, so he

does." Pam hesitated. "Of course, Ted *hates* that, Ted is *such* an intolerant asshole, so small, and he says he doesn't want Eric to do that in New York, and so Eric said, Well, then he won't come back to New York. And with the pandemic he hasn't."

Pam's eyes filled with tears.

But she wanted to get back to her own life, Bob saw that, and so he encouraged her to speak more about her days of being a drunk, which as far as he knew had ended only about two weeks ago. "That's right," she said, when he asked her to clarify that. "About two weeks ago. Huh."

When she told him what she had heard going on between Lydia Robbins and her husband, and she told him graphically, Bob closed his eyes. A sense of heavy fatigue overtook him, and he wished she would stop. "And then he was gasping, calling out Lydia, Lydia—"

Bob put his hand up and said, "Pam, I get what you're saying, I don't need to hear the whole thing."

"Oh, okay," she said. After a moment, Pam said, "Awfully nice to see you, Bobby."

"You too, Pam."

PAM TURNED HER gaze to look out the window. She took her mask off and tossed it onto the bed, and then she looked up at the ceiling and Bob saw that her chin was trembling. When she looked back at Bob her eyes had become watery again. She said, "Bobby, what I'm here to tell you is, I hate my life. I just hate it."

And Bob nodded slowly and said, "I get that."

"I know you do."

And he did. He understood the situation this woman was in. He felt the sadness of it as though an outgoing tide moved slowly through him.

"I brought it on myself," she said, sitting partly up and looking at him. He only shrugged. "No, no, I did. I know that." And he shrugged again and shook his head with a small, slow shake.

He almost said, What are you going to do, Pam? But then he understood that she had come here to Maine for him to tell her what to do. And so he said, "Well, Pam, here's what I think you should do." And her eyes quickened, and she sat up straighter on the bed and said, "Tell me what to do, Bobby."

"First, get yourself into a good AA program, and second, decide whether you want to leave Ted or not. Think about the boys. And then think about what it is you want to do with the rest of your life. You're healthy, and you're smart, Pam. You never thought you were smart, but you are. So think about what it is you want from the next fifteen years of your life."

She put a finger near her mouth and nodded slowly. "Okay."

"Find the best AA program in the city, Pam. Just do it."

She nodded, as though she had already thought of that— which she had.

"What about Ted? Did you tell him what you heard with Lydia?"

She looked at Bob with slight disgust. "Of course not. First, I would have had to tell him why I was in the dressing room, but the real reason I didn't tell him—"—and here Pam shifted so that she was sitting up straight against the head-board of the bed—"—is because I don't really care. I don't care, Bob."

"You don't love him."

She looked at Bob for a long time and then she said, "No, I don't."

"Do you respect him?"

She glanced at the wall and then out the window and then back at Bob. "Why in the world would I respect him?"

*

THEY SPOKE FOR almost four hours. The sun had gone down, and Bob was hungry. But he was also— What was he? He was filled with the deepest sensation of loss and also of love, he loved her, and she was no longer his wife. But she was Pam, and as he watched her walking across the room, he thought that just to have her in his life was enough. When he asked her to come to his house for dinner, she said, "No, Bob. No disrespect to Margaret. But she might think I have Covid, and just— Well, thanks, but no."

As he opened the door to leave, Pam called, "Wait! Wait! I wanted to ask you about Lucy Barton. Did she come up here with William?" She walked over to him.

Bob said, "Yeah, she's still here."

"Do you *know* her?" Pam stood with her hand on the edge of the door.

"I do. She's become a good friend."

"You're kidding me! Bob!" Pam put her hand on his arm. "I met her a few years ago at William's birthday party, but I didn't even know I was talking to Lucy Barton! I just thought she was one of William's ex-wives. She doesn't look anything like her jacket photo. But do you think she would do a Zoom for my book club? Oh my God, that would give me so much social stock if I got *Lucy Barton* to come to the book club!"

And then Bob realized that she was still who she was, Pam.

He simply shook his head and said he would see her tomorrow before she left.

IN HIS CAR driving back home, Bob kept shaking his head. Her *book* club! When they had just spent the entire afternoon talking about her—as she had said repeatedly—her insipid idiot friends. Oh Pam, Pam. Pam.

*

MARGARET SAID, "She's not with you?" And Bob said, No, Pam was afraid you might think she had Covid, and Margaret didn't answer, but when Bob said to her "I'm glad I'm married to you," Margaret leaned over and kissed his cheek.

"How was she?" Margaret asked.

Bob said, "She's become an alcoholic."

Margaret held up the wooden spoon with which she had been poking at a pan on the stove and said, "Nobody becomes an alcoholic, Bob. They are *born* alcoholics."

And then Bob remembered that they had had this conversation before, about the Alcoholics Anonymous group that held its meetings in the church. So he said, "Well, she's quit for the moment. She's going to go to AA."

MARGARET HAD A lot to talk to him about. The locksmith in town who was a heroin addict—Margaret had learned this from a parishioner—had some younger man living with him, and the gossip was that the younger man wanted money from the lock-smith, he was trying to blackmail him, and this younger guy was using fentanyl. Also, Elaine Harwood's husband had fallen on the sidewalk and hit his head and was in the hospital, so Margaret had to deal with Elaine, and so on and so forth.

Bob did not tell her anything more about Pam and her drinking and her son who was wearing women's clothes. He listened to his wife. But it went through his head unbidden: the story that Olive had told Lucy about living with a ghost in one's marriage, because he thought: I will tell Lucy about Pam, and she will care.

*

THE NEXT MORNING, as Bob tugged Pam's rolling suitcase behind him to her rental car, Pam said that she was going to Shirley Falls to see Susan before going back to the airport, she had not seen her in years. It made Bob extremely glad to think of Pam and his sister visiting with each other after so many years. "That's wonderful," he said. He and Pam hugged by the car. "What was *wonderful* was seeing you, Bob, oh my God," Pam said, and Bob told her the same.

A few hours later he had gone to have his midday smoke, which he sometimes did in the back parking lot of an old inn that had closed years before and had vines growing all over it. He had just lit his cigarette when Pam called him. "Bobby? I'm calling you from the car. I'm on the way to the airport and I just left Susan. Listen, I don't know if I should tell you this— Well, I'm just going to." She stopped. "Maybe I shouldn't." Bob exhaled his smoke, and then Pam said, "Okay, Helen is dying. She has—at the very most—one month to live, and Jim doesn't want you to know yet, even though he told Susan a week ago. It's her pancreas," she added.

Bob said, "What did you say, Pam?" She repeated what she had just said. And here was what was so interesting: Bob felt nothing. After talking to Pam some more, he hung up, and he felt nothing. Nothing!

AND THEN, of course, as he finally finished his cigarette, it came swooping down and grabbed him by his stomach, it seemed, and he just kept murmuring: No. No, no no. . . .

7

EVERY THURSDAY, Bob took groceries to an old woman named Mrs. Hasselbeck, and so two days after finding out about Helen—and about Jim's not wanting him to know that she was dying—Bob walked up the steps to Mrs. Hasselbeck's house and rang the bell, carrying one grocery bag that contained cat food and peanut butter and apples and bread and orange juice and instant coffee and a pint of gin and a few other things. The gin he brought her only every other week; it worried him, but then he had figured out to water it down so that it was only half a pint of gin she was getting every two weeks, and she did not seem to notice.

During the height of the pandemic he would leave the food on the front steps, but these days he went in—wearing a mask to protect her—and now she stood there hunched over and smiling up at him, her knobby hand holding tight to the top of a chair. There was something oddly elegant about her, in spite of the utter chaos of her small house. She had huge brown eyes in her old face, and high cheekbones. She was so tiny that Bob could have picked her up in one arm, and she said, "You do know, Robert, that Thursdays are my favorite day of the week." She said this every time he went there. And now he said, "Well, they're a pretty great day for me too." He did not mean this, of course. Her house smelled so strongly of cat piss that he could inhale it through his mask, and there were always dirty dishes on the small kitchen table—everywhere, it seemed—and the place was small and dark—

But today her eyes shone vibrantly as she looked up at him and said, "Robert, the most wonderful thing just happened."

He took the groceries from the bag, setting them on a counter cluttered with used tea bags and cups and dirty silverware, and he turned to her and said, "And what was that?"

She moved toward him, her small arms maneuvering from chair top to chair top. "*Robert.* Two women met on the sidewalk out in front of my house this morning." She pointed toward the window. "And I watched them for maybe thirty minutes or more, and they talked and talked and talked, and I had the sense that they didn't know each other that well, but there they were, talking and talking, and I finally went outside and I said, 'You two women have no idea how happy you've made me. Just to watch you.'" She hesitated and then said, "And they were very nice."

"Hey, that's great," Bob said.

"Can you stay a few minutes?" she asked, and so Bob sat down in a chair and he stayed for an hour. Across from him was the clock on the wall, and he thought that time had not moved so slowly since geometry class in high school.

She said what she usually said: She missed her husband terribly (he had been dead for twelve years), and her five boys had all moved away. "*Away,*" she said, with bewilderment on her face. But then she told him something new. She said, "Do you know, Robert, at one point I had all five boys in high school? *Five.*" And then with the most innocent face he had ever seen (he thought), she said, "And they all hated me, and I didn't know why. I still don't know why."

Silence sat in the room with them.

Then Bob said, "Hey, they were adolescents. Adolescents always hate their parents. I wouldn't take it personally if I were you."

She watched him from where she had seated herself on the couch, whose cushions were flattened enough to look as though they had been beaten for years by a broom. Then she said, "Did you hate your mother when you were in high school?"

Bob had never hated his mother.

He said, "Well, I probably wasn't very nice to her. Maybe she thought I hated her." This was not true. He did not say: When you have killed your father, you are always good to your mother.

He moved as though to stand up, and she said, "Robert, I have one favor to ask you."

"Ah, sure," he said.

She went into the bathroom and then found a magic marker in a drawer in the kitchen, and then she moved toward him and handed him what he thought at first was a small pile of rags. But they were her underpants. "Do you mind writing on the back of these a big B so when I put them on I know which is the back and which is the front?"

So he took them, there were four pair—a tremendously off-white color—of roundish underpants, and he finally found the labels, so worn they were hardly there, on the back, and he took the magic marker and wrote a large B on each pair near the top. "There you go." He handed them up to her where she stood over him, watching.

"Thank you, Robert," she said. "I appreciate that. The pair I'm wearing now you can do next week."

And he said, "Sure, no problem."

When he left, he told her to be careful with the gin, as he always did, and she said, Yes, she would be, and she thanked him again.

As he got into his car, he felt a weight so heavy inside he had to sit for a moment behind the wheel, and then he drove away.

8

OLIVE KITTERIDGE HAD been thinking about all the unrecorded lives around her. Lucy Barton had used that phrase
when she first met Olive and heard Olive's story about her
mother: *unrecorded lives*, she had said. And Olive thought about
this. Everywhere in the world people led their lives unrecorded,
and this struck her now. She summoned Lucy Barton again.

"Come in!" Olive Kitteridge yelled when she heard the
knock on the door, and the door opened and Lucy walked in.
"Hello, Olive," she said. She was more relaxed than the first
time she had been there, months ago now, Olive could see that.
Lucy took her coat off and tossed it onto the small couch, then
sat down next to it. "How have you been?"

Olive flapped a hand. "Who cares. Now, as I told you on the
phone, I have another story to tell you." Olive swung her foot
and leaned back in her chair.

"Go, go. I'm ready," Lucy said. She sat forward, her hands
folded on her lap.

Olive nodded. "Okay. There was a woman in town here
named Janice Tucker. I don't suppose you ever heard of her—"
Lucy shook her head. "Well, why would you. She died a few
years ago, before you came to town. Janice used to cut hair. She
cut my hair, she had a nice little business, and she did this from
her home. There was a place between the kitchen and the ga-

rage, and that was her little hair-cutting place. And she had parakeets."

"Parakeets," Lucy repeated.

"That's right. Two cages with two parakeets each in them, and she really liked those parakeets."

"Was she married?" Lucy asked, sitting back, adjusting herself on the stiff couch.

"Yes, she was. But hold that thought. No kids, by the way. And so, one day—oh, this was years ago now—"

"How many years ago?" Lucy asked.

Olive thought about this. "Maybe ten? I still had my car, but I also had my cane. So I went to get my hair cut one day and there was a woman sitting there having her hair cut, and she looked—oh, you know—like a snot-wot, a bit younger than Janice, so maybe forty-five years old."

Lucy rearranged herself, crossing her legs.

"You could tell this snot-wot had once been pretty and still thought of herself that way, though she'd gained weight, is what I thought, and her face was very hard. Now, Janice was pretty in a different way, a plainer way, but Janice was attractive, always had been, I think. So anyway, snot-wot woman started to go a little crazy."

"What do you mean?" Lucy asked, and Olive nodded and said, "I mean, when Janice put her under the dryer the woman started to muss up her hair and said, Not like this, I didn't want to look like this, and she was really quite worked up and you could see it unsettled Janice. Of course it would."

"But what did she want to look like?" Lucy asked.

"Who knows. She was a nut. So she got up with her hair still half wet and she said, 'I want to pay right now,' and Janice took her credit card and in a few moments Nutty Woman left.

"And *then*"—Olive pointed a finger toward the air—"Janice looked at me, white as a ghost, and she said, 'Olive, oh my God, I think I know who that woman was.'"

THE STORY WAS THIS: Janice Tucker's mother had died when Janice was three years old. Janice could not remember her mother except, vaguely, being picked up out of a crib one time. Her father, who was a plumber, married a woman soon after Janice's mother died, and they had three more babies, and Janice's stepmother was never unkind to her particularly, but Janice understood that this woman did not love her. She loved her own kids. For example, one day when Janice was about thirteen years old, Janice didn't like what they were having for supper and said, "I'd rather have dog food," and so her stepmother made her eat dog food for her supper that night. It didn't bother Janice; she sat there and ate it—it didn't taste as bad as you might think, she told Olive—and she felt—though she knew she might be making this up—a kind of quiet pride coming from her father as she sat there eating the dog food.

"Now. When Janice was a senior in high school, she won a full scholarship to a very fancy college in upstate New York," Olive said. "Janice went off to this college very naïve, and her sophomore year there was a philosophy professor who took a liking to her, his name was Jacques Remerin. Well, you know what happened, one thing led to another, and that poor child had no idea what was happening, but of course Janice fell in love with him, and then—poof!—he was done with her. She walked into his office one afternoon and saw that he was done with her, and she was right. Eight weeks the affair had lasted. Except she wouldn't even call it an affair.

"So. She was devastated. So young and stupid, as she said herself. And of course he was ten years older and seemed very worldly. But the point is this: She had been doing very well academically, and that semester she flunked out. She could not concentrate, so she flunked out of college—lost her scholarship, of course—and she said she felt that she could not come home. The college had told her she could try again the next year, but she knew she would never go back. She told me there were very few women professors there at that time, but one woman, a Latin professor who Janice had had, really looked at her, I mean, *looked* at her—according to Janice—when Janice went to return all her library books; Janice did not care for the look that the woman gave her. Janice told me that she could not face her father and try and tell him what had happened, and so she stayed in that little town where the college was—got a small apartment and a job at the bookstore—and took up with some man called Oliver, who had also gone to that college and had also dropped out.

"Oliver was a genius, it turned out, and he was very peculiar, and one day as they were walking back to his apartment, he just started slamming his head against a tree. It bled—his head, I mean—and he said she was making him crazy."

"Why?" Lucy asked, sitting forward on the couch.

"Because—it turned out *he* was crazy. He had a full-blown nervous breakdown; his parents had to come and get him, and when they took him home to the Midwest he had to go to a hospital, and years later Janice figured out that he may have been schizophrenic. Apparently some of these things don't become full-blown until the early twenties when the brain takes its final shape—" Olive swirled a finger about her ear.

So poor Janice came home, and she ended up marrying the nicest man she had gone to high school with; he had no higher education, but he was very kind to her. Olive said, "And he *was* a nice man. Everyone in town thought so. He was in the antique business."

Olive looked out the window and then back at Lucy. "But this is what Janice told me th˙˙ day after Nutty Woman left. Janice said to me, 'Olive, I think my husband likes men.' And I said, What do you mean, he likes men? And she said, 'You know: that he likes men.'"

Lucy said, after a moment, "What did you say to her?"

"I said, Hell, he likes you, everyone knows that. And as long as he is *with* you in that certain way, who cares if he's thinking about . . . horses?"

"Huh." Lucy made a small gesture with her face that indicated she did not think this was a bad answer. After a moment Lucy said, "Okay, but get back to Nutty Woman. How does she fit into this story?"

"Right." Olive nodded. "It turns out that when Nutty Woman showed up, Janice asked her where she came from, and she said she came from upstate New York and ran the development office at that same school Janice had gone to. And Nutty Woman had apparently gone there as a student as well. And Nutty Woman told Janice she was in Maine to go see her son at Parents Visiting Day at a nearby college.

"And when Janice looked at the credit card, it said 'Emily Remerin.' So slowly Janice understood that this woman had probably *married* that same professor who had gone after Janice, and Janice's theory was that he had left her for a younger woman, and that he and his new girlfriend would probably be at the son's thing that day and it was somehow making Nutty Woman crazy."

Lucy took a deep breath and exhaled slowly. "She was probably right. I mean that Nutty Woman's ex-husband *was* probably going to be there with his new girlfriend."

Olive said, "Who knows. But I suspect she was right."

"So what happened to Janice?" Lucy asked.

Olive nodded and swung her foot. "Janice told me that day that every year she would take a trip to Miami alone. She said her husband hated the place, and yet Janice would go there every year alone. For ten days, she said. He encouraged her to do this, said she deserved the break. And Janice said she would watch the families in the pool, and she would watch the really big ships out on the horizon, and they would make her think of her father, since he had been in the Navy before he had her. He had, apparently, loved being in the Navy, and so Janice would watch those ships and think of her father. And watch all the families with their kids. She said she never read magazines, that she had too many magazines in her hair-cutting place, and so she would just sit and watch. And she finally realized that these trips made her lonely."

"Jesus, of course they did!" Lucy said, sitting forward. "We just got back from Florida yesterday. I would hate to be there alone."

Olive did not want to ask about Lucy's trip, she did not care. So she continued, "And then Janice said that she finally realized her husband liked that time alone because of this guy—kid, almost—that worked with him, called Grunt. That it gave him time to be with Grunt alone."

"Grunt?"

Olive shrugged. "Some nickname he had, I don't think anyone ever heard a sound come out of him. But the kid—according
to Janice, who did not know the specifics—had been terribly
abused, and I will tell you, he seemed that way to me. Poor little
dark-haired guy—maybe twenty-five years old—"

"Wait, so you knew him?" Lucy asked.

"Oh, I don't think anybody *knew* him—" Olive paused and
then said, "But I will tell you this, when I moved out of my
second husband's home I called Janice's husband because there
were some antiques I thought he'd like, and he came over with
Grunt, and he was a lovely guy—Janice's husband, that is—
and as he and Grunt took a sofa down the staircase I saw Janice's husband stop and give Grunt a very sweet hug. And poor
Grunt's face stayed just the same. I'm just saying, that's all.

"Anyway." For a moment Olive seemed to have lost her
steam in telling this, and she and Lucy stayed quiet. Then Olive
sat up straighter in her chair and said, "Anyway, Janice's husband died suddenly. Heart thing. And Janice took in Grunt. He
lived with her like a son."

"He did?" Lucy asked.

"Yuh. And then she gave up her hair-cutting thing and a
few years later *she* died, but it turned out she had left the house
to Grunt, and he lives there now, and he works at Walmart. I
saw him a few years ago working there, and I stopped and
asked him to help me find something, can't remember what,
but that place is such a barn you could walk forever, and he
walked me right over to what I needed, such a sweet guy—
who still looked abused, I must say—and I thanked him, and
he just nodded. And he still lives there in Janice's house, keeps
it up."

"God," Lucy said, slowly. "My God, the lives people live."

"Yuh. So that's the story of Janice Tucker."

Lucy was silent for quite a while. And then she said, "She was a sin-eater."

"What did you say?" Olive spoke this loudly.

"I said, she was a sin-eater."

"What in hell is a sin-eater?"

Lucy shook her head slowly. "Some people on this earth eat other people's sins, and that's what Janice did her entire life, starting with her father and her stepmother and then with that professor creep—who, had he behaved that way now, would be outed and fired—and then crazy Oliver that she got involved with after dropping out. She just kept eating people's sins."

They did not speak for a while. This was not interesting to Olive, and after a moment or so she sensed that Lucy realized this, because Lucy said, "That was a great story, Olive. Jesus, what a story."

"I thought you might appreciate it," Olive said. She was tired now.

They sat together in a companionable silence for a while before Lucy finally got up to leave. "Please tell me a story anytime you want to," Lucy said. And Olive said, "I will."

*

BUT BOB!

Poor, poor Bob. The man's heart was breaking.

Ever since he had heard from Pam that his brother's wife was dying and that his brother did not want him to know (!), Bob's heart had been absolutely breaking. He could not understand, and he kept walking around murmuring, Why, why?

Margaret had been kind about the situation, and considering she had never liked Helen, she was especially kind about the fact that the woman was now dying. About Jim, Margaret only had this to say: "I have never understood your relationship with him, Bob. You have allowed him to be so rude to you for your entire life."

"He loves me," Bob said. "And I love him."

Margaret said, "I know. Do I ever know."

*

WITH LUCY FINALLY back in town, Bob called and asked if she could come for a walk, and she said she was at her studio, but she could head over to the river right now. And she was already there as he pulled into the parking lot, standing by the wooden fence, waving to him. As he walked over to her, he thought how small she was seen from this distance, but how when he was with her he did not think of her as small.

"Man, am I glad to see you," he said.

"Me too! I'm so glad you called."

"How was your trip?"

Lucy shrugged. "Fine. William likes warm places in the winter, it was fine. Also, I saw Olive Kitteridge yesterday. She had a great story to tell me. But—you—tell me everything, Bob!"

"First tell me if Little Annie has survived, then I'll tell you what's been going on."

"Bob! She did! She has survived. She dropped almost every leaf, but then this happened: A tiny green sprout grew from her top leaf. Bob!" She hit his arm lightly with her mitten. "Now tell me what's been happening with *you*."

And so they walked, Bob walking more quickly than he usually did. It was still February and a very cold day, but there was no breeze, and beside them the river was frozen except for far out in the middle where the water could be seen moving; there was a gray blueness to the frozen stretches they walked by. Lucy's nose was red from the cold.

"Start from the beginning," she said. So Bob told her first about Pam's visit, and then he told her—here he had to stop walking—about Jim's wife, Helen, who was dying, and that was why Jim had told him not to come to New York in December. Bob put his arms outward. "But why—why in the *world*— didn't he just tell me the truth?"

"Oh God," Lucy said quietly.

He looked at her, aware of the bafflement in his own face, and they continued with their walk. "Bob, I'm so *sorry*! And you love her, right? I know you do. God, am I sorry." And then Lucy began to ask Bob a lot of questions about Jim, starting with their childhood, many questions she asked, and he answered them all. They came to the granite bench and Bob pulled his cigarette out. "I could practically eat this," he said, looking at it before he lit it.

There were small ice floes moving down the center of the river. A group of seagulls perched on a few of the ice floes, and then they flew back up the river and settled themselves on a different set of ice floes and floated downriver again. Bob and Lucy watched this without comment. After a moment Lucy said, "Here's what I think: Your brother Jim is a tremendously frightened man. He's always been frightened. He killed your father and then let you take the blame your whole life. Think of the fear that guy has lived with since he was eight years old. Think of it!"

Bob said nothing, just smoked hard on his cigarette.

"Remember I told you that Olive was a bully and that bullies are just frightened people? Well, that's Jim right there."

Bob looked at her then. "He sure doesn't *seem* like he's scared."

Lucy shook her head slowly. "Bob. You're not listening to me. Your brother is scared to death. And now that his wife is dying, he's probably *beyond* scared to death. And I think—" Lucy held up her mittened hand. "I think he hasn't told you because you make him feel very vulnerable." Lucy looked straight ahead and nodded, as though agreeing with herself. "Susan doesn't make him feel vulnerable because she's Susan and it's a whole different relationship. But you, Bob Burgess, as you would say, just about bring him to his knees. And so he's not ready to tell you yet." Lucy stared ahead for a while, and then she said, "I wouldn't call him. Wait until he calls you." Lucy reached over and tapped Bob's knee. "When he tells you it will make it all *real* to him. That's what I think."

"Why would telling me make it real to him?" Bob asked.

"I suspect that except for Helen and his kids, you're by far the most important person in his life."

"You do?" Bob turned to look at her.

"Yeah, I do. Think about it. Your relationship with him all these years has sewn you together so tightly. The fact that you love him so much just kills him, and it means you *have* to be just unbelievably important to him."

Bob smoked and looked out at the river. "I never thought of that," he said.

"Well, think of it." Lucy crossed her legs.

"I've been thinking about calling Susan and saying I know."

"You could do that. She's just going to feel bad because she told Pam. But she probably told Pam because she needed to tell *somebody*."

"I hear you," Bob said. He inhaled deeply, and slowly the smoke came from his mouth. "I'll call her." They sat in silence for many moments.

HE GLANCED AT her and felt that she was very deep in some thought. When she finally spoke, she said, more slowly than she usually spoke, "Bob, listen. Years ago, when I was small, I have a memory of reading a book, and it had those black-and-white drawings in it, so it was some kind of book of fables, I think. And all I remember is that there was a picture of a man, he was older, and every time you turned the page, he was a little more slumped. Because it was his job in the world to eat people's sins. And I have—my whole *life*—remembered that. That's what the story Olive told me yesterday was about, about a sin-eater." Lucy looked over at Bob thoughtfully. "And that's what you are."

"I don't get it," Bob said.

"I know. But that's what you do. Starting with Jim, you have eaten his sins—unconsciously, of course—and— It's just what you *do*, Bob. Everyone's sins you take on."

"Other than Jim, what are you talking about?"

"Pam. You take on her sins." Lucy nodded slowly. "Look at the people you tell me about when you work at the food pantry. They tell you things. I mean, I'm using the term kind of loosely, but you *absorb* things, Bob. And that old woman who depresses you so much taking her groceries to her."

"I don't know."

"Well, don't think about it," Lucy said. She gave him a

quick smile to indicate their joke. And then she added, "But I see you around town and everyone who has a problem seems to come to you."

They sat quietly while Bob finished his cigarette, and then he stuck the butt back into its pack.

Bob said, "Thank you, Lucy."

"Of course," she said.

9

SUSAN WAS EXTREMELY glad when Bob called her. "Oh Bobby, I was worried that Pam told you—and she did!—and I'm just so sorry about the whole thing. But, Bobby—"

"How did Jim sound when he spoke to you about it?"

"He sounded like Jim, frankly. I mean, he sounded slightly pissed-off, which I guess is normal enough. But, Bobby, she's *dying*, and he just sounded . . . oh, I don't know. He's very upset, clearly. But he's not quite right. Well, who would be quite right."

Bob was sitting in his car with his cellphone to his ear; he was in the parking lot of Walmart, where he had come to get some kind of thing to fix the chimney with. It took him a moment to realize what Susan had just said to him. "What do you mean, not quite right?"

"I don't know, Bob. I really don't. I wish he had called you. I didn't like having the pressure of this news. But I mean, honestly, Bob, he sounded like—sorry—an asshole."

"You mean he sounded like himself."

"That's what I just told you."

"Okay, I hear what you're saying. I'll give him another week and then I'm going to call him. Take care of yourself, Susie."

———

BUT JIM CALLED him that night. He called Bob around ten o'clock, just as Bob was getting ready for bed, and Bob took his phone and went downstairs with it because Margaret was already asleep.

"Did Susan tell you?" was the first thing Jim asked.

And Bob said, No, but Pam told him, because Pam had gone to visit Susan.

Jim's voice was very low, quiet. "It's happening, Bobby."

Bob shut his eyes. "I know."

"She's doing it really well. She got all the kids around her, and she told them very calmly—I mean, she wept, but Jesus Christ, Bob, I keep thinking, When is this going to hit her? But I think it has. And she told me she wants to do it well, and she is."

"Tell her that," Bob said, and Jim said, "Oh, I have."

And then Jim said he was going off his antidepressants.

Bob said, "Jim, *seriously*? Jesus, are you sure you want to do that right now?" And Jim said, Yes, he wanted to be able to feel it, he said ever since he went on the antidepressants a few years ago he hadn't been able to really feel anything deeply. "And I need to feel this," he said.

"Okay, just go off them really slow. Oy, Jimmy."

"I know. I am. I'm not being stupid about it. I'll probably just finally be off them by the time—by the time she's gone."

"Where are you right now?" Bob asked, and Jim said he was in the bedroom, that they had just had a hospital bed brought into the living room for Helen. "She's going quickly," Jim said. And Bob asked about nurses, and they had them, and Bob asked about the kids, and Jim told him. "Larry seems to be having the most trouble."

Then Jim said, "I don't think she wants to see you. She loves you, she really does love you, but she doesn't want to see you. She hasn't even seen her friends, says she doesn't want to, but she'll speak to you on the phone sometime soon." He added, "It's only the kids she wants to see."

"And you," Bob said, and Jim said, "I guess so." And that's when Bob heard Jim's voice start to break.

A number of years before, Helen had almost thrown Jim out of the house because Jim had had a couple of stupid affairs. Later, it was Helen who insisted Jim go on the antidepressants; she said they made him easier to be around. Helen, to Bob's knowledge, had always been kind to Jim, except of course when he'd had his affairs, although even then she—it had seemed to Bob—handled it with some dignity. But this is what had worried Bob: if she would be kind to Jim during her dying. He did not ask Jim directly.

Bob said, "Jim. Listen to me. Are you listening?"

"Yeah."

But it turned out that Bob could not say what he had been going to say—which is that Jim had been a good husband to Helen for years before his screwing up. Bob stopped himself because he did not know if in fact Jim *had* been a good husband to Helen for years. Even before the affairs. How could Bob know what their marriage had been like? And why had Helen insisted on Jim going on antidepressants for the last few years to make him easier to live with?

So Bob said, "Jimmy, you must be feeling so alone right now. But you're not alone. The kids are being nice to you, right?"

"Oh yeah, the girls have been great." Jim paused and added, "I don't think Larry can stand me, though, who knows, I'm not sure he's ever been able to stand me."

"You guys will work that out," Bob said, but he thought: I am lying to Jim. I have no idea if he will work it out with Larry. And I have no idea if he feels alone.

After another moment of silence had passed, Jim said, "Don't worry about finding the right thing to say. I really mean that, Bobby. Honestly. There *is* no right thing to say. It's just good to hear your voice. Shit, I've missed you. I don't know why I didn't let you know. I really don't know why. I guess because it would make it feel real to me, but it's real, all right."

"Jim, you can do this however you want to."

"Thanks, Bobby. Just trying to say I'm sorry." He paused and added, "But I've missed you. Big-time."

"I'm right here. Anytime you need me, call and I'll be there," Bob said.

Jim said, "Thanks. I'm going to hang up now, but thank you."

BOB COULD NOT remember Jim's ever speaking to him so kindly. He sat down on the couch and put his elbows into his stomach, leaning forward. When he went upstairs to bed, he did not fall asleep for hours. It was not until the next day that he remembered Jim saying that to have told Bob would have made it feel real to him, and that Lucy had said that same thing to Bob.

10

AND SO TIME passed by as it does—often strangely: so slowly and then a chunk is gone. March had arrived and there was mud everywhere, it seemed. Certainly in the fields outside of Crosby and in the park in the middle of town and alongside the roads: mud everywhere. Bob Burgess moved unhurriedly as he took his boots off in the foyer, trying to scrape the mud from them. He felt this about himself: that even when he got up in the morning and went down the stairs, he moved down them more deliberately than he used to.

A few weeks before, Helen had finally called him. She sounded weak as she said, "Bobby, you've been *awfully good* to me my whole life, and I love you very much." Immediately tears came to Bob's eyes, he could not believe that she was dying, that they were having this conversation. And she said, "Don't be mad at me that I didn't want to see you. I didn't want to see anyone except the kids, it's not pretty to die."

"That's okay," Bob said.

"Now promise me something," Helen said, and Bob said, "Of course."

"Larry does not like his father very much. And I want you to help him. And help Jim. Jim is going to be a mess, and so is Larry, and so if you could keep that in mind, and help Larry especially." She paused and then said, "And also Jim."

"Of course," Bob said.

"I'm going to hang up now, Bob. I will see you in heaven. I love you very, very much. Oh, and I've planned the funeral—meticulously—so no one has to worry about that."

Bob said, "I love you too, Helen."

And she hung up.

FOR MANY DAYS Bob walked around as though not really here in the physical world. When he went into the grocery store, he would stop and people would bump into him and he would say, "Oh sorry, sorry."

ON ONE SUCH day as he stumbled around the grocery store, he heard his name called out, and it was William. "Bob!" called William, raising an arm above his head to wave to him—Bob saw a person turn to look, because William was so enthusiastic—and Bob walked over to him and said, "Hey, William, how are you?"

"Great," said William. He was wearing thin reading glasses far down on his nose, and his white hair stood up as it usually did. "Just great. Man, this work I'm doing at the University of Maine—" And off he went on his parasites. In a certain way Bob could not believe it. And yet through his fog he understood this to be true, William liked his parasites and his work. His big white mustache moved as he spoke. Finally, William said, "So how are *you*?"

And Bob said, "My sister-in-law is dying," and then William's face changed. He looked hard at Bob and said, "Oh my God, Lucy told me that. I'm so sorry. You're quite fond of her, right?"

And Bob said, "Yeah—she's, well, she's Helen."

William asked how long she had been sick and then he spoke to Bob about the length of time it usually took a person to die of this disease, and in a way, Bob liked that. It made him sort of feel cared for. "So sorry," William said, shaking his head. "So sorry about this, Bob." He pushed his hand through his hair and said, "Where are the pickles in this place?"

After they parted, Bob thought again of how he had told both his wives his memory of saying to his mother that he had never really liked Christmas and how both of them had been kind but not—to Bob's mind—*really* been able to care. And he thought now as he bought a jug of orange juice, That's just how it is, that's all. He thought: God, we are all so alone.

BUT—LUCY. SHE DID not make him feel alone. He realized this as he walked to the register.

Book Two

...

Book Two

I

IN THE FOURTH week of March, the body of Gloria Beach was discovered in a quarry pool outside of Saco, about two hours south of Shirley Falls. There had been warmer weather for a few weeks, and her body was discovered by a hiker walking past the quarry. The body had floated to the top of the water apparently from a car that was pulled out by the state police the next day; the body was badly decomposed, and they had used dental records to identify the body as that of Gloria Beach. The car was the missing rental car from Saco, the car that had allegedly been rented by the woman named Ashley Munroe. There was a photograph of Ashley in the paper. She had bright red hair and a squint. The car had been rented the day that Gloria Beach went missing, and back when the car had not been returned, Ashley Munroe had been accused of auto theft, but her defense—as you might recall—was that her driver's license and her credit card had been stolen, and she had not been charged. And also she had those excellent alibis, having given birth to her baby during this time—right there in Shirley Falls. People had seen her there on the very day the car was supposed to have been rented in Saco.

The car rental place did not have Ashley Munroe on camera; their security cameras only stored things for sixty days, so there was no visual record of her in the place. Also, the cus-

tomer service person who had apparently dealt with Ashley
Munroe at the car rental place had since moved to Florida and
had no recollection of the event.

This time only Matthew Beach's photograph was in the
paper next to Ashley Munroe's. And he still looked unfortu-
nate. The newspaper said that investigations were ongoing. No
one had yet been named a suspect.

*

WE MIGHT WANT to take a moment to wonder who this Gloria
Beach woman was. But the full story of Gloria Beach remains
shrouded in mystery. There are some "facts" as she recorded
them in a journal—in two notebooks she kept at various points
in her life, a journal that only her son Matthew had access to.
The journal would eventually come to Bob Burgess, who
shared parts of it with both Margaret and Lucy; later, Katherine
Caskey, a social worker in town, would have contact with it as
well.

But the "facts" seem to be these: She was born Gloria Labbe
in a very small town called Selby, far north in Maine, an only
child. A photograph—the only known childhood photograph
of her, on the back was written *Gloria 14 yrs*—shows her to be
a short, strikingly attractive girl: She gazes at the camera with
her face tilted down and her eyes looking up. By the age of sixteen she had given birth to a baby boy. Who was the father? We
do not know. But in her earliest journal entries she makes references to an uncle, her father's brother, who would come to visit
on occasion. She writes, "I dread the visits . . . the smell afterward." When she became pregnant her parents reacted poorly,

and this is when we learn that her mother was a drinker, because Gloria writes, "I hate the smell of my mother's drinking more than anything except" (The sentence is not finished.) Her father told her that she was a deep embarrassment, and she writes: "The words sliced through me, I will never forget them." By the age of seventeen Gloria Labbe was living in a motel on the road that went from Selby to Milo; she was given a room at this motel in exchange for working the front desk. She was extremely stressed at this point in her young life: She had a baby to look after, and she would put him in a playpen by the desk during the day. There are also a few references to her having to "please" the owner of the motel so that he would not kick her and the baby out, and she records these incidents with a matter-of-fact yet sorrowful distance. "I know how to do this but it makes me sick each time," she writes.

When Walter Beach walked into the motel one day—he was from Shirley Falls and he had come for a few days to Selby to see an accountant he wanted to have join his firm—he was taken with Gloria's beauty and her child, and with the whole pitiful and touching situation. He married her four weeks later and she moved with him to Shirley Falls along with Thomas, her small son. The very moment she was married she began to gain weight. She refers in her journal to "the sex act," which she hated, and she ate more and more and became quietly hysterical, and then not so quietly. She later gave birth to Diana and Matthew, and very little is said about that. But as her children grew older, she went to work in the school cafeteria. She was aware that she was known as Beach Ball or Bitch Ball by the kids there. She writes, "The more frightened I become the more awful I behave. No one [and this is underlined three times] can

hate themselves more than I do." In a later entry—there appear
to be none for a few years—she refers to Diana's beauty, adding, "But she's tall." She also records being "pathetically" dependent on her husband. When Matthew was ten years old he
became ill with leukemia, and she writes of this with great love,
of giving up her job at the school and devoting herself to her
"Small Angel," as she called him. At this time she lost all the
weight she had gained, because her anxiety—which was different from the anxiety she had suffered previously for so many
years—was such that she could not eat. Almost nothing is said
about Thomas and Diana.

Her husband left her without warning. According to her
journals she was both relieved and devastated, and also confused. But he had a large life insurance policy with her named
as the beneficiary, and he wrote to her that even though they
were divorced she would still receive the money when he died.
"I cried for two hours when I heard that."

That is really all we know of Gloria Beach at this moment.
But the point is that she had her story, as we all have our stories.
And we will return to it in time.

*

SUSAN OLSON, as she sat at her kitchen table on that next morning after Gloria Beach's body had been discovered, looking at
the newspaper that had landed on her doorstep in the plastic
wrap that was still slightly wet from the rain in the early morning hours, said quietly, "Oh my *word*." She stopped eating her
toast and read the article two times. "Oh my *God*," she said.
There was no one with her, she was used to talking out loud to
herself.

But this was a Thursday, and she was to meet Gerry O'Hare—her friend, the former police chief—for coffee later that morning on his porch. She could not wait to discuss this with him.

"Holy, *holy* crap," Susan said softly to herself as she peered at the paper on the table.

*

FORTY-FIVE MINUTES AWAY on the same morning that Susan was reading about Gloria Beach in the Shirley Falls newspaper, here, in the smaller town of Crosby, Bob was having a cigarette. It was a windy day with muted sunlight that was trying to press through the cloud covering, and Bob was standing beside his car in the back parking lot of that same old inn that had gone bankrupt and had vines growing over its windows. Last night his wife had sniffed his shoulder and said, "Bob? Don't tell me you're doing that again. *Please* don't tell me you are smoking again."

And he had lied!

He had lied.

Now Bob thought, Keep moving, so that the smoke wouldn't stick to him, although the wind seemed to twirl itself around and not go in one direction. As he took a step forward, his phone in his coat pocket started to ring and he stepped right into the smoke he had just exhaled, and he thought, You idiot. Meaning himself.

He did not recognize the number. He squinted at it, swiped, and said, "Hello?"

"Bob? Is this Bob Burgess?" It was a woman's voice.

"It is."

There was a pause, and then the woman said, "Bob, this is Diana Beach. We went to school together a million years ago."

Bob closed his eyes briefly. He had read the newspaper article that morning. "Hello, Diana," he said.

The woman said, "Bob, I'm in town, and my brother needs a lawyer. Now."

HE WALKED back and forth, hoping that the wind would get the smoke off him, but he doubted it would, and so he leaned against his car and called the number that Diana had texted him.

It rang and rang and rang and Bob finally hung up.

*

AN HOUR LATER Bob was walking up the steps to Mrs. Hasselbeck's house when his phone rang again, and so he put the groceries down and saw that the number was the one he had called earlier. "Hello?" He saw Mrs. Hasselbeck at the window, ready to open the door, her face filled with gladness. He held up a finger to indicate just one minute, and he heard a man's voice say, "Is this Bob Burgess?"

"It is," Bob said.

"It's Matt Beach, and thank you, Mr. Burgess, I was outside with my dog when you called," said the man "Thank you so much for taking my case. Thank you, Mr. Burgess."

And then Bob understood: He would take the case.

"I'll call you back in half an hour," Bob said, and Matt Beach said, "Thank you, thank you, thank you."

———

MRS. HASSELBECK WAS beaming at him: "Hello, Robert!" And Bob said "Hello," and then he was inside, unpacking her groceries once again, and he said that he was sorry but he could not stay long, and he saw the disappointment on her face and he said, "But I'll stay for a little while."

She told him at great length the funny things her cats had done that week, the apparent dispute they had with each other, and Bob could not stand stories about cats, but he sat there and said, "What a thing."

She had apparently not remembered the time—weeks ago—that she had asked him to write the letter B on the back of her underpants, and he did not remind her that she had one more pair—the pair she had been wearing—which needed the B; he did not want to embarrass her. But as he finally stood to leave, she said, "Robert, my oldest boy called me last night! He lives in Oregon, and he's heard of that psychiatrist, what's his name, you know—the Beach man—Thomas Beach, the older brother of the guy who killed his mother here in Shirley Falls. My son read about the case."

Bob turned and said, "It's in the Oregon press?" And she said, "No, my son read it online because a friend here told him about it. And Greg, my son, wanted to know if I knew of the case. And I said, Only what I know from the papers." She beamed up at him with her shiny large brown eyes. "He told me that the guy, Thomas Beach, the psychiatrist, has a wonderful reputation."

*

AS BOB WAS driving to Shirley Falls to see Matt Beach later that
morning, his sister, Susan, was sitting on the front porch of
Gerry O'Hare's house and they were talking about Bitch Ball.
Gerry was wearing sweatpants with his white socks and
flattened-in-the-back moccasins, and also his blue cap. Susan
was saying, "I don't understand the mechanics of it. I mean,
how does an old woman end up in a car in a quarry? I mean
literally, how does that happen?" A huge stack of old newspapers sat in the corner of the porch, and by the corner near the
door were various boots of Gerry's, rubber boots and work
boots. Above them along the wall were cobwebs weaving a
light lace.

Gerry said, "Well, whoever did it probably put her body in
the passenger seat and drove the car to the edge of the quarry,
and then—most likely—the person took a big stick and stuck it
through the front door onto the gas pedal." Gerry was wearing
a fleece vest this morning, unzipped. He stuck one hand into a
pocket and took a sip from his coffee with the other hand.

"Really," Susan said slowly, shaking her head in quiet
amazement. But then Susan said, "Remember that woman who
did that to two of her kids, I can't remember where it was, but
somewhere in the country, huge national news, drove her two
kids into a lake."

"Oh yeah, yeah, I know what you're talking about."

"Wait! That woman blamed it on a Black man, do you remember that?"

Gerry tilted his head. "She did? Oh, you're right, she did.
Jesus, that was foul stuff."

Gerry had been planning on asking Susan if she wanted to
have dinner with him some night, but—oddly—the words
would not come from his mouth. He pondered this. And then it

came to him: Susan had an innocence that somehow protected her. She did not understand that a man might want to have dinner with her. But he did.

Susan said, "You know what I was thinking the other day? I was thinking about when Zach got into so much trouble." Zach was Susan's son. "Those were horrible days." She sipped from her coffee mug. "Just horrible," she said.

Gerry remembered those days well from back when he was the police chief in Shirley Falls. Zach had thrown a pig's head through a storefront Somali mosque in town. A really screwed-up strange guy, Zach had been back then. It had been a truly awful thing for the Somali community, and Gerry had felt very sorry for them, but also for Susan throughout the whole ordeal; her ex-husband was the one who had been filling Zach with that kind of hate. "But he's all straightened out now," Gerry said.

Susan nodded. "Yeah. Yup. I think he might marry his girlfriend, Kelly." She stood then and swiped with one hand at the cobwebs above his head. Then she flicked her hand trying to get the cobwebs off and sat back down again. "Whoa, that mother who drowned her kids, trying to blame it on a Black man. It was in the South, I think I remember now."

Gerry was about to say, It could have been right here in Shirley Falls, but he did not say that because of what Zach had done fifteen years earlier to the Somali community. So he only said, "Well, you like Kelly, so that would be good."

And then they spoke of Gerry's kids: One was a state trooper in New Hampshire, the other had moved to Massachusetts and was working as an investigator of insurance fraud.

Again, Gerry opened his mouth to ask Susan if she wanted to have dinner with him—it had touched him, her removing the cobwebs; there was an intimacy, he felt, to the gesture—but

Susan had just remembered something about state troopers and was telling Gerry how her brother Jim—the famous one, years back—had put a state trooper on the stand one time and just blown him up. "So to speak," Susan said.

And Gerry remained quiet. But he took his cap off and placed it on the small table beside him.

2

MATTHEW BEACH'S HOUSE, to remind, was on the outer edge of Shirley Falls, two miles down on the end of a narrow road where the family had always lived. Diana Beach was not staying there with her brother; she was staying at the hotel in town by the river. She had wanted to accompany Bob on his visit to see Matt, but Bob had said no.

As Bob drove along the road his heart was heavy. He was not sure why he had agreed to represent the man, but—again, only partly consciously—it seemed to have something to do with the fact that Bob had for most of his life thought he had killed his father, and this man had perhaps killed his mother. Bob steered the car carefully along the narrow road; it was potholed and muddy, and you would not think that anyone lived at the end of it. Evergreens and bare trees leaned above his car as he drove. But then there was the house: a medium-size white house, three stories high, whose paint had long ago been waiting for a new coat, and the shrubs in front of the windows had not been clipped for years. A straggly forsythia bush wagged in the wind, its branches skinny and bare, close to where Bob parked his car.

FROM BEHIND THE house came a big black dog, and the dog barked with a kind of hysteria as Bob stepped from the car.

After a moment, Matt Beach emerged from his house through the side door and tried—with no effectiveness—to call the dog off.

Bob said, above the barking, "It's okay. My sister used to have a dog who barked all the time, no problem."

"You sure? Well, come in." Matt Beach was a small man, short and thin, with graying hair. He wore black glasses that appeared too big for his face, and he was wearing jeans that looked filthy and a T-shirt that had a rip from the neckband partly down one side.

Inside, the house was dark from all the trees surrounding it and the shrubs that pressed against the windows and from the fact that there was no sun. Dirty dishes were piled in the sink. "Sorry about the mess, not used to having company," Matt said, his hand fluttering through the air.

The guy was killing Bob. He saw immediately an innocent face, but he knew from experience that this was not a legal term. *Without guile* is what went through Bob's mind. But the man was tired, Bob saw this, he had gray circles beneath his eyes, and he was stifling a yawn.

WITH THE DOG still barking outside, Bob sat at the man's dining room table, which was covered with papers and unopened envelopes, and Bob quickly understood: This was a fellow who could not remotely organize himself.

In the dim light, Bob said, "Matt. What did you tell the state policemen who came here?" The house held a weariness within it, and Bob felt a shudder go through him; he did not want to be here.

Matt said that he had told them about the last time he'd seen his mother. Which was on November fourth. Matt had gone to the grocery store; it was a Friday—he often went early in the evening on Fridays to get groceries for the following week. He was at the grocery store maybe forty-five minutes, he wasn't sure—and when he came home his mother was not there.

"What did you do then?" Bob asked.

"I freaked. I mean, I kind of couldn't believe it." Matt's face looked really surprised as he recalled this. "I went outside, I went out and kept calling to her, but I knew she couldn't walk far, at that point she really couldn't walk much at *all*. So I called the police."

The police had come over and looked around with their big flashlights and filed a report, and then Matt had called his sister, who didn't answer, but when she finally called him back, she sounded very upset.

Bob asked, "What about the cops who came over after her body was discovered? When did they come here?"

"Yeah, two days ago. They came and told me they'd found my mother. They were super nice to me. And then as they were about to leave, one of them pulled out this piece of paper. Hold on, let me find it." Matt looked around the table and then pushed a piece of paper toward Bob. Bob saw that it was a search warrant. Matt said, "They said something about taking my computer. And they took it."

Bob glanced over the search warrant. "They took your computer?" Bob thought: *Fuck.*

"Yeah." Matt looked at Bob with bewilderment on his face.

"What's on your computer, Matt?"

"Nothing," Matt said. "I mean, I have an account with Amazon to get things, but I never bought much from them. I don't have a Facebook page or any of that stuff. I never email. Truthfully? Mostly what I did on my computer was to play Solitaire."

Bob sat, considering this.

Outside, the wind was picking up, and against the window of the dining room a bare shrub squeaked. Matt said, "But sometimes I would write a letter to myself or something like that. Because my mother would be annoying me and so I would write about that on my computer."

"Did you ever write that you wanted her dead?" Bob asked quietly.

"No. I don't think so. I just wrote that she was making me a little crazy. But just sometimes."

Bob stood up and went to a lamp in the corner of the room; he switched it on and nothing happened. "Turn it again," Matt said. So Bob turned it two more times and the lamp went on. He seated himself once more at the table, his shoulders thrust forward. "Did they take your cellphone too?"

"I don't have a cellphone," Matt said.

"You don't have a cellphone?" Bob asked.

"No." Matt looked down at his lap and then back up at Bob, and he said tiredly, "Look, I don't really have any friends or anything at this point. And I don't have a cellphone. Is that really that weird?" His question seemed to be an honest one.

"Well, for a guy your age not to have a cellphone might be strange, but it's certainly no crime." Bob noticed the water-stained wallpaper behind Matt; it was dark green with birds on it.

"When I told them I didn't have one, I saw one of the cops

look over at the other. And then I realized they were probably just *trained* to be nice to me."

"They are. Exactly." Bob sat back.

THEY SAT IN silence for a moment and then Matt said, "One of the cops asked if my mother had a will."

"Did she?"

Matt's eyebrows went up. "I said I didn't know, because I didn't. It never occurred to me that she might have a will." And then Matt said, "But she did. I haven't told the cops that I found it. I mean, I just found it last night, because after they asked, I got to thinking, and after looking around I discovered it tucked far back in a drawer in her room."

"Can I see it?"

Matt got up and went into his bedroom, and he came back and handed Bob a will; it had been signed ten years earlier. The will had not been prepared by a lawyer; Bob recognized the standard form of a will that people could do by themselves, and this was the case with Gloria Beach's will. But it looked legitimate to Bob; it had the witnesses' signatures and so forth. The will left Matt one hundred thousand dollars from his father's life insurance policy; Gloria had been the beneficiary of her ex-husband's life insurance, and now it was Matt's. The will also named the bank she had put the money into and left Matt the house and an additional fifty thousand dollars from his mother; that was what she had.

"Oy," said Bob. He put the will onto the table in front of him. "Did you know she had that much money? That your father's life insurance money was coming to you?"

"Why did you say 'Oy'?" Matt asked, and Bob looked up at him.

"It's Yiddish. Years ago I worked at the Legal Aid Society in New York, and there were many people who worked there who were Jewish and the phrase just stuck in my head. So I say it."

"Okay," said Matt.

"Did you know this money was coming to you?" Bob asked.

Matt said, "Not in a million years. But I did know that my father had a life insurance policy and that when he died my mother got the money. I sort of remembered her telling me that, but I never, ever thought it was so much. Or that it would be coming to *me*."

Bob thought: That hundred-thousand-dollar policy must be worth a lot more now; Matt's father had died so long ago. He said, "Do you know the value of the policy now?" And Matt just looked at him with apparent puzzlement. Bob said, "Do you have statements from the bank?"

Matt glanced at the piles of papers on the table and shrugged. "No idea. If it came to my mother, I never opened it."

"Tell me about your employment history," Bob said.

Matt said he had worked at the ironworks, starting when he was twenty, for thirty years; he had retired when he was fifty to be there more for his mother; his mother had been living in an apartment, but then she came back to the house so that Matt could care for her. He said, "I figured I'd apply for Social Security when I'm sixty-two, I'm only fifty-nine right now." He yawned openly, then said, "Sorry, I haven't been sleeping since they found her."

"So what have you been living on?"

"My savings, my pension. And my mother. She would write

me out a check every month for three hundred dollars." He paused, then said, taking off his glasses and rubbing his eyes, "She was sort of cheap. She made me take coupons to the store each time I went." And then he added, "But she hadn't been raised with much money at all, so you can understand why." He put his glasses back on and looked around and said, "This house was paid for in full years ago, back when my father was still living here. My father had a successful accounting firm. So we didn't have a mortgage or anything."

"What was he like?" Bob asked, and Matt only shrugged.

BOB OPENED HIS laptop and typed some notes into it. Then he looked at Matt and said, "Listen. About the will. Let's pretend for a moment that you and I did not have that conversation."

"What do you mean, you mean *lie*?" Matt asked.

"No, not lie." Bob felt offended. "I just mean we're going to let it sit there for a while and you are not to mention it to anyone until I tell you to."

"All right." Matt gave a small shrug.

After a few moments, Bob said, "Can you tell me about your childhood? How did you feel about your mother?"

"I loved her," Matt said, and then he added, "She could be a little difficult at times, but I loved her. She saved my life, you know. When I was ten years old, I had leukemia and she saved my life."

"How did she save your life?" Bob asked, sitting forward in the chair.

"She took *care* of me. And it seemed only right that I would take care of her too." He shook his head. "But my sister hated her. And I haven't heard from my brother in *ages*, he moved to

Oregon. He's my half brother, you know. My mom had him when she was sixteen, but then my father married her when Tom was almost two years old."

"Who was the father of Tom?" Bob asked, and Matt shrugged. "Dunno," he said.

"You don't know?"

"Nope."

"Does your brother know who his father is? Was he ever curious?"

Again, Matt shrugged. "No idea."

Bob typed these details into his laptop.

Matt looked around the room and he finally said, quietly, "In the last few years, it was almost like taking care of a baby. I've never *had* a baby so I don't really know, but I would, you know, change her, feed her, take her into the shower."

Bob waited but Matt did not continue, he just looked down at his fingers, which only now did Bob notice had been picked raw, each of Matt's fingertips was red. Bob said, "Okay. No more talking to anyone without me. Understand?" And Matt nodded.

"CAN I LOOK around your house?" Bob pushed his chair back. "Remember that I'm your lawyer. I am on your side."

"Sure, sure." Matt stood up quickly and held out his hand in a gesture to indicate that Bob could go anywhere.

IT WAS ON the second floor that Bob came across the paintings. Two sizable, connected rooms appeared like a painter's studio.

There were two easels set up, and on each easel was a large canvas of a nude pregnant woman. "*Jesus,*" Bob said. "You're *good.*" The paintings were done in different colors, and the figures, with their large middles, were really things of beauty. Leaning along the walls were more paintings, each done in a different stage of a woman's pregnancy.

"Seriously? Do you think so?" Matt asked.

"I'm very serious. These are fantastic, Matt." Bob almost said that they should be in a gallery in New York, but he did not say that—although he could easily picture them there. He kept staring at them: They were sort of abstract, the women's faces not done with realism, the bodies not done with realism, but they were, to Bob, stunning. He looked carefully and understood that a variety of brushstrokes had been used, and the colors were subtle yet astonishing. "Where did you learn to do this?" The room smelled of oil paint and turpentine and seemed to have a freshness that the rest of the house so distinctly did not.

Matt went over to the corner of the room and showed Bob a tall stack of large books each about a different painter. The books were clearly old, their covers were torn. Matt said that for years he had studied what the artists did and how they did their different strokes, and then he had practiced, it had been his obsession. "Has anyone ever seen these?" Bob asked.

Matt looked puzzled. "No. My mother wouldn't look at them because they were nudes. Oh wait, yeah, my sister has seen them. She's always been nice about them. You know, encouraging to me."

"Nobody else?"

"No. Well, just the models, and they don't really care."

———

A SMALL BEDROOM DOWNSTAIRS, right next to Matt's bedroom, was the room his mother had lived in. Even now, so
many months later, Bob detected a smell: not of urine, exactly,
but a smell of decay, is what went through his mind. The single
bed was carefully made up, but when Bob opened the closet
door there were no clothes in there.

Matt said, "I threw it all away. It just spooked me out after a
while seeing her stuff, so I finally threw it away. There wasn't
much." He added, "I just kept hoping she'd come home, but I
somehow knew she wouldn't, so I threw her stuff away."

Back at the dining room table Bob opened his laptop again.
"Matt?" He felt uncomfortable with this question. "Ah, Matt,
do you have *any* friends?"

And the poor man looked down right away. He said, quietly,
"I didn't really have any time for friends all these years with my
mother."

"Right," said Bob. "But any of the guys you worked with at
the ironworks? Anyone who could give me an idea of what a
good guy you are? Maybe an old girlfriend or two?"

Matt looked up and gave a small smile. "Sure." He looked
around the room and then finally said, "Fred LaRue. Also,
Johnny Tibbetts." And then, after a long moment, he said, "I
didn't really have any girlfriends. But I sort of went out with a
couple of women years ago. My mother liked them for a while,
but then she didn't."

"Why didn't she like them?"

"Who knows." Matt sat with his shoulders slumped and
then he yawned. "I think they both moved away, though." His

eyes watered from the yawn, and he removed his glasses again and rubbed his eyes.

"What were their names?" Bob asked, and Matt told him, and Bob typed the names into his laptop. Then, as he stood up to go, he said, "Matt, do you have a gun in the house?"

Matt looked surprised but said immediately, "Yeah, I have a rifle."

Bob sat back down. "Okay, I need to know. When was the last time you shot the gun?"

Matt looked blank for a moment and said, "A few weeks before my mother disappeared. Actually, my sister shot it. She was up from Connecticut, and she shot it because my mother saw a raccoon outside her window and she always hated raccoons and she kept mentioning it, getting more agitated, and my sister said to me, 'Matt, would you take your gun and fucking kill that raccoon?' But I didn't want to, so Diana did. She opened the window and shot it, and then I went outside and shot it again to make sure it was dead. God, the poor thing."

"Where do you keep the rifle?" Bob asked.

Matt said, "In the closet in my bedroom." After a moment he said, "You want to see it?"

Bob nodded. He went into Matt's bedroom and saw, in the closet, the rifle lying across the top of a shelf high up.

"And your sister knows it's there? Is that where she got it to kill the raccoon?"

"Yeah. That's where she took it from."

"Is it loaded right now?"

"Yeah," Matt said again. "Is that a bad thing?"

"You have no plans on using it, right?"

"Right."

"Well, I'd unload it," Bob said, and Matt said with a small shrug, "Okay," and they walked out of the room together. "So that was the last time your sister saw your mother? A few weeks before she disappeared?" Bob turned to ask this.

"Yeah," Matt said, looking down. He shook his head slowly, and when he looked up at Bob his eyes were wet. "You know what hurts me the most? God, this just *hurts* me." And he sank down into a chair back in the dining room. "That my mother must have been so scared when she was taken." Matt drew a hand across his nose and his eyes. "She would have been so *frightened,* and that's what hurts me so much. To think of her so small, and so scared, being driven away."

Bob waited, sitting back down in a chair himself.

Matt finally said, "I used to sort of wish Diana wouldn't come. She didn't come much. But she made things worse every time just because they hated each other so much."

"Why did they hate each other so much?"

Matt looked away and said nothing for many moments. He kept running his hand through his hair; he was no longer crying. He put his glasses back on and said, "Well, my father always liked Diana, and my mother hated that he liked her more than he liked my mother. Diana was always pretty, you know. I think my mother resented that." He still did not look at Bob. He raised his shoulders and said, "They just hated each other."

AS THEY WALKED toward the side door of the house, Matt said, "Ah, listen. You should probably know." He pointed upstairs to where the studio was. "One of those models was Ashley Munroe."

3

AT THE VERY same time that Bob had gone to see Matt Beach, Olive Kitteridge was sitting in her wingback chair waiting for Lucy Barton to show up. Of all things, Lucy had called Olive and said, "Olive, now *I* have a story to tell *you*!" And Olive had said to come over anytime, and so today was the day Lucy was going to tell her own story to Olive.

There was a rap on the door a little before ten o'clock and Olive yelled, "Come in!" and in came Lucy; these days she wore a puffy black winter coat, which she took off right away. She was wearing a thick black sweater and sat down on the small uncomfortable couch. "Hello, Olive," she said, with a smile that made Olive feel warmly toward her.

"Hello, hello," said Olive. "Now. Tell me your story."

Lucy nodded. "Okay," she said. She unzipped the big zippered boots and took them off and said, "Sorry, I should have taken these off earlier," because there were small drops of brown water on the floor, but Olive waved a hand and said "Forget it," and so the boots stayed on the floor next to Lucy's feet; she was wearing one red sock and one blue, Olive noticed.

"Now." Lucy looked over at Olive, her legs were crossed, and she said, "Okay, so I had to go to Washington, D.C., for a gig last week."

"A what?" Olive asked, leaning toward her.

"A gig. An event. I had to do an event in D.C."

"What was the event?" Olive asked, and Lucy sighed and said, "Oh, it was just the stupidest thing. I sat in a huge auditorium and only five people were there. Oh Olive, it was so stupid." She waved a hand as though to dismiss it.

"Five people in a huge auditorium?"

"Yeah. I mean, it was also Zoomed to people, oh, who knows. That's not the story. The story is this."

Olive sat back in her chair.

"I took a train from New York to Washington, and I met this *man* on the train." Lucy looked straight at Olive.

Olive had a reaction to this.

Olive thought: Lucy, honestly, you are too old to be boy-crazy. Lucy already had Bob Burgess—remember we have mentioned before that Olive believed those two to be in love—and Lucy also had her ex-husband, William. And she was still walking around looking for men? And only five people showed up to see her? Some small rearrangement was going on in Olive's mind about this woman.

"Olive, it was a strange thing. But— Okay. So, I'm sitting in the Red Cap area at Penn Station—"

"The what area of Penn Station?" And now Olive was afraid she would not be able to follow this story.

"Oh, the Red Cap area, where if you need special help they take you down to the train early."

"Why do you need special help?" Olive asked.

Lucy seemed surprised. "I don't. But if you tip these men, these Red Cap people, they'll get you on the train before everyone else. And of course, some of the people really *do* need extra help, I mean they might be in a wheelchair or something. But

some people just do what I do, which is to go down to the train
that way because it's so much less confusing than waiting in
some long line at the last minute when they finally say the gate
number."

Olive said, "Go on. So you met this man."

"Well, I *noticed* this man, who also came to the Red Cap area
and sat down. And there was nothing about him that distin-
guished him in any way. Nothing. He might have been fifty-five
years old, I really don't know. But as I glanced at him, I
thought—I just kind of thought this—I like you. Then he got
up and threw something away and sat down again. He was a
tiny bit slumped over, wearing glasses, not one thing unique
about him at all. But I thought: I like you. That's all. But it was
interesting to me—after—that I had even thought that.

"So they tell us to get ready, and we all followed a Red Cap
guy down this elevator, all squished in together, and I saw that
this fellow and I were the only people wearing masks. Anyway,
the point is: It turned out we were sitting next to each other in
the quiet car. You know, they reserve seats now."

"The what car?" Olive asked. She was confused by many
parts of this story.

"Oh, the quiet car, where you're not allowed to talk or to be
on your cellphone. And his seat was by the window and my seat
was by the aisle, and he said something about wishing *his* seat
was the aisle, and I said, Oh, I'll sit by the window, no problem,
and he said he liked to sit by the aisle so that when he got up he
didn't have to bother anyone, and I told him I knew just what
he meant, that's why I always preferred to sit on the aisle, in
case I had to get up, but I told him it was no problem, I'd sit by
the window. So I did."

Olive watched her. Lucy's face looked intense as though deep into her memory of this.

Lucy continued, "And after I got settled, I said to him, Well, I'm going to move past you in about an hour because I'll have to go to the café car, and he said, Oh, that's okay. Then he said, 'I'll split my lunch with you, if you'd like. But I won't split my halva,' and we sort of laughed. I have no idea what halva is, by the way. And when the conductor came by, I had to stick my phone in front of this man's face so that the conductor could read the ticket off my phone, and I said, Sorry to stick that in front of your face, and he said, Oh, that's okay."

Olive was about to say: I thought you weren't supposed to be talking in this quiet car, but she did not say it.

"Then he took out his lunch from a paper bag. And, Olive, he had all kinds of sliced meats prewrapped in cellophane from some deli probably, and a plastic container of mixed fruit, and then another plastic container of just *grapes,* and then a plastic container that had HALVA written on it with a magic marker. But he didn't eat his lunch, he just sat there with it. So I said, Go ahead and eat, because I won't be getting out past you for an hour, and he said, Oh, okay, and so he started to eat. He'd obviously—I think—been waiting for me, so he ate and ate and ate, and then he put the wrappers and the containers back in his paper bag and the train moved along. And after a while I went to the café car and got hummus and some water, and when I got back, I could just tell he was thinking: That's all she's going to eat? But of course we couldn't talk because we were in the quiet car.

"But it felt like we were talking, it's hard to explain. I mean, when I looked out the window and saw how swollen the rivers and inlets were with all the rain, I felt that he was noticing this too, and it was sort of like we commented on these swollen waters together. That kind of thing.

"And then, Olive— It was so strange. I thought: I love him! Because I did. You know, I used to know a writer who wrote something about looking around every room she was in and thinking: If I was caught in a bunker with these people, which one would I want to have sex with? And I thought of that. I didn't want to have sex with him, but I thought: If we were in a place of real danger, you are the person I would want to hold on to. And I could sort of feel his arms around me, very comfortably."

Now Olive was simply put off. A friend who talked about who she would have sex with if they were all stuck in a bunker? And Lucy was so— Olive didn't know what, but she was disappointed in the woman.

"This never happens to me, by the way," Lucy said, uncrossing her legs and crossing them again the other way. "But it did, and I thought again, with even more clarity: Why, I love this man!

"And then he got off at Baltimore. He just had the bag his lunch had been in and also something in a frame that was partly wrapped in bubble wrap, and he brought that down in a bag with two handles, and sat down again waiting for the train to stop, and I said, 'Well, it was nice sitting with you'—we could talk quietly at that point because the train was stopping—and he said, 'Yeah, it was so nice.' And then he said, 'I'm no photographer, but you want to see a picture I took?' And I said, Oh yes. So he brought out his phone and showed me this picture. He said it was daybreak and the sky in the picture was purple as

the sun broke through and it was in the country and there was a
bird sitting near the front of it, and I said, 'Oh, that's just *beautiful*!' Then I asked where had he taken it, and he said, 'A field
near where I live. And look at that bird. That bird just kept sitting there!' And I said again it was just an absolutely gorgeous
photo, and he looked at me and said, 'Yeah, I sent it to my
mother.'"

Lucy shook her head slowly. "I mean, Olive."

"Do you think he was married?" Olive asked this after a
moment.

"No," Lucy said. "He had no wedding ring, and he seemed
the kind of man who would have worn one if he was. His phone
went off a couple of times and he hurried to silence it, I did notice that. No idea who was calling him. Maybe his mother. So
anyway, he stood up and we wished each other well, you know,
and as he walked past the window of the train, I saw that his
jeans looked like he could have come from Maine, and he had a
large low-slung stomach that I hadn't noticed before."

After a moment she looked again at Olive and said, "But I
loved him. And he loved me."

OLIVE DIDN'T KNOW what that remark meant about the jeans
that could have come from Maine. She finally said, "Did he remind you of Bob Burgess?"

Lucy said simply, "No, he wasn't like Bob at all. He just was
whoever he was."

"And you fell in love with him."

"*No!*" Lucy said this vehemently. "No, you're missing the
point!"

Olive said nothing.

And then Lucy said, "How often has that happened to you? That you sit by a stranger—without even really talking—for a few hours, and you realize that you love him?"

Olive thought about this, and she said, "Never."

"That's my point." Lucy said this quietly, with a certain kind of defeat.

"Is that the whole story?" Olive asked.

"Yeah," Lucy answered. She didn't look at Olive, and Olive could sense her disappointment. But Olive was disappointed as well. And she didn't know how she would tell this story to her friend Isabelle Goodrow later this afternoon when Olive went to visit her.

After a long moment Lucy looked over at Olive and said, "Let me try another one. It's not very long."

"Go right ahead," Olive said.

"Okay, so the last time I was in New York, I hailed a cab near where our little place is, it's on a big two-way street, and this cab across the street stopped, but the sun was in my eyes and I couldn't tell if his white light was on—which indicates he's free—and other taxis drove by me on my side of the street but they were all full. But the guy across the street waited for me, it was not a short wait, I needed the light to finally change, and it did. So when I got into his cab I said, 'Thank you for waiting.' "

"Go on," Olive said.

"And he was young, no more than thirty years old, I think. He was wearing a mask, not all of them do anymore, and he had a woolen hat pulled low on his forehead and he seemed kind of tired, I mean he was hunched over slightly, and he was small, and as we pulled into the traffic he said to me—sort of quietly, but really sincerely, 'How has your day been so far?'

"And I almost said, Oh fine, but it hadn't really been fine, and something about the way he asked me I thought he deserved an honest answer, so I said, 'Oh you know, not that great,' and then I said to him, 'How has your day been?' And he said, 'I'm just really hungry.'

"It was about one-thirty, and I said, 'I get it. I'm sorry.'

"And then we drive through all this heavy traffic in what I felt was a very companionable silence, and then we got to where I needed to go, and I said, 'Just pull over wherever it's safe for you to stop, and I'll get out.' So he pulled over and I paid him and tipped him, and I said, 'I hope you can have your lunch soon.'

"And he turned to look at me then, these enormous brown warm eyes, and he said, 'God bless you.' But he said it—oh how can I tell this—like he was giving me a benediction or something, and I said thank you, but then I realized that wasn't enough, so I said, 'God bless you, too,' and he smiled a little behind his mask, and he said, his brown eyes so warm, 'I will see you again.' And I was so surprised, and I said, 'Oh I hope so, that would be lovely.'

"And that was that. It took me about five full minutes to realize he had really made my day. I mean, you know, he was sort of touched."

"Touched? You mean he was crazy?" Olive asked.

"No, I mean he was touched by God."

Olive rolled her eyes. "I don't believe in God. That's all rubbish," she said firmly.

"Okay, but think of this, Olive. If God is love, then this man was touched by God."

Olive rolled her eyes again.

"And maybe you don't believe in God—which is fine, I

don't care—but you have been loved. And you love. You love your friend Isabelle Goodrow."

"Yes, I do, you're right about that," Olive said.

Lucy gave a small shrug.

And then it came to Olive; she had an understanding. She said, "Lucy, you're a lonely little thing."

Lucy looked up at her quickly. She said, "Who is not lonely, Olive? Show me one person."

Olive said, "Plenty of people. All the snot-wots who live here and gather every day in the lounge for their glass of wine with each other. They're not lonely."

"How do you know?" Lucy bit on her lower lip, and then she said, "How do you know what those people think about in the dark when they wake up in the middle of the night?"

Olive had no answer for her.

Lucy stood up and pulled on her coat. "Those are my stories," she said, and then bent down to put her boots back on. "But you're right. They are stories of loneliness and love." Lucy stepped into the tiny kitchen for a moment and returned with a paper towel and she bent down and soaked up the drops of water on the floor left from her boots. Then she picked up her bag and said, "And the small connections we make in this world if we are lucky."

And then to Olive's amazement, Lucy said, smiling at her with a gentleness on her face, "And I feel that way about you. A connection. Love. So thank you." She moved toward the door.

Olive said, "Wait." As Lucy turned, Olive said, "Well, phooey. I feel connected to you too. So *there*." She stuck out her tongue.

Lucy's face opened in a full smile. "Bye-bye for now, Olive Kitteridge."

Olive raised a hand over her head. And the woman was gone.

Olive sat for a very long time in her chair. It was a really, really long time that she sat there.

And then she called her friend Isabelle and she said, "Have I got a story for you."

4

IT JUST SO happened that in March a woman in the attorney general's office had returned to practice after a maternity leave, and she was eager to get back to work. She had—before going on leave—unsuccessfully prosecuted a man who had allegedly killed a young girl and disposed of her body in a garbage bag. The woman's name was Carol Hall and she had worked in the attorney general's office for nine years and was known to be the best they had. The unsuccessful prosecution had rankled her, and she had decided to take the Matthew Beach case and do it well. Bob Burgess had heard this the day before, and thinking of this now, he thought: Oh Christ.

SHORTLY AFTER BOB left Matt's house and was back on the main road to Shirley Falls, he pulled into a gas station parking lot and made a few phone calls. First he called the attorney general's office's criminal division, getting Carol Hall on the phone. He told her he was taking the case of Matthew Beach. "Good," she said. He told her that the seizure of Matt's computer was unconstitutional and that he was going to file a motion demanding it back. "Fine," Carol Hall said. But then she said, "As soon as they ping his cellphone and find out he was in

Saco that day—and they will find that out any minute now—
I am bringing him in and charging him with murder."

"Good luck with that, he doesn't have a cellphone," Bob
said.

He heard her receive this, and then she said, "We'll be in
touch, Bob Burgess."

Then Bob called the state police and then the local police
and then the sheriff, and he said that he was taking the case of
Matthew Beach, and no one was to speak to Matt outside of
Bob's presence. All of them, he noticed, answered with their
dry, almost sardonic Maine tones. "Okay then, Bob." Bob told
them all that he was going to file a motion that anything on the
computer could not be used as evidence and that the computer
should be immediately returned to Matt. And they said, basi-
cally, Okay, do what you need to do.

And then he called Diana Beach and told her he had seen
Matt, that he was taking the case. "Oh Bob, thank you *so* much.
I feel *so* much better now," she said.

She said that she wanted to meet with Bob, and he told her
to come to his office in Shirley Falls the next day.

And then, still in the gas station parking lot, Bob, searching
on his cellphone, found the number for Ashley Munroe, and he
called her. She picked up immediately, and he asked if he could
come see her. "When?" she asked. And he said, "Now."

HE FOUND HER in a trailer on the other side of Shirley Falls.
The sun was trying to break through the clouds, but the wind
from the north had picked up; the trees near the trailer park
were bare, and their thinner branches bent over in the wind.
Bob parked his car and walked around the trailer park. He saw

two trailers that still had Christmas wreaths on them, and then he found Ashley's home.

Ashley came to the door holding a baby in her arms. She was a tall woman with bright red hair, so bright it had to be dyed, Bob thought, and she had glasses on that kept slipping down her nose. There was a sweetness to her, he felt, and she was thin, but the middle of her had a few folds that could be seen over the tight stretch pants she wore. "Come in," she said, and Bob saw that one of her front teeth stuck out; they went and sat at the small table. The mobile home was very tidy. There were fake flowers hanging above the kitchen sink, and a certain quiet festiveness to the place. It was one of the wider homes in the park.

Ashley sat across from him, jiggling the baby on her knee. Her nails were painted turquoise. "What do you want to know? I had nothing to do with this, not one thing, I told the cops that already." She looked straight at Bob as she spoke; her eyes were hazel behind her glasses, and her lips were cracked from dryness. "I was in labor when that car was rented, and my driver's license and credit card had been stolen, like, I don't know, maybe a few days before. It was a new credit card, my mother had just given it to me to help out with things for the baby, even though my boyfriend works as an electrician. I keep my things in a tiny zipped bag, and I didn't know until after I gave birth that they had been stolen, because I hadn't used the card for a few days, and when I reported it stolen they said the last thing charged on it had been that car." She glanced around. "My boyfriend lives here now. What else do you want to know? You want to know about Matt?" She bent and kissed the baby's head.

"Yes, tell me about Matt." He liked the frankness of this

woman. He found her to be believable, and the baby kept smiling at him. The baby had one curl on the top of her head, and
the curl was held by a bright pink ribbon.

Ashley pushed her red hair back, and Bob saw a tattoo on
her neck, a small rose. She said, "I modeled for him all during
my pregnancy. Some guy my boyfriend knows had heard that
Matt liked to paint pregnant women and paid twenty-five dollars an hour, so I went once a week for two hours at a time.
Sometimes it wasn't that long, but he'd always pay me for two
hours."

"What was he like?"

The woman's face became slightly soft. "Oh Matt." She
shook her head a few times. "Matt. He was a sweet guy, I think.
He made me sad."

"In what way?"

"So eager about his painting. The first time I went there I
was a little nervous, but when I saw the other paintings upstairs,
I realized, No, he's serious about this, and he was. I mean, he
gave me a robe to put on, and I realized he wasn't going to hurt
me. He was going to *paint* me, and he did. He was a nice guy, he
just was. Still is, for all I know."

"And what about his mother?"

Ashley closed her eyes briefly, then said, "She screamed at
me one time when she saw me coming down the stairs, and
when that happened I thought, I'm never coming back here,
but Matt said to me as he followed me to my car something like
Oh, don't let her bother you, that's just who she is. Something
like that. So I came back. It must have been the second time I
was there that she did that, and it scared me. After that, I would
just rush up the stairs, and sometimes before Matt got upstairs I
would hear them hollering at each other. Really hollering."

"What kinds of things would he say to her?"

Ashley got up and put the baby into its crib. The baby waved her arms and Ashley made clucking noises over her, and the baby stopped waving her arms.

"She's a really good baby," Bob said, and Ashley smiled. "Isn't she? She's a dream baby." Ashley came and sat back down and spoke quietly, indicating with a finger to her lips that they needed to be quiet so that the baby could take its nap. "What was the question?" she asked, almost in a whisper.

"What kinds of things would Matt say to his mother?" Bob tried to whisper back.

"Oh." Ashley looked surprised and said, "Gosh, I can't even remember. Hold on. Well, his mother screamed things, like calling me a cunt and saying, You have that cunt upstairs waiting for you, and Matt would scream back, Shut up! She's a model! That sort of thing." Ashley shook her head slightly, pushed her glasses back up her nose with a finger, and said, "Frankly?" And she ducked her head and whispered even more quietly to Bob, "I wouldn't blame him if he killed her."

Bob stood up from the table and thanked her for her time.

"Sure," she said.

AS HE DROVE to the center of Shirley Falls, Bob thought of how his sister and Olive Kitteridge had said the same thing: They didn't blame Matt if he had killed his mother. Once in town, Bob went to the county superior court and filed a motion challenging the seizure of Matt's computer as a violation of his Fourth Amendment rights.

By the time he arrived home he was exhausted. Margaret talked and talked about her day—who was in the hospital, who was not—and he finally said, "Don't you want to hear about my day?"

And she said, "Well, of course I do, Bob."

So he told her, but he told her with little affect to his voice, he was that tired, and she did not ask him many questions, and that caused a dreariness to rest in him. She just said, "Are you *sure* you want to be taking this case?" And for some reason that made him almost angry. He stayed quiet after that. But he thought—oh, it was a terrible thought to have about your wife—about Lucy telling him so long ago about narcissists. Margaret did not seem interested in his day. And then he thought about living with a ghost in the marriage, because although he knew he would not tell Lucy about the case, he very much wanted to, but it was all privileged stuff, between his client and himself. He could have told Margaret because she was his wife. But Margaret did not seem to care, and he did not feel like telling her anyway.

5

AT THREE O'CLOCK that morning Bob was woken by a phone call from Jim. "She's gone," Jim said.

*

JIM HAD BEEN sitting beside Helen's hospital bed in the living room when he heard her take her last breath. Jim was not aware that he was waiting for any breath at all, but then her breathing stopped. It just stopped. And he was absolutely stunned. He kept staring at her, and her eyes were partly closed, and she did not take another breath. Where was she? She was right there, but she was gone. He could *not* believe it.

It was by coincidence that the nurse was in the kitchen making herself a cup of tea when this happened, and so later Jim figured he had been with his wife for about eight minutes alone before the nurse came back into the room and said quietly, "Oh, there we are."

Jim went upstairs to call Bob, who answered on the third ring, and Jim said, "She's gone." Bob said, "I'll fly down in the morning."

Jim then woke up his daughter Margot, who had been staying with them at the house with her husband and their two children, and Margot went downstairs and sat by her mother, and she wept and wept, and Jim held her; her husband was with them as well. They decided not to wake the others, it was not going to bring Helen back. The others were not staying at the house: Emily with her baby and her husband, and Larry with his wife. They were all staying at a hotel in Brooklyn Heights.

About an hour after Helen died, Margot said, "Dad, I can't watch her anymore, it's just killing me, but please, please, please don't leave her here alone. I mean, even with the nurse." And Jim said that he would sit with Helen, and he did so for the rest of the night, until it was morning.

*

FOR BOB, who had not been in New York for more than two years, there was a sense of unreality as he landed in LaGuardia Airport. The airport had been reconstructed and become huge, and this disoriented Bob. He made his way—it took a very long time—to the taxi area to take a cab to Park Slope. The cab-driver had a gray beard and wore a twisted scarf on his head, and he asked Bob, through the glass partition, "How are you?" And Bob told him that his sister-in-law had just died, and the man said, "Oh, I am sorry to hear that," and he shook his head many times, and Bob wondered about all the stories this man had heard. "I'm just going to spend a couple of days with my brother, I'll come back for the funeral in two weeks," Bob said, and the man nodded and repeated how very sorry he was.

But in the not-yet-dusk—it was five o'clock on the first day of April—New York looked different and yet the same, it was the oddest feeling. Bob's cabdriver dropped him off at Jim's house in Park Slope: It was a brownstone on a block of mostly brownstones, the buildings looked serious to Bob in a way that he had not remembered. There were daffodils blooming in front of many of them. "Thanks a lot," Bob said, tipping the man thirty percent, which is what Bob tipped every cabdriver he ever had.

As he walked toward Jim's house a forsythia bush, its yellow blossoms partly out, reached toward him and he had to push it partly back to get by.

ALL THE THANKSGIVINGS here, all the Christmases that Bob had been to in this house—

BUT THE MOMENT Bob walked through the grated door below the stoop, he felt the huge and gaping lack of Helen. She was gone, and he grasped the sense of this as Jim closed the door behind him.

Even the hospital bed was gone; they had taken it that morning, Jim told him, after they had taken her body. "They zipped her up in a bag," Jim said. Bob stood dazed in the living room. The white painted horsehair wallpaper sparkled against the dark wooden frames of the room, it was a beautiful house, he had forgotten this in a way. His nieces and his nephew seemed so glad to see him that it bewildered Bob. Emily said, "Uncle *Bob*! Uncle *Bob*!" And she came over quickly to give him a huge hug, as did her sister, Margot; Margot's older son, who was skinny with pimples, also gave him a hug. Even Larry hugged Bob, as his wife, Ariel, stood politely next to him. Margot and Emily had both had a baby during the pandemic, and one of these children, Margot's, was now walking, a little boy who kept putting his wet fingers into his wet mouth and beaming at

Bob, just beaming at him. The other baby, Emily's girl, was much younger, and when Emily said "Oh, here, Uncle Bob, hold your grandniece!," Bob took the swaddled child in his arms, and within seconds her placid face became wrinkled, and she screamed and screamed until Emily took her back, and she still kept screaming. Bob felt very bad about this, even though Emily kept saying "Don't worry, Uncle Bob." He noticed that Jim took the baby then, and the baby stopped screaming, and the way Jim held her, bouncing her in the tiniest way as he walked back and forth, Bob thought: He is so comfortable with that child.

Neighbors had brought in food, it was sitting on tabletops throughout the living room, and every so often one of the kids would scoop up a handful of nuts or slice a piece of cheese and pop it into their mouth. It was the oddest thing, almost like a celebration. But Helen was not there. Jim sat on the end of the couch holding Emily's baby, and the girls told Bob where they were living now—Margot in Philadelphia, Emily in Providence—and they got Bob all caught up, and their husbands seemed to be kind, grown-up men who took part in all the conversations. Larry and Ariel lived in Manhattan, on the Upper East Side, and Larry did something from home that Bob could not quite understand, something with computers; Ariel worked in cosmetics for a large retailer.

With great sadness, Bob did not know what to do. Every so often one of the girls—Margot or Emily—would start to cry, and then stop, and there was laughter as well. But Bob felt really out of place. This is how central Helen had been to this family, he realized. He would not have felt out of place had she been there. But she was gone. And the house itself seemed to know this: There was a sense of darkness in the home, even though all the lights were on.

LATER, IN JIM'S study upstairs, Bob sat alone with Jim. It was nine o'clock in the evening, and except for Larry and Ariel the kids had all gone out for a walk through the neighborhood; they had said they would be back soon. So Bob sat with Jim, who looked remarkably like himself, only very tired, and Jim said, swiveling around in his chair, "Bob." Bob said, "Jimmy."

"I'm just so weirded out," Jim said, and Bob said, Of course he was.

And then Larry entered the room, and Jim looked at him and said, "Larry." Larry's eyes filled with tears, and he said, "Dad, I just have to tell you this." Tears began to really run down the boy's face—to Bob he looked like a boy, though he was thirty years old. But nothing about him made Bob feel that he was full-grown, unlike Larry's brothers-in-law. Larry squeezed his eyes shut, and he said, "Dad, I just have to tell you: You sucked as a husband to Mom."

Bob looked quickly at Jim, but Jim seemed to receive this remark with equanimity. "I know that, Larry," he said. "But it was not at all as bad as you think it was. We had many good years, especially when we were in West Hartford and you were just a small kid."

Larry said, "And you were famous, you were freakin' *famous* at the time with that stupid Wally Packer trial, and—" He seemed unable to continue, and he finally said, "I'm going to get Ariel, and we'll be back."

Jim just nodded his head.

But as the boy turned his back to leave the room, Jim laconically pulled his hand from his pocket and raised his middle finger at his son, and Bob was amazed. He was even more amazed when Larry turned and said, "Did you just give me the finger? Dad. You are such a cretin. I can't stand you, Dad. Jesus Christ."

"Do you have eyes in the back of your head?" Jim asked his son calmly, and Larry said, pointing to the large mirror across the hall, "Do you have no eyes at all?" His face was contorted, and he said, "Dad, you just gave me the finger, you are *such* a piece of crap. I can't *believe* Mom had to live with you."

"I am." Jim said this kindly. "You are absolutely right, Larry, I am a piece of crap."

And Larry left the room, calling for Ariel; he could be heard going down the stairs, slamming the front door as he went out.

"Whoa," said Bob quietly.

Jim sighed. "Yeah," he said.

It came to Bob then that Larry had been born to the wrong father. He was a son that Helen would love—and she had—but he was not a son that Jim should have had. The girls were different, they were softer and warm, both with their father and with Bob. But Larry had always been different, and Bob thought: He should not have had Jim as a father.

Well.

There you are. A lot of people feel this way about their parents, and probably, thought Bob, a lot of parents feel this way about their kids. He thought then, briefly, of Mrs. Hasselbeck and how—to his knowledge—not one of her five sons ever came to visit her, they had all moved to the West Coast, and what was that about?

Bob, who, as we know, had no children, felt a sense of awe

and sadness at this whole thing as he sat in front of his dry-eyed
brother, Jim.

"Oy, Jimmy," he murmured, and Jim said, "Oy, indeed."

AFTER A WHILE Jim said, "Bob, tell me about this case you've
just taken. Matt Beach. Talk to me about it." And Bob said,
"Sheesh, Jim, that can wait. We don't have to talk about that
now."

But Jim sat forward with his elbows on his knees, and he
said, "Truthfully? I'd like to hear about it. I think it would help
me. Get my mind someplace else. So tell me." He sat back.

And Bob—who had no trouble with the confidentiality of
his client's information, because it was *Jim* he was speaking
to—told his brother about Matt, the amazing paintings, and the
model Ashley Munroe, and Jim interrupted and said, "Does
Matt get any money as a result of his mother's death?"

"There's a one-hundred-thousand-dollar life insurance policy from his father. The man died years ago, so it has to be
worth more than that now. And about fifty thousand from his
mother's estate. Plus the house."

Jim raised his eyebrows. "You might be fucked," he said.
He stood up, and Bob followed him out of the room.

Bob said, "But you don't throw your mother into a quarry if
you want the money. Because if she'd never been found, it
would take five years for her to be declared dead."

"Good point, but does Matt know that?" was all Jim said.

6

TWO DAYS LATER Bob was sitting in his office in Shirley Falls waiting for Diana Beach to show up. Even though it was the first week of April, it had snowed a couple of inches the night before, and while the snow was (sort of) melting, it still covered the streets and the sidewalks. A lot of sidewalks hadn't been cleared yet, and Bob's feet, in his sneakers, were feeling wet. Today was another gray day, and Bob switched on his desk lamp and also the tall lamp in the corner of the room. Then he sat down at his desk with his laptop open, glancing over the notes he had taken from his visit to Matt Beach. In his mind, he thought: *Go away, Jim.* Because he needed to stop thinking about Jim and Helen; he needed to concentrate now on Matt and Diana.

He kept picturing Matt—what was it about him? His anxious face had settled itself deeply into Bob's mind. And those paintings! The guy had really taught himself to paint. Bob didn't know that a person could teach himself to paint like that. But Matt's paintings were sophisticated, is what went through Bob's mind. With the strokes controlled and yet free—the colors vibrant and right. And Bob thought of that stack of art books, with the tattered covers, that had been in Matt's studio, the guy had been seriously teaching himself to paint. Bob shook his head slowly. He thought then of Margaret, when she had been speaking of Lucy, saying that artists are childlike, and Matt had that quality. It was difficult for Bob to remember that Matt was fifty-nine years old. But he also, Bob thought, had never really learned to socialize, and that was part of it as well.

At exactly two o'clock Bob heard the elevator door open, he heard the sound of a woman's heels heading down the hall away from his office and then heading back; people often did this. There were no signs telling them where the different offices were. He got up and opened the door.

"Bob."

Bob stepped back and Diana Beach walked in. She was a tall woman, well-dressed, wearing a navy blue blazer and a blue tweed skirt that went just below her knees, and then brown pumps; the edges of her shoes were wet from the snow. She did not look like she came from Shirley Falls, as he had expected she would not. And she looked much younger than he had expected; he thought of Susan recently telling him that the women in town thought Diana had had plastic surgery and he realized this was most likely true; he had seen women in New York who looked this way.

"Hello, Diana. Have a seat." He indicated with his hand a chair across from his. Bob sat down slowly, heavily, into his swivel-backed chair behind his desk. "Sorry I had to cancel our meeting the other day." Bob had not told her the reason why.

Diana placed her handbag on the floor next to her and, crossing her legs, said, "Oh, that's all right. How have you been, Bob?"

"I've been fine. What about you?"

She really was a pretty woman. Her hair was dyed a pale brown and tucked up neatly on her head, and her skin was smooth. She had large eyes and wore no glasses. He would not have recognized her. But then he had never really known her so many years before when he was in school with her.

She said, "Are they going to arrest Matt?" She leaned forward as she asked this.

"Not sure. They have to have something to pin him to the crime and they don't really—yet."

"Bob, this whole thing is just making me sick." Diana crossed her legs the other way and smoothed her skirt.

"How often did you see your mother?" Bob asked, and Diana said, "Maybe once a year? Twice? I would drive up. But it was so unhealthy, their situation."

"In what way?" Bob asked.

"Oh, she was so old, and he could barely do all the care for her, and I kept saying, You must get someone in to help you. And he just wouldn't." She added, "Honestly, I could barely stand to see them. But my older brother cut himself off from the family years ago, and I'm all that Matt has."

"When was the last time you saw your mother?" Bob asked, and she said, right away, "About a month before she disappeared."

"What about Matt's paintings?"

Her face changed; it became excited. "Aren't they *good*? Did you see them? I think they've kept him going all these years. It's all he would talk about when I saw him, I mean he would tell me which artist he had just been studying and—"

Bob said, "Did you ever meet any of his models?"

And her face changed again. She held up a finger, as though to indicate that she needed a moment to compose herself. And then she said, "Only once or twice, they would usually be leaving as I got there, just a very few times over the years would I see one. And my mother would scream at them, she hated them."

"She would scream at them? Actually scream?"

"*Yes.* She called them terrible names, things I'm not even comfortable repeating to you. I think she hated the fact— I *know* she hated the fact—that they were posing for Matt in the nude. My mother hated anything to do with sex."

"And how did the models respond to this?"

"They just ducked out of the house. I think they all just really needed the money."

"Did you ever meet Ashley Munroe?"

And something in Diana's face changed again, he could not say what, but she became very cold-looking, and she said, "No, I never did."

BOB WAITED, his fingertips pressed together while his elbows rested on the arms of his chair, and he turned his chair to look out the window. Silence was in the room. Then Bob turned back and said, "I understand you're a high school guidance counselor?"

Diana said, "Yes. Yes, I am. It's been a great job for me." She paused and then said, "I had a guidance counselor in high school. Do you remember Miss Donnelly?" Bob shook his head. "She was the first person in my life that I trusted. I asked her—before I told her—I asked her to keep the things I was going to tell her private. And she did. She changed my life, that woman, and so I became a guidance counselor as well."

"What were the things you told her?" Bob asked, and Diana said quickly, "Private things."

"Have you worked in the same school your whole career?"

She looked at him with a certain squint in her eyes and said, "Well, no, after my marriage ended—my first marriage— I moved and took a job elsewhere in Connecticut. I was there almost twenty years and retired recently. You know, Bob"— and her voice changed slightly to one of almost confusion—"it used to be that my work was aspirational, I mean my job was to *inspire* these kids, but in the last few years I began to realize that people, young people, see themselves as victims, and this was discouraging for me. They get stuck in that victim mode, and it became harder for me to help them. But still, I think I was a very good guidance counselor. There were times when I'd have one of my memory lapses, but people were very good to me."

"Memory lapses?"

Diana gave a brief laugh and said, "It's a condition I've had from childhood, but no big deal."

Later Bob understood that he should have asked more about this condition, but he did not. Instead, he said, "Do you have any children, Diana?"

Without looking at him, shaking her head furiously at the floor, she said, "I would never, ever, ever have children."

"Got it." Bob said this without expression. And then he said, "Did your mother leave a will?"

Diana seemed surprised by this question. "I have no idea." Her face changed just slightly again; again, she held up her finger as though to ask for a moment to collect herself, and then she said, "She had our father's life insurance policy. But surely Matt told you this."

"I'm asking *you* right now. What Matt tells me remains confidential at the moment." He was surprised at the authority in his voice.

Diana nodded quickly. "Yes. Right. Well, she had that life insurance policy from my father. And since he died—oh, it must have been thirty-five years ago—I always assumed that's what she and Matt were living on, because, you know, Matt quit his job at the ironworks some years ago."

Bob sat quietly for a few moments. "When did your father leave the family?"

"When I was fifteen years old," Diana said. "He simply walked out of the house one day and we never heard from him again until he showed up dead in North Carolina, where he had set up another accounting firm. I mean, I suppose my mother must have heard something, because he divorced her once he left. She never contested it."

Bob said, "Was it hard for you, when he left?"

Again, her face seemed to twitch, and her voice got very low as she said, "I loathed him. But I was off to college two years later—scholarship, mind you, I went to Brown—and I seldom came home again." She looked around, as though slightly frightened. And then she looked back at Bob and said, "So Matt was stuck with her his whole life." She added, "Honestly, it was a prison sentence for him."

"Are you married now, Diana?"

She glanced down, and her mouth moved before she spoke. It was evident to Bob that she was once more trying to compose herself, and it took her a few moments. "My second husband and I are divorced. We had been married almost twenty years." Again, her face moved, her mouth turned down. She added, "My first husband was the friend of a psychiatrist I went to when I first lived outside of Hartford. I went to him for help. And— Well, anyway, I met this friend of his and we ended up getting married. I met my second husband when I was still married to my first, and meeting him, my second husband, felt like the greatest gift I had ever been given. I finally felt *safe*."

"When was the divorce?" Bob asked.

She looked up at him. "Last August he announced that he was seeing another woman. She was a friend of mine—my *best* friend, if you can believe that. And the divorce went through last week." Diana's face was moving with great emotion as she spoke these words.

Bob felt very sorry for her then; he recalled Jim saying that she had seemed poignantly sad as she walked home from school so long ago, and he could see this now.

"WE'LL STAY in touch," he told Diana. As she was leaving, she took his hand in both of hers and said, "Thank you, Bob. Thank you so, so much."

*

AS HE LEFT his office that day—he had waited to be sure that Diana Beach was out of the building—Bob bumped into Katherine Caskey on the street. "Bob!" she said, and he said, "Hello, Katherine." She was holding a package and she set it down on the pavement to give him a hug, and Bob thought that this dear Katherine Caskey was the only person in Maine who hugged him every time she saw him. He had known her for years—she was a social worker in Shirley Falls, though, like Bob, she lived in Crosby—and yet it was not until the pandemic that they had discovered this *really* amazing coincidence: that right after Bob's father had died, his mother had gone to a minister in West

Annett, about an hour away, to see if he would officiate at the funeral; Bob's mother, for whatever reasons, had been on the outs with the Congregational minister in Shirley Falls, and she had driven to the house of the minister in West Annett and asked him to do the funeral—and he had. But here was the thing: That day, as a small child, Bob had stared out the window of the car, he was in the backseat with Susie, and he had stared at the little girl who was standing on the porch of this Reverend Caskey's house next to her father. He had stared and stared at her, and she had stared at him. And he had never, ever forgotten her.

It was Katherine Caskey. And it was during the pandemic, as they were eating outside one evening in Crosby with Katherine's husband and William and Lucy, and also with Margaret, that Bob and Katherine put this together. She had never forgotten him either! Her mother had died the year before, and these two children had been locked in a stare that neither ever forgot. And that day, more than two years ago now, Katherine had said to Bob, "When this pandemic is over, I'm going to hug you so hard, I can't *tell* you how hard I am going to hug you!" And so there was now this bond between them.

"How *are* you?" Katherine asked him now, picking the package up, and Bob said, unexpectedly, "I am so weary."

And she looked at him. She was an attractive woman with auburn hair (it would have to be dyed, Bob understood this, she was a year older than Bob), and she said, "Tell me."

Bob said, "I've taken on the Matthew Beach case, and it makes me tired."

Katherine shifted the package she was holding to her other hip, and she said to Bob, "I heard you'd taken the case. Oh Bob."

"No, no, I'm fine. How are *you*? How are the kids, and how is Elton?"

"We're all fine." Katherine looked away. Then she looked back at Bob. "I'm a little worried about Elton. Ever since he retired, he's been . . . oh, I don't know. But I'm worried about him, Bob. He's just—I think—a little depressed."

"How depressed?" Bob asked. He really wanted to know.

"I don't know. I can't tell if he's just depressed or if there's something cognitive going on. But he won't see a specialist, so I guess we'll just have to roll with it." Her face was worried, she looked older as he watched her. And then she said, "I'm getting ready to retire myself, but I have clients I care about, and so I can't just say, Okay, that's it, good luck."

At that moment Katherine reminded Bob of Lucy—it was her genuineness, he realized. "I get it," he said. "Well, you sure have helped a lot of people."

"Thanks, Bob." She said this quietly.

"Come on, I'll walk you to your car. Let me take that for you." And she gave him the package, which was not so much heavy as bulky. It turned out that they were both parked in the big parking lot, and as they walked, Bob said, "My sister-in-law, Helen, just died."

"Oh Bob!" Katherine stopped walking and turned to him and said, "Oh, you loved her, didn't you? And didn't Margaret not like her, or who am I thinking of?"

"No, Margaret met her and my brother once a few years ago when they brought their grandchild up here to summer camp, and you're right, Margaret was not impressed. And also, Susan was never able to stand her either."

They continued walking till they reached Katherine's car. Katherine unlocked the car and took the package from Bob and stuck it into the backseat, then turned to Bob. "It's because she was rich, right?"

Bob thought about this. "More than that, I think. Helen was . . . limited, in a way."

"Who's not limited?" Katherine said.

"I know."

They stood in silence for a moment, and then Bob said, "You must be really good at what you do, Katherine."

She shrugged. "Who knows."

"I know," Bob said. And he added, "Let me know about Elton."

"I will." Katherine opened her arms to him, and they hugged once more before she got into her car. He felt her bones against his bulk. And as he walked away, he thought, I am so grateful for her.

*

AT THIS POINT in time the nature of Bob's relationship with his wife was vaguely puzzling. Did she hold him? Did he hold her? In truth, not that often. They did have an intimate life, although Bob felt that Margaret was not always as interested as she used to be, and in fairness, Bob was not as interested either. And when they *were* intimate, afterward Margaret only held Bob a few minutes and then she would get up while Bob fell asleep. She had joked about this for years. "Sex *energizes* me," she said, "and it puts you to sleep."

But in terms of holding each other: No, they did not do that much anymore. And this is one reason that Bob was grateful to Katherine Caskey, to feel her arms around him. He was just appreciative of those moments.

It may be that not enough is said about this sort of thing, older people and how much they might appreciate the touch of another human being. Mrs. Hasselbeck, for example: How did she live without any human touch to her skin? Charlene Bibber? Somehow they existed without it, many people do. Yet one has to wonder about the toll it takes, the lack of being touched or held. So many people are not.

Bob was thinking about this as he drove back to Crosby.

7

THE FUNERAL OF Helen Farber Burgess was held at St. John's Episcopal Church in the neighborhood of Park Slope in Brooklyn. Bob could remember Jim and Helen going there at Christmas, though he couldn't remember that they went there a whole lot more during the year. In any event, this is where Helen had wanted her funeral to be, and she had planned everything, right down to the white roses that adorned each pew entrance. Margaret went with Bob, and Pam was there. Pam had asked Bob to ask Jim if she could come, and Jim had said, "Sure, who cares."

So Pam sat on one side of Bob and Margaret sat on the other; the two women were very kind to each other, never having met before. And the funeral went on forever: This is what Bob thought. In front of him sat Jim with his three kids and their spouses, and his eldest grandchild; the two babies had been left with a neighbor. The girls—women now, of course, Emily and Margot—both spoke about their mother, Margot weeping copiously, and Margot spoke of when they were little, and their mother would make pancakes in the shapes of their initials. "A big M," Margot said, drawing it with her hand, tears wetting her face as she pushed back her long dark hair with her other hand.

Bob thought: Oy, Helen.

Then Emily spoke; she was slightly more controlled. She told a story about how kind her mother had been when a boy in middle school had broken up with her. "She was just the *best*," Emily said, blowing her nose. "The best in the whole world."

When Larry got up, Bob's heart folded over. The kid was a mess. His eyes were so red that they appeared smaller. Larry went on and on about summer camps he had been sent to as a kid and how he had hated them, and his mother had been so kind about that, she had always wanted him to come home. "But I didn't," Larry said, glancing down at his father. "And my mother sent me a letter every single day." He wiped his face with his arm. "Mom, you're in heaven right now. And I want—" His lips quivered. "I want you to save me a place."

Jim did not speak, he just sat there dry-eyed, and as Bob turned to look behind him, he saw that the church was at least three-quarters full, and many of the women were weeping; these would be Helen's friends. Bob was impressed with their weeping. He did not weep, he did not feel much of anything as he sat there (except for being so sorry for Larry), and glancing at Pam he saw that she was dry-eyed too. She glanced back at him, and a kind of quiet acknowledgment passed between them: This was sad, but it was empty—for them—of real feeling. Why?

But when the priest described how Helen had planned every detail of the funeral, Bob felt deeply sad for Helen; he could not feel her presence in the church. The organ played and there were white roses everywhere, especially all over her casket, and Bob could not stop himself from thinking: Oh Helen! It's your funeral, and yet— He did not know how to finish his thought.

———

WHEN IT WAS OVER, they drove behind the hearse nearly two hours to Connecticut to the town in which Helen had been raised. Pam rode with Margaret and Bob, and she kept thanking them profusely for allowing her to do that, and Margaret—God bless her, Bob thought—was very nice to Pam, turning in her seat to look at her, asking straightforwardly about her AA meetings, and Pam answered straightforwardly in return. They were great, Pam said, they were changing her life. "When I heard myself say, My name is Pam and I am an alcoholic, boy, that was something." Then Pam said that part of recovery was going around to people who had been hurt by her actions and making amends, and that was hard, Pam said. Adding, "But so meaningful," and Margaret nodded.

When they arrived at the cemetery, everyone gathered around the open plot—it was mid-April by now—and Bob watched Jim, standing there in his long black coat, who seemed very alone.

On the drive back to the city, Bob said to Margaret and Pam, "I felt nothing, but I loved her very much."

And Margaret said, "Don't worry, Bob. Grieving is a strange thing." And Pam, in the backseat, said quietly, "It sure is."

BACK AT THE HOUSE, Jim sat with his small grandchildren, who had been returned by the neighbor. A few of Helen's friends had come straight from the funeral and brought over food. There were little sandwiches and platters of cheese and prosciutto, and wine was served, and a decanter of whiskey sat on the shelf across from the fireplace.

Margaret surprised Bob. She went from friend to friend, asking how long they had known Helen, and listened as these women talked to her. Pam stood by Bob's side; she was wearing a mask, had been wearing one all day. He looked at her with irony. "I bet you want a drink."

"Always," she said.

"You're doing great, Pam. I'm impressed."

"Thanks, Bobby." Then she leaned in and said, "I don't really care for these women friends."

"I hear you," Bob said. Then he added, "Sorry. But I'm going to have a slug of whiskey." He walked over to the decanter, remembering how Helen had always poured him a whiskey as soon as he walked through the door, and he felt a sickness as he poured it into a glass and drank a swallow. Pam had followed him. "Don't be sorry. That's part of the deal, not drinking while other people are."

"What's been going on with you, Pam? Who are these people you had to apologize to for being a drunk?" Bob held his glass of whiskey and looked at her.

"Oh," she said, with a sigh big enough to make her mask move slightly. "First of all, Ted, because I would get really nasty to him some nights after drinking."

"And how did he take these apologies?" Bob asked.

Pam said, "With surprise, to be frank about it. He's amazed I'm in AA."

"Who else did you apologize to?"

"Oh, you know, a couple of women friends." She rolled her eyes. "And they were—of course—very supportive. Said I had never said anything mean to them, blah blah." Pam's eyebrows went up. "And maybe I hadn't, maybe I had just thought about the things I wanted to say to them, who knows." And then her eyes watered, and she said, quietly, "And the boys. I guess I used to call them drunk." She shook her head. "But they were great. Especially Eric." Pam touched Bob's arm. "He came to see me, Bob. And he was dressed in women's clothes, and I'm not going to lie to you, it was very hard at first. Well, awkward. You know the fucking doormen and everything, I mean of course they didn't say a word. But he's such a great kid, Bob. And he said he really misses me, and he'll come again as long as Ted's not there." She looked around. "Oh, Bobby. What a mess everyone is." Then she looked at him and said, "What about *you*?"

"All good, thanks. What's going on with Ted?" Bob asked.

"Well." Pam twirled a piece of hair by her face with her finger. "I'm still trying to figure out what to do about him. I've been actually . . . pretty okay living without him. I mean, he comes back to the city sometimes, but otherwise he's still in the Hamptons. Has been all winter."

"With Lydia? She still out there? You didn't apologize to her, did you?"

"Never," Pam said. "Oh, she's still out there." She added, "Fuck them both."

JIM HAD DISAPPEARED.

Bob found him sitting by himself in the study upstairs, and Bob walked in tentatively and said, "Jim?" His brother turned to look at him, his eyes were without expression. "Ah, Jimmy," Bob said, and sat down across from his brother. They sat without speaking. And then Jim said, leaning forward with his elbows on his knees, "You know what I'm thinking? I'm thinking I don't want to be buried in that horrible plot next to her in

Connecticut, I don't *want* that, Bob. But we have two plots, Bob, it's making me a little crazy."

"Where do you want to be buried?" Bob asked.

Jim said, "I don't. I want to be cremated and I want my ashes spread over the Androscoggin River in Maine. That's what I want."

8

ODDLY, THE MEMORY of being in the car with both his wives became a very special thing to Bob; he had felt understood by them both—such different women!—and the fact that they were generous and benevolent to each other sort of slayed him. This is what brought tears to his eyes as he told Lucy about it later on their walk by the river. Not the death of Helen. "I guess I can't believe she's gone."

Lucy said, "Probably not."

"Except their house itself is so different, so empty."

Lucy nodded and looked over at him. "Oh Bob, I'm sorry. Tell me more." And so Bob said how alone Jim seemed at the burial, how attentive he was later to the little grandchildren, and Lucy listened, shaking her head. They walked in silence for a while.

"Everything okay with you?" Bob turned to ask her.

Lucy smiled at him. "You already asked me that. You poor thing. Yes, everything's fine, Aiden is fine, Chrissy is fine. Becka's seeing some philosophy student."

And then she told him about her experience with Olive Kitteridge. "She was very confused by my stories, but so what."

"So what," agreed Bob. "But tell me the stories."

Lucy squinted at him. "You sure? You don't need to hear my stupid stories."

"I want to hear them," Bob said, and he did.

And so Lucy told him about the man on the train and also the taxi driver. Bob kept looking over at her as she talked. He tried to think of anyone else he knew that would tell such stories, and he could think of no one. "That's so curious," he said, meaning the man on the train. "That you felt like you were commenting together on the swollen rivers."

"But we *were*, Bob. I swear to God we were."

"Oh, I believe you," he said, and he did. "You're something, Lucy."

She laughed. "William always says, 'You're a strange one, Lucy.' "

"You're not strange, you're *Lucy*." He added, "William says he thinks you're a spirit. That's all he means when he says you're strange."

"Thanks, Bob." She kept walking without looking at him.

IT HAD SNOWED once again a few days earlier, and the path they walked on was slightly slushy. "I can't stand this snow in April," Bob said, and Lucy said, "Oh, me too!" But they already knew that about each other.

"I wish I could tell you about this case I've taken," Bob said as they walked. "But I can't because it's all attorney-client privilege."

"I understand," Lucy said. "I went out with a lawyer for a while between my two marriages, and he told me that. Except he was *always* telling me stuff he shouldn't." She waved a hand dismissively. And then she stopped walking, and her eyes became warm as she looked at Bob and said, "David was such a lovely man, Bob. You know, my second husband."

"I know exactly who you mean. God."

"He was the best thing that happened to me, except for my girls."

"Ah, Lucy." After a moment Bob asked, with tentativeness, "What made you think of him?"

"Oh, I think of him a lot. Lots and lots I think of David. But just now remembering that lawyer who would tell me stuff he shouldn't have— Well, David was very different from that sort of person." She glanced up at Bob and said, "But keep talking. Please." And she started to walk again.

So now Bob told her that Jim did not want to be buried with Helen, that he wanted to be cremated and have his ashes spread over the Androscoggin River.

"Aha, of course he does," Lucy said.

They had reached the spot where Bob always had his smoke. "Why of course?" Bob asked.

"It makes perfect sense to me. Returning to the scene of his crime, and because frequently people return to their child-hoods." Lucy sat down next to him on the granite bench. "Why do I feel so bad for your brother?" And then Lucy poked Bob's leg a few times and said, "This is why. Because when you were telling me about him that day, when he confessed to you that he thought *he* was the one who killed your father— You know what I've never forgotten about that story?"

Bob squinted at her above his smoke. He was happy—he felt happiness—just to be in Lucy's presence.

"The fact that he said that every day at school he would think, I'm going to go home and tell her, meaning your mother. Today I am going to do that. Starting at the age of eight, Bob. Your brother kept thinking: Today I am going to tell her, today I am going to confess. And then he couldn't. And as time went by he couldn't do it even more, and meanwhile your mother was so loving to you because she thought *you* had done it, and so this was confusing to the small boy Jim, maybe he thought he wouldn't be believed. And then in college, and then at Harvard Law School, he *still* kept thinking, I'm going to tell her. I'll write her a letter." Lucy shook her head and sighed. "Oh Bob. What a tortured way to live. No wonder he had to become one of the best defense attorneys in this country. He thought of himself as a criminal."

"Oh, I know. I know. I hear you." Bob sucked long and hard on his cigarette. And then he had to stand because the wind was blowing the smoke straight at him. He walked around in circles before squishing the cigarette out. He held it up before putting it back into the pack. "Thanks, Lucy," he said.

"Of course," Lucy answered.

AS THEY WALKED back to the parking lot, Bob felt again that just to be in the company of Lucy gave him a respite from everything; this went through his mind. So he told her that. He said, "It makes me glad to be with you, Lucy. You give me a break from . . . well, you know, life."

"A break from your sin-eating," she said, with an open smile. "I'm so glad." Then she added, "I feel the exact same way. Only I'm not eating sins."

When they reached their cars, Bob opened his arms and said, "Big hug to you, Lucy."

And she opened her arms and said, "To you too, Bob."

But they did not hug.

Book Three

...

Book Three

I

BY THE MIDDLE of April, the forsythia bush out in front of Bob and Margaret's house had still not begun to bloom. But the purple crocuses had come up by the basement edges of the house, and other houses had tiny sprinklings of purple and yellow crocuses. There were no daffodils yet as there had been in New York, although their stalks were up and the buds were there, and certainly no tulips, although their stalks were showing through the ground now as well, deep reddish green.

BOB CALLED UP Olive Kitteridge and asked her about the person she had gone square dancing with who had said something about the Beach family; the memory of Olive's calling him in his office months ago to speak to him about the Beach case came back to him one day. Olive sounded listless on the telephone. "I can't remember now. Something about sex, I think."

"Sex?" Bob asked.

"Bob, I'm sorry, I just can't remember."

"What was the name of the person who said this? The person who was at square dancing?"

"It was years ago, Bob. I just can't remember. Goodbye." And she hung up.

*

OH, OLIVE.

Here is what was happening with Olive. Her best friend—at this point in her life, the best friend she felt she had ever had in the whole world—Isabelle Goodrow, who lived "over the bridge" in a horrible room with the aides going in whenever they wanted to, or more likely they didn't want to go in and so stayed away—Isabelle Goodrow was going to be leaving to live in California near where her daughter lived. This is what Isabelle had told Olive the day before, even before Olive had settled herself down, intending to read the newspaper to Isabelle from front to back.

Amy Goodrow, Isabelle's daughter, was some high muckety-muck doctor out there in California, and she was married to some other high muckety-muck doctor, and apparently Amy and her husband had decided to have Isabelle come live in a facility near where they lived. This is what Isabelle had reported to Olive the day before, on Thursday. They were flying in this weekend, and they would take Isabelle back with them. They had this new place all arranged.

Isabelle had wept as she told this to Olive. Olive had not said a word. She had not been able to say a word. When she finally got up to leave, she said, "I will miss you, Isabelle."

When she got back to her apartment, Olive sat for a very long time. She thought to herself: Isabelle was meek and mousy the first time I met her, and she's still meek and mousy, she'll do whatever she is told to do. Olive sat until it got dark outside, and then she rose and put a light on. She did not fall asleep that night until it was almost dawn, and when she woke four hours later, she felt wretched. She called Isabelle up and said, "When do they arrive?" It was now Friday. And Isabelle said, "Later this afternoon."

"Okay," Olive said. And she hung up.

Isabelle called her back. "I'm sure Amy would love to see you," she said, and Olive said "Ay-yuh" and hung up.

Around two o'clock that afternoon, Olive wrote down on a piece of paper: LUCY BARTON SAYS— And then Olive stopped. She didn't really know what Lucy had said. But she picked up the paper again and continued: THERE ARE VERY FEW PEOPLE IN THE WORLD WE FEEL CONNECTED TO. I FEEL CONNECTED TO YOU. LOVE, OLIVE

She put the piece of paper into an envelope and walked over the bridge to the nurses' station without passing by Isabelle's room. "Will you please make sure you deliver this to Isabelle Goodrow before she leaves?" Olive asked, and the aide looked surprised and said, "She's leaving?"

And then Olive walked back to her own apartment. It was like waiting for a death. She simply wanted Isabelle gone now. Although she did not want Isabelle gone at all. Olive was as distressed as she could remember feeling since Henry had his stroke. But then she had had something to do, which was to visit him in his awful stroke home, every day she had gone there, she had even—when the weather permitted—taken their dog, and she would wheel Henry into the parking lot so that the dog could lick his hands. And Henry had sat in his wheelchair with a smile on his face, not able to say a word. He had never spoken a word again after he had the stroke.

But now Olive had no place to go, she had absolutely nothing to do. All Friday afternoon she waited to hear from Isabelle, and she did not, and when she got into bed that night she began to swear in a way that she had not—could not remember, anyway—sworn for years. "You goddamn asshole," she said quietly into her pillow, meaning Amy Goodrow. "You stupid, stupid goddamn pig." These are the sorts of things she said as she lay sleepless on her bed.

Amy Goodrow had never liked her mother. She *loved* her, Olive knew that. But Olive also knew the history told over and over again by Isabelle, that Isabelle had been a single mother with no parents or family alive to help her, and she had moved from a small town in New Hampshire to Shirley Falls, Maine, when Amy was just a baby. . . . Olive knew every bit of it. Amy's loneliness, Amy's affair with a teacher, and how when Isabelle found out about the affair she cut off the girl's hair, Olive knew the whole story. And Olive had met Amy a number of times these last few years, and her husband, and their one son (totally unimpressive to Olive), but Olive knew this: Amy was doing her duty to a mother she loved but had never liked. Why did a child move so far away if she did not want to live a whole new life? Even Isabelle had said that, and she and Olive had that in common, Olive's son, Christopher, was living in New York City when he could have stayed so much closer—

Olive sat up. These words went through her mind: I will kill myself. Christopher will be sad, but not that sad, he'll get over it. I will kill myself. She thought how she would do this. With a knife and her wrists? That was too frightening. And then she thought of her father taking his gun. And she thought of her mother, so young—fifty-seven at the time, and then dying just a few years later, so young—and she thought about herself and what her father's suicide had done to her. In fact, she did not know what his suicide had done to her, but deep within herself, she knew that it was not good.

———

SATURDAY THERE WAS still no word from Isabelle.

And Olive thought: I am not going to walk over and say goodbye.

AND THEN ON SUNDAY—at noontime—Olive's phone rang, it was Isabelle's number, and Olive stared at it, and then she picked it up and said flatly, "Hello?"

"Come over here," Isabelle said. "Olive, I told them no. I just told them, *finally,* as they were signing all these forms and stuff, I just said, 'I am not going.' And you could tell at first that they didn't believe me, and finally I asked Arjun to leave the room, and I said to Amy, 'Listen to me, Amy. I know you want me near you. But Maine is my home. It has been my home since you were a baby, it has been my home with my husband. And this is now—even here in this nursing home—my home. I have my friend Olive who I will never be able to replace, and, Amy, I am not going. You will have to declare me incompetent—and maybe you can, but I will fight you on that—and I am telling you, I can't go, and I am not going."

Olive said nothing.

"Did you hear me?" Isabelle said.

"Tell me again," Olive said.

And Isabelle said, "Olive, I am *exhausted,* and you are telling me to tell you everything again? No, I'm not going to. But they just left. They left, Olive!"

And Olive said, "I will be right there."

2

EVEN BY THE third week of April, Maine is still chilly, though at least the forsythia had finally, in some spots, just barely begun to bloom. But many people in the town of Crosby, so ready for spring, are more out and about than they have been so far all year. Also, the sun does not set until seven-thirty, and this gives people a kind of deep breath without their even quite knowing it. Curtains are drawn later.

And so it happened that one evening during this time the curtains had not yet been pulled in the home of Margaret Estaver and Bob Burgess, and while only a few people witnessed what happened, it went around town very fast: The couple had a big fight. The one person who first saw this was walking his dog by the house and—feeling unconsciously sheltered, as we have said, because of the sense of safety this couple provided to the town—looked into the lit windows and slowed down. Margaret Estaver was facing her husband with a look of absolute hatred.

A few minutes later an older couple walking by on the opposite side of the street saw Bob Burgess suddenly raise his arm, and he appeared to be yelling. This couple walked across the street to get closer to the house, and they did, in fact, hear yelling, and yet they could not make out any words, and they strolled on past, alarmed. And then Margaret flung the curtains shut. This news made its way through the small town, but probably not as much as you might think; people were uncomfortable reporting this about Bob Burgess and Margaret Estaver, and so in the end, only a dozen or so people heard about what was seen through the windows in the large brick house in the center of town.

IT WAS QUITE an altercation: Margaret, earlier that very day, had given a sermon at the Arlington Street Church, the Unitarian church in Boston. The day before she and Bob had traveled to Boston, Margaret had ordered a car for them because she did not want Bob worrying about the Boston traffic even though he had said he would be fine driving there. But no—she wanted to hire a car. This is how excited she was about being invited to speak at that church. "We'll take an Uber!" she had said.

No trees had leaves yet, and the streets of Crosby seemed dirty as Bob and Margaret left town. As the car pulled onto the highway, Margaret reached into her briefcase and brought out the sermon she was to give the next day. Bob could not read in a car, it made him carsick like a kid, and so he sat beside her and watched the trees go by, listening to his music with his earphones in. He had already heard Margaret's sermon—four times—and told her he thought it was brilliant. A slight uplifting came to him: He realized he was glad to get out of town. The combination of Helen's death and the Matthew Beach case weighed on him continually, he understood this now. And by the time they reached New Hampshire the highway seemed cleaner, more cheerful somehow. But the sky was gray, and it remained gray until they came to Massachusetts, and then the sky cleared and the sun shone down. Margaret reached over and squeezed Bob's hand. "I think it's pretty good," she said, and he pulled out his earphones and said "What?" And she repeated what she had just said. "Of course it is," Bob answered.

The truth is, even in their small church in Crosby there was often a very slight sense of unease for Bob as he watched from the third-row pew, his wife standing before the congregation in her long white robe and speaking to them all about Love and Charity and all the other stuff. His unease, he realized, was because there was a certain manner that overtook her at such times, though he would be hard-pressed to say exactly what it was. But sometimes he had the image of a child playing dress-up and being excited by her importance. So it wasn't always easy for Bob to watch. But people loved her. Bob loved her.

He looked out his window as the Boston skyline appeared.

IN THE HOTEL, he felt a gladness. He liked the spaciousness of their room; he liked seeing people in the lobby and in the hallway. They had dinner in the restaurant downstairs, and Bob asked Margaret again if she was sure it was all right that he did not attend the service, and she waved a hand and said it was totally fine with her, she was just glad to have him along. She had already told him not to come to the service, and he had been privately relieved. As we have just mentioned, there was often a vague discomfort he felt when he watched her preach. She said now, "Really, Bob, you wouldn't be comfortable, especially at the coffee-hour reception after, don't worry." So Bob was going to meet an old friend who lived in Boston, and the next morning Margaret said, "Okay, I made sure we have late checkout at two, so I'll come back to the hotel by one and I'll pack up and then we have an Uber waiting for us at one-fifteen."

The service was at eleven followed by the coffee hour, and Bob said, "Yeah, that's more than enough time, Margaret."

AND SO THE next morning, after Bob had seen his friend Koby, who talked almost without stopping about his divorce and the new woman he was seeing, and who after two hours had finally said "Tell me what's new with you, Bob," and Bob found he had little to say, Bob went back to the hotel and he lay on the bed, and a secret sadness moved through him. He understood that this had to do with the friend he had just seen. (He would tell Lucy about it.) He often had waves of soft sadness move through him; he knew this about himself and accepted it. But also, he knew it was because of Helen and because of Matt Beach and how much Matt was depending on him.

Then he sat up and looked around and saw that Margaret's clothes were piled on her suitcase, and her overcoat as well; the day was a nice one and she had not needed to wear her coat. He hoped her sermon had gone well; he assumed it had.

At one o'clock, Margaret had not returned. He called her, and she did not pick up. Bob folded up her clothes and put them into her suitcase. He made sure to get all the chargers, the phone charger and the charger for her computer and the one for his, and he put them into the small brown bag he always transported them in, and he zipped up his own suitcase. He called her again at one-fifteen, and again she did not pick up. He texted her, and she did not answer.

On his phone was a locator app, and he checked to see where Margaret was, and she was still at the church, two blocks away. He could not figure it out. Anxiety swam through him. He left a twenty-dollar bill on the desk for the chambermaid, and then bumping his way through the room he was able to get the door open and he rolled their two suitcases out, Margaret's overcoat folded across his arm. Down he went in the elevator.

BOB WAS A person who was not comfortable being angry. Years ago, his therapist in New York City told him that this was because of his childhood and the fact that he had killed his father. His therapist—oh, what a kind woman she had been!—had explained that he never dared to get angry because he carried within himself this vast guilt. But now his irritation grew into real anger. He was worried about the Uber that was coming to pick them up, and he kept leaning down into cars and asking if it was theirs, and the drivers all shook their heads. And when Margaret finally sauntered through the front door of the hotel at twenty minutes past *three*, pulling her phone from her bag she announced, "Oh, the Uber canceled."

They had to wait for another one; it took more than half an hour to find a driver who would drive them to Maine, and Margaret talked constantly about the event she had just attended. "They loved me, they just absolutely loved me, Bob. And when I got to the part— What's wrong?" She frowned at him.

"You said you would be back at one. We had to check out, and you didn't answer your phone, and I couldn't figure out what had happened."

"Oh Bob, honestly." And then she continued to talk about how well her sermon had gone over. Bob did not speak all the way back in the car except for once when Margaret said, "How was Terry?" And Bob said, "Koby." And Margaret said, "Oh, right, Koby. How was he?" "Fine," said Bob, and he looked out the window.

He could not for the life of him understand why he was so angry at this woman. But it seemed to bubble inside him— bubble, bubble, it went. And it did not go away.

AS THEY ENTERED the town of Crosby, Bob finally understood. He had felt abandoned. That is why he was so enraged. He remembered how, as a child, he had once gone to a Cub Scout meeting and his mother had forgotten to pick him up after. For over an hour he sat on the steps of the church where the meeting had been, and he began to cry. He was small, six or seven years old, and then his mother finally showed up. "Stop crying," she said as soon as he got into the car. But he had not been able to stop. "Where *were* you?" he asked, and she said, "Oh come on, Bob. I was visiting Jeannette and I forgot the time. Stop the crying!"

As Bob looked out the window now, he realized that this is what had happened, and he thought: When we get back, I will explain this to Margaret, and it will be okay.

BUT IT WAS not okay.

HE SAW, as he was speaking to her across their kitchen table, that her eyes became small. No kindness appeared on her face. When he stopped speaking, she said, and her voice was very tight, "Bob Burgess, I am not your mother. That's the first thing. The second thing is, I know full well about your childhood trauma and I live every damned day of my life trying to negotiate around that, I am always, *always* trying to make you feel safe, and when you say that an ordinary person would apologize, any ordinary person knows that sometimes people are late. It happens! It's called *life*!"

He raised his arm; it was a gesture of futility, but she said, "Don't you dare raise your arm at me!" And then he became livid. "Oh for Christ's sake, Margaret, don't be an idiot," he said. Margaret rose and closed the curtains with a fury. He turned and said with anger, "Jesus, Margaret, you are just gaslighting me."

IN A DAZE he drove to the local 7-Eleven and bought two packs of cigarettes and a bottle of wine with a screw top. Then he drove to the river, and in the parking lot he took three large swallows from the wine bottle, and then he put it back in its paper bag and walked down to the river—it was dark now— stepping off the path to go down closer to the water, where he stood smoking a cigarette.

"THEY NEVER CHANGE." Lucy Barton had said this when she told him that her younger daughter was convinced that her ex- husband was a narcissist. "They never can change their behav- ior."

And then Lucy had told him about gaslighting, that this was something narcissists do, and he had not exactly understood the concept. But he understood now, when Margaret had turned it on him, saying that she lived every day of her life aware of his childhood trauma.

They love being the center of attention.

They cannot take criticism.

They are controlling.

They talk about themselves all the time.

They are not empathic. Though this one gave Bob hope: Margaret was very compassionate about her congregants. In fact, about many people.

But then this: They like to think that they can save the world, there is often a grandiosity to them, and when they do good things for people they do so because it makes them feel bigger.

HE DROVE HOME, not caring that he smelled like smoke, and when he walked in, Margaret said, "I *was* an idiot about you raising your arm." But she did not say it nicely, he thought. He sat across from her at the dining table. Finally, he spoke. "You're pretty self-absorbed at times, Margaret. You haven't even really asked me much about this Matt Beach case, and you gaslighted me this evening when I told you why I was upset. I think that's what gaslighting is—turning it around on the other person." He stood up and walked upstairs to their bedroom and lay down on the bed, and still, he felt stunned.

TWO HOURS LATER Margaret came up. She sat on the bed beside him, and she said, "I just googled gaslighting and you're right. You're right, Bob, God, I'm so sorry." She took hold of his arm.

And in that way their altercation ended. But it had really shaken Bob.

———

IN THE MORNING Margaret asked him to fill her in on the Matt Beach case, and so he did. He told her that he was waiting to get Matt's computer back, that Matt had no cellphone, and that Carol Hall was just crouched like a crazy person waiting for one more piece of evidence to tie him to the crime and then she was going to have him arrested on murder charges. He also told Margaret about the will. "We have three years to probate a will in Maine, and I'm not going to mention it to anyone until we see if they can find anything else to tie him to the crime."

Margaret listened, asking him questions, and he answered them all, but he did not know how he felt. Margaret really did appear to be sorry about their fight the night before, and she really did appear to be interested in what he had to say this morning. It's not that he didn't trust her—they had been married for many years now. But he was aware of the age-old sadness inside him.

Margaret said, "Have you spoken to those two men who worked with him at the ironworks?"

And somehow Bob felt better by her asking that. "Got two appointments lined up this week with them," he said.

"Good," she said.

3

THE NEXT DAY, the state police called and said that Bob could pick up Matt's computer. "You found out he doesn't have a cell-phone, right?" Bob asked, and the guy didn't answer. So Bob went into Shirley Falls and picked up the computer, and then he drove to Matt's house with it and said, "Now let's see what's on this."

Matt looked worse than usual; Bob wondered fleetingly if his cancer had returned, but Matt just said what he always said, that he had not been sleeping. At the dining room table, Bob looked at Matt's computer while Matt picked away at his red-tipped fingers, and Matt was right: there was almost nothing on it.

Except for this: *I can't stand her, she makes me so crazy, I can't stand it stand it stand it.* And a few more entries in which, over the course of the last three years, he repeated things like this. But there was also this: *Oh Mommy I love you.* And then this: *I remember coming home from school one day I was maybe eight years old it was before I got sick and my mother was sitting on the couch and she was crying, and I said Mommy what's wrong and she said that the kids at school called her beach ball because she was fat and then they called her bitch ball when they got older and she looked at me oh my God she was really crying and she said Matt honey I don't know why I'm the way I am and I said Mommy you're perfect and she said Oh honey come sit on my lap but I didn't be-cause I felt I was too old for that.*

And more: *She is making me crazy. I am losing my mind.*

One more, which killed Bob: *All I want to do is hold a woman I love, to really hold her.*

Bob pushed back his chair and said, "None of this ties you to the crime, and I'm not going to let them use any of it if I can help it. There's not enough probable cause to bring you in, Matt."

And Matt sat with his shoulders slumped, staring at the table.

"Matt," Bob said. "Do you ever have thoughts of hurting yourself?"

Matt looked up at him quickly. "What do you mean, like off-ing myself?"

"That is what I mean."

Matt looked away again, and he said quietly: "No." And Bob thought: He is lying.

"OKAY," BOB SAID. "Let's get that rifle out of your house." He started to move toward Matt's bedroom, and Matt stood up and said, "Bob, if I really want to shoot myself I can just go to Walmart and buy another gun."

Bob stopped walking and watched Matt. "You know I can," Matt said, with a small shrug. "So leave the rifle where it is. Please."

Bob thought about this. Then he said, "Listen, I want you to call me every morning and every night until this case goes away. If you don't call me, I'm going to call you. And please don't hurt yourself, Matt. There is not enough evidence to go charging you with murder. Do you understand me?"

Matt just nodded from where he stood by the wall. Bob sat down again in the dining room chair. "Is there anything you want to tell me about this case that you haven't already told me? Anything at all?" Bob asked this slowly.

Matt looked over at him. He looked dazed, and he did not answer for a few moments. "No," he said quietly. And again Bob thought: He is lying.

As Bob left the house, it was the first time he felt certain that Matt had had something to do with his mother's death. Nothing had especially changed. It was something in the manner of Matt.

*

AS BOB DROVE HOME, Carol Hall called him. "I'm getting ready, Bob. I bet I could bring him in right now and make it stick. I'm offering you a chance to avoid the press and have him surrender himself to the police."

"Carol, stop it. You don't have probable cause. When you do, you let me know. I'm sure you're aware by now that he does *not* have a cellphone, just like I told you? Did they bother to tell you that?"

"They did. But I also know that he wrote on his computer that his mother made him crazy. We have three years' worth of notes to himself on that computer, Bob."

"You're going to embarrass yourself if you think that's enough for probable cause. And I'm going to make sure it's not even going to be allowed into evidence," Bob said.

She hesitated just long enough that Bob knew she was not yet certain, and then she said, "All right, but I have the police watching him. Just so you know."

"They can watch him all they want. He's not going anywhere."

But after he hung up, he was deeply worried. If they should discover that Matt was now the beneficiary of his father's one-hundred-thousand-dollar life insurance policy, then Carol Hall might have enough to bring him in. If the bank where that money was should somehow notify someone—he knew it was illegal for a bank to do so, but that did not mean that some idiot who worked there wouldn't do it—he should prepare for a Harnish bail proceeding, which was Maine's way of getting bail for a client in homicide cases.

Would Matt show up for his court date?

Probably, where else was he going to go?

Would Matt pose a substantial risk to anyone in the community?

No.

Was there substantial risk that Matt would commit another crime?

No.

BUT IT ALL had to be prepared, and it made Bob very tired.

*

JOHNNY TIBBETTS ARRIVED in Bob's office looking defensive. It took Bob a while to get the guy to relax enough to tell him what he remembered about Matt Beach. Johnny Tibbetts was a tall man, very thin, with thinning hair, and his teeth—Bob noticed—were bad. "I don't remember him much at all," Johnny Tibbetts said. "But he was okay. A good enough guy. Strange."

"In what way strange?" Bob asked.

Johnny shifted on his chair, his hands stuffed down deep into his old coat pockets, and he said, "Dunno."

Bob sat back and sighed.

And then Johnny Tibbetts said, "Something about naked pregnant women. He liked them. Was always wanting to paint their picture." Johnny Tibbetts opened his mouth and laughed, showing those bad teeth. "Fuckin' whack job, Jesus Christ. *Pregnant* women?"

In another ten minutes Bob let the fellow go.

And Fred LaRue, when he showed up, had not one extra thing to offer.

4

LUCY WAVED TO BOB from where she stood waiting by the wooden fence in the parking lot, and he thought there was an innocence to her that she probably did not understand about herself. As he got out of his car and walked toward her, the sight of her standing there made something gold-colored flicker inside him; it was joy.

AND THEN HE had to stop walking, because—at that precise moment—he understood exactly how much he loved her.

"OH BOB," she said, as she walked to him. "Oh Bob, Bob, Bob. The sin-eater."

He did not look at her, and she said, "Never mind. Sorry. Tell me what's wrong. You looked so happy to see me, and then your face fell."

Bob said, as they began to walk, "Margaret and I had a doozy of a fight." As he spoke those words, he was aware that he was betraying his wife. But Lucy just listened as he told her of their argument, and then she said, "You don't think William has those tendencies? Come on, Bob. How long do you speak to William before he starts in on his parasites? I'm serious.

Sometimes I think if I hear the word parasite one more time I will die. Just *die*."

"Do you think she can change?"

"She can change." And after a moment Lucy said thoughtfully, "And so can William. There's a difference between being self-absorbed and being a narcissist."

He felt the joy of Lucy's presence return to him. "Well, we're stuck with them," he said, and why did he say that? Was he hoping she would say No, we're not—let's run away together?

But Lucy said, "Yes, we are, and it could be a whole lot worse."

Bob said, "I wish I could talk to you about this Matt Beach case. But it's unethical, so I can't."

"I understand," Lucy said. "But do you have any idea how much longer it will go on?"

"No. Just waiting."

"Oh Bob," and she looked at him as she said this; her voice was quiet with understanding. And then she said, with excitement in her voice, "Look at the dandelions, Bob, *look* at them!"

And so he did. And they were just dandelions. He said nothing.

Lucy tapped him on his arm. "But, Bob, they're *beautiful*! Don't you just love them? I always remember when I was young and they would show up in the grass by the side of the dirt road we lived on."

He stopped walking, and so did she. "Lucy, what *exactly* is it you like so much about these dandelions?"

She said, "Well, they're yellow, and they grow in green grass, and the combination of the green and yellow— Oh, I just love it!"

He stood looking at the area where the dandelions grew, and then he saw what she meant: their spots of yellow in the green. "Got it," he said. And they kept walking.

THEY REACHED THE place where Bob had his cigarette, and as they sat down together on the granite bench he said, "Remember how I told you I'm always terrified?"

"Oh yes," Lucy said.

"It's a terrible way to live."

Lucy said, quietly, "I know that. I know exactly what you mean." Then, after a moment, she said, "For me, it's when the sun goes down. God, do I get scared. I can't help it, I just get so *scared*."

He lit his cigarette and watched her. "I'm sorry," he said, and she said, "Yeah." He wanted to ask her if William was kind about that—her getting so scared when the sun went down. But he did not ask her. Instead he asked, "What is it that makes you so frightened?"

She looked at him with surprise. And then she pursed her lips as she stared at the river, and she finally said, "Honestly, I don't know. I really don't know." She shrugged slightly and said, "Probably stuff from my childhood." She glanced at him quickly and then away, and she said, "No one has ever asked me that before. Even that shrink I saw for years in New York. Maybe I never told her how scared I am when the sun goes down. But the answer is, I don't know."

"That's okay," he said quietly, and for a moment he placed his hand on her knee. They sat together without talking, and then Lucy said, "It's a strange thing to get older. I mean, thank God the girls seem okay, Chrissy with her baby and Becka with her new fellow. Except as I told you before, Chrissy having that baby has somehow changed her relationship to me. I mean, it almost feels like sometimes she doesn't even like me anymore." Lucy waved her hand. "I've told you all that. But I think: Something bad is going to happen to those girls after I die, and I won't be there for them."

"They'll have each other," Bob said, and Lucy said, "Yes, I've thought of that. They'll have each other."

"I hate getting older," Bob said. "I think that adds to my terror. But honestly? The way the world is going . . . I wonder if that's just because I'm old, or if we really are in a mess."

"Oh, we're in a mess."

They sat together quietly for a few moments. Then Lucy said, looking at him, "Bob, have you ever envied people?"

"*Envied* them?" he asked.

"Yeah. Like, who is it you envy?"

He glanced at her. He said, "It's funny you ask that. Because back when Jim was so famous during that Wally Packer trial, people would say to me—some people would say this— 'You must envy your brother.' But I didn't. I didn't envy Jim at all. I *loved* him. Oh, he was an asshole, but I loved him, and I never envied him, even with the life he had with Helen. That wasn't *my* life. So I never envied Jim at all. And it was—it is, now that you're asking this—interesting that people thought I would. But I just *loved* him." After another moment he said, "And I still do."

Lucy said, "I've been thinking about Jim, because you told me once that he said, People always tell you who they are if you just listen—they will always eventually tell you who they are. Do you remember his saying that?"

"Yeah, I do."

"And I was thinking about that this morning because I got an email from a person I've known for years, and the word envy showed up at least five times in her email, and all of a sudden I realized: Oh, she envies people. And I think she might even envy me, because of my success."

"She probably does."

"You say that so easily. But it took years for me to realize that." Lucy shook her head and sighed deeply. "Actually, I only realized that this morning as I read her email."

He waited.

"I remember when I envied that poor girl who was marrying the prince in England, I was so young, but I remember feeling envious." Lucy tapped Bob's arm. "And you know why? Because she had so many clothes! I'm serious. I can remember exactly where I was, when I realized, Oh my God, she has people coming to her to deliver all these clothes! My envy lasted, I'm serious, probably ten minutes. And of course it turned out she was probably the loneliest person on this planet. But I don't remember feeling envious a lot, Bob, and I don't understand that. You would think, *I* would think, that I would have been envious of people from the start, all these mothers who seemed to love their children as they picked them up from school, all those kids who seemed to have normal lives, but I just somehow understood: That's not my life. And I was always inside my head, and I remember thinking: I'm glad this is my head."

Bob smoked and squinted out at the river. Lucy kept on talking. "Even as I was working so hard to become a writer, I wasn't envious of the ones who had success. I would just read their books, and if I liked the book I would think: Wow! Good for you! And if I didn't like the book but they had gotten a lot of recognition for it, I would think: Well, I'm glad I didn't write that book, so who cares?"

He watched her while he smoked. She was struggling to say something and finally turned her face to look at him. Then she said, her voice quiet with an understanding, "I think there must be an arrogance involved."

"What do you mean?" Bob asked, squinting at her through the smoke.

"I think it's because I'm secretly arrogant."

Bob shook his head. "I think—since you asked me—I think that being envious is just not a part of your personality."

She said, "But being secretly arrogant is."

Bob said, "I used to be envious of people with kids."

Lucy looked at him quickly. "Oh, of course," she said.

"But it was kind of a generalized envy. I didn't want to be those people, I just wished I could have kids."

"I get it," she said.

As he continued to smoke, a thought arose in Bob's head, he was really thinking about this, and then he said quietly, "Honestly, Lucy? The only people in the entire world that I feel envy for are your daughters."

"My *daughters*?" And they looked at each other then, he saw her looking straight at him, as though her gaze had gone inside of him, and then she said quietly, "Oh, because I love them so much."

"Exactly," he said. He felt a blush come to his face, and he looked away and took a last deep drag from his cigarette.

For many moments they were silent. Then Lucy said, "But you're not jealous of William?"

"Nah." And he meant it. "Sorry," he said.

She looked at him again—it was hard for Bob to have her looking at him so intensely—and she said, "I get it. I'm not jealous of Margaret either."

Bob squished out his cigarette and put the butt back into the pack.

LUCY STARED STRAIGHT OUT at the river for a long time, and then she said, "Bob, I think that we are all standing on shifting sand." She did not look at him as she spoke. "I mean, we don't ever really *know* another person. And so we make them up according to when they came into our lives, and if you're young, as many people are when they marry, you have no idea who that person really is. And so you live with them for years, you have a house together, kids together—" She stopped and said, "Sorry."

"No, no, go on," Bob said.

"But even if you marry someone later in life, no one knows who another person is. And that is terrifying. You know how you said you were terrified? As far as I'm concerned, everyone should be. I mean, every so often a couple has a fight and things get said, and it scares them both profoundly, and yet in a heartbeat they pretend that fight never happened, because they *can't* proceed with what they just learned. And I understand that. I do." Lucy nodded, still looking at the river. "What I'm trying to say, Bob, is that people just live their lives with no *real* knowledge of anybody—like that woman who emailed me this morning and might be filled with envy, but I don't know if she is!" Lucy said, looking at him now, "My *point* is that every person on this earth is so complicated. Bob, we're all so complicated, and we match up for a moment—or maybe a lifetime—with somebody because we feel that we are connected to them. And we *are*. But we're *not* in a certain way, because nobody can go into the crevices of another's mind, even the *person* can't go into the crevices of their own mind, and we live—all of us—as though we can. And I respect that, Bob, I do.

"But none of us are on sturdy soil, we just tell ourselves we are. And we *have* to. And I get that, and as I said, I respect it. I'm just saying . . ." She stopped then and looked at him with eyes that had become red-rimmed.

And then— Oh, she had more to say: He could see it in her face, in her body as she sat forward. "But maybe I do envy people and I just don't know it." She looked at the river again and said, "Because back in New York, when I was young and William sent me to my first shrink, I remember telling this man—he was a sweet man—I remember saying to him, 'I'm not lonely.' But what I *remember* about that, the whole reason I remember it, is that I saw something move across his face when I said that to him that day, and it wasn't until probably years later that I realized: Oh, he saw that I was really lonely, but I just didn't know it. I mean, Bob, you don't come from my background without being lonely."

She looked back at Bob with fear on her face.

"Well, if you're *you*, maybe you do," Bob offered.

She didn't answer him, she had gone somewhere in her thoughts, he could see this. So he said, "When *did* you first know that you were lonely?"

And she became deflated then, he saw her energy leave her, and she said, "When I found out about William's affairs. It was as though some bubble I had lived in my whole life just burst, and I realized: Oh."

He wanted to wrap his arms around her and say, Oh Lucy.

———

SHE TURNED AGAIN to him and said with a sense of acceptance, "I'm so good at being lonely, though. I'm just so good at it."

HE LOOKED OUT at the river, which was low today.

And then she said, "You know who I envy? All of a sudden I envy someone, Bob!"

"Who?" He turned to look at her.

"I envy a person who is my age who can just leave her life and go on to another." She was silent then.

And after a long moment, Bob said, "Ah, Lucy, that's a made-up person. You can't envy a made-up person."

"Well, I do," she said.

"I hear you." (But he thought: She wants to leave her life?) He added, glancing over at her, "I *think* I do."

She said, "You do."

He held up his cigarette pack. "Thanks," he said.

"Of course," she said.

AS THEY WALKED BACK, Bob felt a sense of dislocation, and they did not speak as they would have in the past. Bob felt— what did he feel?—a quiet inner lifting of exhilaration. He finally said, "Say something. Anything. Just tell me anything."

Lucy said, "Okay. Charlene Bibber's dog has dementia. She told me the last time I saw her. We were supposed to take a walk together that week, and I met her in the grocery store, and she told me that her dog—it's a rescue collie named Boober, very big, I've seen him, long thin nose, slanted blue eyes, gorgeous fur—and Charlene has had him five years and she's just crazy about him. But now he can't get up unless he can place his legs on a mat, and even then she has to help him. And he really doesn't understand what is going on. But he does recognize Charlene. Anyway, Charlene can't leave the house for too long or the dog sort of loses it. His bowl has deep ridges in it so that he can't eat too fast—he has to lick the food out of the ridges."

Lucy looked at Bob and continued.

"Charlene has a vet who gives him acupuncture for now, but she knows she'll have to put Boober to sleep soon, and she's just not ready to do that yet. The vet says he'll put the dog down when she's ready. Oh, and she has a neighbor, some strong man, who said he will pick up the body when the vet puts the dog to sleep."

They stopped walking and looked at each other. "The vet gives the demented dog acupuncture?" Bob said. "Seriously?"

"That's what she told me."

"I'm sorry," Bob said, because he had started to laugh. "I don't mean to be insensitive, but, Lucy, what a story."

"I know," she said. "I know. I've been meaning to tell you."

THEY WERE AT the parking lot now, and Bob turned to her. "Lucy—" And then he did not know what to say.

"I hear what you're saying," she said, brushing back her hair from her face.

"I didn't say anything."

"I know. But I heard you," Lucy said.

*

WHEN HE WAS eating with Margaret that night, Bob said, "I'm sorry about the fight we had, Margaret." And why did he say this? Because of his walk with Lucy? Margaret only reached over and touched his arm.

BUT AFTER THAT latest walk, Bob thought of Lucy almost constantly. He kept going over their talk, trying to remember it accurately and worried that he did not. She became a golden blur to him. But she had said she envied someone her age who could just leave their life? What did that mean? She had said, I hear you. She had said, I hear what you're saying. I heard what you said.

AND WHO—*who who who* in this whole entire world—does not want to be heard?

IF HE WENT an hour without thinking of her, he gave himself a treat—say, a donut—which he ate with pleasure. It did not happen very often. Meaning he did not eat very many donuts.

5

A FEW DAYS later Bob drove out to see Matt Beach. The sky was clear, and it was not cold. Bob pulled into the driveway, and Matt came out of his house while his dog barked hysterically beside him. "Matt," Bob called. "Let's go get you a cellphone."

Matt stood there looking perplexed. "Why?" he finally said.

"Because." Bob gestured for Matt to get into the car. "Come on, let's go do it."

Matt turned and put the dog back inside the house. Then, as he got into Bob's car, he said, "Who am I going to call?"

"Me," said Bob. "You're going to call me."

*

IT PUT BOB's mind (partly) at rest to get the cellphone for Matt. Matt was like a twelve-year-old kid when he finally had the phone. "Look at all the things it *does*!" Bob asked Matt if he would mind being on the locator app of Bob's phone, and Matt said he wouldn't mind, it was okay. "It'll mean I know where you are every minute, so don't do it if you want your privacy," Bob said.

"Oh no, that would be *great*!" Matt said. "You are the only person in the world who cares where I am." But he said it cheer-fully. Then he said, "Can I see where you are too?"

"Sure," Bob said. So he set that up for Matt as well. "Now you're the only person who can track me," Bob said. "I don't even let my wife track me."

"Why not?" Matt asked, and Bob said it was because some-times he went off to have a cigarette.

"She doesn't know you smoke?" Matt asked. "Even *I* know you smoke."

"How?" Bob asked, and Matt said, "Because I can *smell* it."

"Oy," said Bob, and Matt said, "I like how you say Oy."

BOB COULD NOT wait to tell Lucy all about it.

*

OLIVE KITTERIDGE CALLED Bob Burgess back. "The people were named Donnelly. And their daughter had been a guidance counselor at the high school those Beach kids went to. And the guidance counselor's mother told me, although she was not supposed to tell me, that Diana had been sexually abused by her father. Apparently that's why Diana went on and became a high school guidance counselor, because she felt like that Don-nelly woman had saved her life."

BOB FOUND THE name of Patricia Donnelly, who had been the guidance counselor of the school at the time Diana was there, he remembered the woman now. But she had died twenty-two years ago. And her mother was in the memory care unit at the

High Farm nursing home. There were no other family members to be found. He did an extensive search to see if the guidance counselor had reported any abuse, but there was no record of such a thing.

*

THAT NIGHT, when Matt called him, Matt said, "I'm calling you from my new cellphone," and Bob said he knew that. Matt said, "And guess what? I'm tracking Diana now too! She let me. But when I asked her if she wanted to track me, she laughed and said, 'You never go anywhere,' and that kind of hurt my feelings."

Bob said, "Forget it. She's got stuff on her mind, like her divorce and stuff."

"Yeah, you're right," Matt said.

Then Bob said, "Matt, did anything happen between your father and your sister? Anything, you know, like—ah—inappropriate?"

Bob heard Matt hesitate. And then Matt said, "I'm six years younger than her. I really don't know what happened."

"Okay," Bob said in a nonchalant manner. "Just don't go dark on me."

"Dark on you?"

"Don't disappear."

"I'm not going to disappear," Matt said. "Because you're tracking me!"

*

TO BE IN LOVE when the outcome is uncertain is an exquisite kind of agony. This is how it was for Bob. At times he felt he was living his very largest life, as though his soul were billowing before him like a huge and rippling sail. For the next few days after that last walk with Lucy, Bob slept profoundly well; he felt in the darkness as though Lucy were lying next to him, close against him, and this was extraordinary for Bob. When he woke, the world seemed magical to him, and he felt that he was experiencing some Large Awareness. But then he would crave Lucy, just to see her, just to be with her, and to really crave anything one might not ever get in this world is a difficult thing. For anybody. But Bob was a patient fellow. He simply waited until their next walk together.

*

BUT BEFORE THEY had their next walk together, this happened: Bob stepped through the automatic doors of the big grocery store in town, walking over the large sheets of cardboard laid on the floor to catch the grime of people's boots, and he went down an aisle filled with various oils and pickles and then he saw Lucy looking at the meat section. She seemed small, diminished somehow, and Bob stopped walking as he watched her. Lucy bent over the chicken and then dropped a packet of it into her shopping cart. As she did this a woman walked over to her. Bob knew who the woman was, Arlene Cleary, she had worked in the local bookstore years ago, and her husband was head of the school board. As Bob watched, Arlene stopped and spoke to Lucy. It looked as though Arlene was hesitant at first to speak to Lucy, but she did. Much taller than Lucy, Arlene bent down slightly to say something, and Bob—he would never forget this—saw that Lucy had only a faint smile for the woman. Even from where Bob stood he could tell that Lucy was being barely polite. They spoke briefly, and then Lucy turned away. It went through Bob's head that Lucy had called herself arrogant, and she seemed that way to him right now. Arlene Cleary walked away, Bob felt, with a slight sense of insult.

But then another woman—and it took Bob a moment to realize it was Charlene Bibber—rushed over to Lucy and flung her arms around her, and Lucy kept hugging her back. They hugged and hugged, and Lucy pulled her head back at some point and wiped a few hairs away from Charlene's face and then hugged her again. And Bob saw that Charlene was weeping; her dog must have finally been put to sleep.

Bob left the grocery store without buying anything, and he kept thinking about what he had just seen. Many people in town would not have cared so much about Charlene Bibber, because her political views were very different from most people in this mostly liberal town. But Lucy, who had essentially snubbed Arlene Cleary, was hugging poor Charlene as the woman wept. This part did not surprise Bob, but he had been shaken by Lucy's response to Arlene Cleary.

Bob was aware—as Lucy herself had said—that he did not know her as well as he thought he did. Isn't that what she had said? We are all standing on shifting sand.

It shook him.

*

EVER SINCE THE evening of her fight with Bob, Margaret had felt an uneasiness. She did not fall asleep until late most nights, because these thoughts always came to her in the dark. Her marriage was not what she had assumed it was. But what did she mean by that? And then her mind would follow: *She* was not what she had assumed she was. It really frightened her. One night as she lay there next to a sleeping Bob, she thought: You're an actress, Margaret. Quietly, she got up and went down the stairs and sat by the small lamp they always left on at night.

What had crossed Margaret's mind to reach this understanding was her memory of when Bob had raised his arm and she had said, Don't you dare raise your arm at me! Thinking about this now, she understood: It had been a false note. She knew that never in his life would Bob be violent toward her and yet she had said that, knowing even as she said it—she understood now—it had been histrionic, it had deflected from the real matter at hand, that she was self-absorbed. Although she still could not quite believe that was true; she rebelled against it inwardly.

But one morning not too long after their fight, as they were having breakfast, Margaret, tightening her bathrobe belt, said, "Bob, do you love me?"

He looked at her with genuine surprise. "Margaret!" He placed his hand on her arm. "Of *course* I do."

6

AND THEN CAME Bob's weekly walk with Lucy, and she waved as she so often did from the fence, and she came to him quickly and said, "Oh Bob, Charlene had her dog put to sleep." He listened as she went on about this, and he said, "That's heartbreaking," and Lucy said, "But it *is*!" Only later in the walk did he ask Lucy what she thought of Arlene Cleary, and Lucy waved her hand dismissively and said, "Oh, she's only interested in me because every so often my name is in the paper. I hate people like that." She added, "There aren't many of them in Maine, though, which is good. Why do you ask?" she said. And Bob said, "I just wondered."

"But something made you ask," Lucy persisted, so Bob said, "I saw you blow her off in the grocery store."

Lucy stopped walking. "You did?" She stood there looking at Bob. "Why didn't you come over and say hi?"

"Because then Charlene showed up and she was upset. I figured it was about her dog."

"It was," Lucy said. Lucy didn't say anything else.

"What?" Bob said. "You think I was spying on you at the grocery store?"

"A little bit."

"I guess I was," Bob said.

Lucy frowned and gave a very tiny shake of her head and started to walk again.

"Don't be mad at me," Bob said, walking with her.

"I'm not *mad* at you, Bob. Jesus." After a moment she said, "I just don't *get* it. It kind of makes me feel creepy to think that you were just standing there watching me." She looked at him, her face was pained.

Bob thought: I could die.

He stopped walking again, and so did she. "Lucy, I'm sorry. I completely get why that would make you feel weird." And then she smiled at him and reached and touched his arm. "Don't worry," she said.

"But I do."

"I know. But don't. I was just being an asshole. Seriously, Bob."

They walked again, and Bob said, "No, *I* was the asshole."

"It's really okay. Don't think about it." And she smiled at him to indicate their joke about how they both thought of things too much.

"I bought Matt Beach a cellphone," Bob said, and Lucy said, "He doesn't have a cellphone?" And Bob said no, and he told her about buying one with Matt, how happy it seemed to make him, how he was killing Bob with his innocence of the world. "But I can't say any more about it," Bob said, and Lucy said, "Don't."

Then Lucy spoke of her daughters. She said, as she had before, that maybe in a certain way they didn't like her anymore, but she wasn't sure. But she *was* sure they didn't need her anymore, and Bob said, "They probably don't in a certain way," and she said, "Oh, I know," but still, she told him how it made her sorrowful. "But not so much anymore," and again she smiled at him, this time with her full face. He thought that she was beautiful.

SO THERE THEY WERE, walking and talking. When they reached the spot for Bob to have his cigarette, Lucy said, gazing out at the river, which was high and moving rapidly today, "That was a great talk we had last time. About envy."

His heartbeat sped up. He said, "I know."

She turned her face to him again, she was happy, he could see this. "I'm just so glad you're in my life," she said. And he said, "Me too."

He took a drag of his cigarette and said, "Lucy, I'm so sorry about seeing you in the store and—" But she was already shaking her head, and she touched his arm lightly and said, "Bob, please don't give it another thought, I was just being a jerk."

They sat there looking at the river. There was enough of a wind to make small whitecaps appear in the middle of it, and also the wind blew the smoke over Bob as he sat. But he did not get up, as he would have in the past.

Lucy was restored to him.

On the shifting sand they stood on.

"Thanks, Lucy," he said, as he put the cigarette butt back into the pack.

"Of course," she said.

Book Four

...

I

JIM BURGESS SQUINTED against the sun slanting sharply across the street and against the buildings on the block where he lived. It was a Saturday afternoon at the end of April, and the tulips on his block were in full bloom. Magnolia trees had earlier opened their blossoms to the world; in some cases, their petals were already falling off. The neighborhood of Park Slope in Brooklyn was at full throttle: Children were on the sidewalk next to worried parents as they went off to a birthday party, or non-worried parents whose confidence was seen in their steps, or people just taking the hands of their children as they crossed the street. One young man—he seemed young to Jim, everyone seemed young to Jim—said to his two daughters, "Okay, let's think what to get Mommy for her birthday," and both girls jumped and clapped their hands and said, "Oh, let's get her—" And Jim walked past them, thinking, *God*, they make me want to throw up.

He had left the house without his sunglasses.

What was he to do?

HELEN. HELEN. HELEN. Helen. Helen. Helen.

This is what his mind did so often, and what it was doing now.

———

OH JIM BURGESS! What are we to do with you?

*

AFTER HELEN DIED—we are talking about the moment she stopped breathing and then when her body was taken from the house—after this transpired, what happened to Jim was this: He was silently catapulted into an entirely new country, one he had never known existed, and it was a country of quietness and solitariness in a way that he could not—quite seriously— believe. A terrible silence seemed to surround him, he could not feel himself fully present in the world, even as he dealt with Helen's friends and with the occasional man who said, Let's have lunch—throughout this, Jim understood that he had been exiled to a place that was, before, unimaginable to him. And yet it was now where he lived.

A woman friend of Helen's gave him a book about a man, some minister, who had lost his wife, the book took place in the 1950s. Jim did not read it. But one night, out of exhaustion, he opened it and read the lines "Because his wife had died in sum- mer, he waited for winter to come. And when it came, he saw that it made no difference."

Jim thought: How did the writer know this? And he under- stood then that this was a private club, and a quiet one, and no stranger passing him on the street would know that he was a member, just as he would not know if they were a member. He wanted to stop people he saw, older people especially who were walking alone, he wanted to say— Did your spouse die? Now that Helen was gone, he was a panicked and petrified man.

*

AND SO JIM flew to Maine. It felt like the only place where he could have the tiniest sense of respite. He stayed with his sister in Shirley Falls. Helen had hated Susan, had hated the small house and the orange curtains that had been hanging in the kitchen windows for years. But now Jim felt the most minuscule bit of comfort in being here. He could have stayed at the hotel by the river, but he did not; he would test it out at his sister's, and so he stayed in Zach's room—Susan's son had moved out years ago. He found it worked. As well as anything could work these days.

*

BUT IF JIM had found the tiniest sense of refuge in the state of Maine, Pam Carlson, back in New York City, was having a time of it. To start with, we should note that Pam had thought she was doing pretty well. She had been sober for three months and had been acknowledged at her AA group for this; she had felt a real sense of pride, and also—relief. She could do this!

And then a few things happened: The first thing that happened was that Lydia Robbins stopped by Pam's apartment on a Thursday afternoon. In the area of New York City in which Pam lived, no one just stops by. People call, or they meet somewhere, but when Pam's buzzer buzzed and the doorman said, "Lydia Robbins to see you," Pam felt so surprised (and mixed up) that she said, "Oh, send her up."

Up came Lydia Robbins and in she walked, her glossy hair had grown longer, and she said "Pammy!" and gave her a hug, and then sat herself down on the pale green couch in the living room. She looked around and said, "I've always liked this place." Then she said, conspiratorially, "You know, Itsie said one time that she thinks it looks like cheap Long Island in here, but I don't agree. I love it." And Lydia looked around at the pale green walls and the glass table in the corner while Pam tried to absorb this. Itsie McCullough had *said* that? And Lydia was *telling* her that Itsie had said that? "We all *really* miss you," Lydia said now. Pam was very, very nervous, waiting, as she later told Bob, for the other shoe to drop, but it never did. Lydia chatted on: about different parties she had gone to, how she felt so comfortable in the Hamptons these days, it was surprising to her that she felt more comfortable there than in the city, and then she finally got up and kissed Pam on the cheek (which made Pam crazy, because Pam was still a germophobe) and then she left.

So, what was that all about?

The only thing Pam could think was that Lydia had come to see if Pam knew anything about her goings-on with Ted. And, while she was at it, to give her a jab about the apartment. It left a terrible taste in Pam's mouth. She was furious with herself for letting the woman in, and then talking to her as though they were still friends. Although Pam had been slightly cooler to Lydia than she would have been months ago, she was not sure that Lydia had even noticed. Anyway, it was unsavory, the whole visit, and Pam did not go to her meeting that night. Why not? Sometimes she did not go on Thursdays, and that night she did not go.

On Friday she was to have met Daphne, a new friend from her AA group. Pam loved Daphne, she was a smoker and a little crazy and laughed a great deal, and she was about ten years younger than Pam, and Pam could tell her anything, like about Eric wearing women's clothes, and Daphne didn't care. Her own daughter had married a man in prison (!) and brought no end of distress to Daphne, which Daphne shared with laughs, and also with tears popping from her eyes. But this very daughter had called Daphne that morning and said she needed her, and so Daphne, with reluctance, went to spend the day in New Jersey with her. This left Pam alone. She went to a museum, and she felt lonely in it, because she thought: I am a woman alone in a museum in New York.

Who cared?

Well, Pam did.

And then Saturday night she went to her meeting, although not as many people attended on Saturday nights, and then on Sunday—Sunday descended with a quietness that Pam had long ago learned to distrust. It was *awful*. By one o'clock in the afternoon she had eaten two candy bars, and she knew she was in trouble. She should have called her sponsor, a lovely woman—a retired lawyer—who had been sober for thirty years. But Pam did not call her.

Outside, the day was glorious, sunny, and not too hot or too cold. The weather seemed to mock her. Pam walked through her apartment, and the quiet was dreadful. She gazed into her sons' rooms, the trophies they had won, Eric from his debate team in high school, Paul from his lacrosse team, and she closed their doors. Then she went into her bedroom, a big square room painted white, and she thought now that it had little warmth to it, and she also thought about how Itsie McCullough had said the apartment looked "like cheap Long Island." Pam thought, What the fuck. She went back down to the living room and sat on the sofa, and she thought, Yes. No. Yes. No. Yes.

And she got her bag, found her keys, and walked to the li-quor store in the bright sunshine, passing by people she barely saw. She bought a bottle of wine and a bottle of vodka. When she returned to her apartment, she drank the bottle of wine within half an hour and then took some gulps from the vodka bottle and then she fell asleep on the couch. When she woke up, she saw that she had urinated on the pale green couch. "Oh *fuck*," she whispered to herself. "Oh, fuck, fuck, fuck."

In the shower she almost fell, and that scared her beyond belief, and so she made her way to her king-size bed, and she looked at the ceiling, which was spinning, and she thought: I should die now.

The next morning, she called her sponsor.

And then she called Bob.

BOB HAD BEEN about to go out the door to see Jim at Susan's house in Shirley Falls, but now he sat down in the chair in the living room he usually sat in, and he listened to Pam and thought about this. "I'm so sorry," he said. "But I think this happens."

Pam said, "Oh, it does. I just wish it hadn't happened to *me*."

"What triggered it?" Bob asked.

"That's just it. Lydia? Christ, what a mess I just went through for that piece of shit, Jesus."

"Don't you have a sponsor you call when that starts to hap-pen?" Bob asked.

"Yes. The most wonderful sponsor. But I didn't call her be-cause I wanted to get drunk. I make myself sick."

"Did you tell your sponsor?"

"Oh yeah," Pam said. "Right away this morning. And she was good about it. Kept asking me what had happened, and I just don't *know*. I mean, Lydia of course, but my *God*."

Bob said, "That's scary. I mean that you don't know exactly why you did it."

"Precisely!" Pam said, "Bob, that scares the shit out of me. Because it could just keep on happening."

Bob was quiet for a moment, and then he said, "I don't think it will keep on happening, Pam. I think you can do this. Frankly, I know you can."

"Seriously, Bobby? You think I can do it?"

"Completely serious. You can and you will."

"Thank you, Bobby." She said it quietly. Then she said, "I'm going to move out of this place. I hate it here, especially after what just happened. I'm going to get my own place."

"You should. You absolutely should. Get yourself a nice small apartment, Pam. That makes sense."

She said, "I know. I don't know why I've stayed here."

Bob said, "Because it's your home. But now it's time to get a new home."

"Thank you. I appreciate everything you said. And I'm thinking of leaving the pee stain right there on the couch. Now, what's new with you?"

And Bob, glancing around his living room, the old white sofa that was not as white as it had once been, and the coffee table piled with books and phone chargers and pens, told Pam that Jimmy was up in Maine for a week and that he—Bob—had taken a case that was making him crazy. He even told her about Margaret and the church board, which now included Avery Mason, who slept through each service, and how this caused an uneasiness for Margaret. Margaret had mentioned it again the night before: that Avery Mason had managed to get himself on the board.

"Oh man. That sucks," Pam said.

He told her once more that he believed in her, and she thanked her. "That really helps," she said. She added, "Say hi to Jim for me. And to Susie too. Tell her I miss her. It was so good to see her a few months ago."

*

WHEN BOB WALKED into Susan's house his heart positively overflowed at the sight of his brother sitting in the living room easy chair. Jim raised his hand in a hello. Susan was walking between the kitchen and the living room, bringing Jim a cup of coffee. "Thank you, Susie," Jim said, and Susan raised her eyes at Bob to indicate (this is what Bob thought): Look at how polite he is.

And he was polite. It unnerved both Susan and Bob that their brother could be this considerate; Jim asked Susan many questions about what it had been like to recently retire from her work as an optometrist, to which she answered: "Pretty much great. Not lonely like I worried I would be." And then Jim said, "What about Gerry O'Hare?"

Susan, who had sat down on the couch, looked immediately at Bob, and then back to Jim. "What about him?" she asked.

"Well, you said you saw him on his porch for coffee a few times a week. I just wondered how that was going," Jim said.

Susan raised a hand just slightly, and then let it fall back into her lap. "Fine."

"You like him?"

"I do."

"He ever mention the fact that he dumped you in high school after two dates?"

Susan laughed easily. "Three dates. No, he has never mentioned that, and neither have I."

"You ever see each other for dinner, or anything?"

"No." Susan seemed vaguely confused by the question.

"Why not? Is he seeing some other woman?"

"No." And then Susan's face had a blush come over it. "At least I don't think so."

"Well, just ask him."

"Ask him?"

"Ask him, Susie. Just say, Gerry, is there any woman you're seeing? And if he says no, then invite him over for dinner. Seriously. Just do it."

Susan stayed quiet, apparently thinking about this. After a moment she looked over at Bob and said, "Bobby, when Bitch Ball disappeared, Gerry mentioned to me that Matt was sort of known in town as a perv. That's what he said. And I should have told you that, I just kept forgetting."

"A perv?" Bob felt a sweat break through under his arms.

"Yeah, a pervert. That he wanted to paint women naked in their stages of pregnancies. I think that's what it was."

"Oh, okay, thanks," Bob said. And he thought: *Phew.*

After a moment Bob said, "Well, here's a piece of news. Pam fell off the wagon." And again, Jim surprised him by looking at Bob and saying with apparent real concern, "That's too bad." And then Jim stared straight in front of him as though thinking about this. "But just tell her to put her big-girl panties on and get back on the wagon."

"I did," Bob said.

"Oh man, I hope she can do it," Susan said. "We had such a nice visit that morning when she came up here."

"She'll do it," Jim said.

And then Susan turned to Jim and said, "Now listen, Jim. Just so you're not taken by surprise. I probably shouldn't tell you, but Larry and Ariel are going to ask you to go to some Caribbean island with them next month as a conciliatory birthday present to you."

Jim looked at her, then out the window. "I'd rather slit my throat," he finally said.

2

"COME IN, COME IN," Olive Kitteridge yelled from her wing-back chair, and Lucy Barton came in, still wearing her puffy black coat even though April was almost over. She unzipped her boots and took them off, and took her coat off, then sat down on her coat, which she spread over the little couch.

"I'm ready. Let's hear it." Lucy clapped her hands twice.

Olive said with a nod, "Okay. Now, *this* is a love story."

"And a loneliness story?" Lucy asked teasingly, and Olive held up a finger and said, "Oh, I suspect there was a lot of loneliness along the way, ay-yuh. Now hush up and listen."

Lucy settled back on the hard little couch, sticking her feet forward. Her socks matched each other, Olive noticed. At least they were both a dark color.

"My first husband, Henry—" Olive pointed at the photograph of Henry there on the hutch. Lucy nodded. "My husband Henry had four aunts, and one of them was named Pauline. Now they all lived here in Maine—Henry's grandmother had come over from England with her husband to start a tea shop in Portland—and after the grandmother died—all four of the girls adored their mother, by the way—after she died, these four sisters all stayed close to each other. Three of them lived right here in Crosby along some little road, one little house

after another they lived in—when their husbands had died—
are you following this?"

"Yes," Lucy said. "Three old widows in little houses lined
up on a little road."

Olive said, "Good. Now, Pauline was slightly different.
Pauline stayed in Portland her whole life, and oh, she would
come to visit her sisters here in Crosby, but she had her life
in Portland, and Pauline was— Well, she was a very lovely-
looking woman. To be fair, all those girls were striking, but
there was something a little different about Pauline. I wouldn't
call it an elegance, but she liked nice things, she *always* kept her
figure, even when she got old, she had a small waist and full
breasts and she dressed nicely. Not fancy. But just different
from her sisters.

"Now, I got to thinking about Pauline the other night, who
knows why. But I remembered this: When she was a young girl,
I don't think she was more than twenty years old, she taught for
one year on an island off the coast, Cliff Island, in a tiny little
one-room schoolhouse. And every morning a fisherman drove
her in his boat to that island. Every morning."

"And—" Olive gave a meaningful nod. "She fell in love
with him. And he fell in love with her."

Lucy said, sitting forward, "Oh, I can picture this. A beautiful young woman with a sort of longish coat, and nice shoes,
being helped into his boat each day, I mean he must have taken
her arm to help her get in and out of the boat. Did he pick her
up afterward as well?"

"Oh yes. Twice a day they saw each other." Olive gave a
firm nod of her head.

Lucy said, "Wait—was he married?"

Olive nodded again, and said, "He was. I think he was about ten years older than she was. And she was really quite in love with him, which of course her parents found out about, her mother must have known, because, as I said, they were all close to their mother. And so the minute school got out in June, they sent Pauline off to England for a year. Off Pauline went, back to England to cool her heels."

Lucy waited and then she said, "So when she came back it was over?"

Olive nodded. "Ay-yuh. But there's more to the story."

"*Tell* me," Lucy said.

"She came back, and she married a man who was—more than her sisters had married—a man of some money. He was invested in a grocery store, or a line of them, I guess. Anyway, Pauline came back and married this man and that was that. She did very well for herself."

"That's the story?"

"No," Olive said. "The story is this—as far as I can see, the story is this—her husband, can't remember his name, oh, it was Frank, Frank dropped dead of a heart attack in his early sixties." Olive waited a moment, and then she said, "But *my* husband, at that point, had a boat. You know, not a big boat, but he had a boat, and a few years later he said to Pauline, 'I'll take you out to Cliff Island if you want to see that school again,' and she said, Yes, she thought she would like to see it. She hadn't been there for over forty years.

"I was there, I will never forget it, we drove in the boat with Aunt Pauline, well into her sixties herself by then, but healthy, you know. And pretty—as I've said—still an attractive woman with her white hair. And Henry dropped her off at the wharf, and he said, 'We'll just wait in the boat while you go see the schoolhouse'—which was no longer a schoolhouse. And we waited and we waited, and we waited, then Pauline *finally* came back, and she was very red in the face, and she said, 'You'll never believe who I saw.'"

Olive nodded and said, "It was that same fellow who had taken her to and from the island so many years ago."

"Seriously?" Lucy asked.

"Perfectly seriously," Olive said.

They were both quiet for a moment. Then Lucy said, "Did she say what they had talked about?"

And Olive said, "Not a word. But that woman sat in our boat with her face red as a ripe strawberry. She did not say one word. We dropped her off and she thanked us, and off she went."

"Do you think she ever saw him again?" Lucy asked.

"Nope. Not that I know of. No, I don't think she did."

After a moment Lucy said, "I think she was right not to marry the fisherman. Back then a divorce would have been— you know, not good—and also you said she liked nice things. It's hard to think of her with a fisherman."

Olive shrugged. "Well, she didn't marry him."

Lucy asked, "Had she any kids with this husband of hers?"

Olive nodded and said, "Yes, and that was a tragedy right there. Because one of the kids came out crazy, tried to stab her mother, the girl was sixteen, tried to stab her with a fork one day, and off she went to a psychiatrist in Portland."

"Oh Jesus," Lucy said.

"Yuh," Olive said. After a moment she continued. "So the girl—what was her *name*?—I can't remember the *name* of that woman—anyway, she was sort of on and off crazy for the rest of her life, she'd go off her medications and all hell would break loose, and then she'd go back on them. She moved out west, never came back home much at all."

"Oh my God," Lucy said. She sat up straight. And then she said, "So what is the point of this story? Pauline should have married the already married fisherman?"

Olive laughed. She really laughed at that. "Lucy Barton, the stories you told me—as far as I could tell—had very little point to them. Okay, okay, maybe they had subtle points to them. I don't *know* what the point is to this story!"

"People," Lucy said quietly, leaning back. "People and the lives they lead. That's the point."

"Exactly." Olive nodded.

3

IT WAS EARLY May now, and the leaves were starting to come into being, bright little green leaves like young girls, shy in their beauty. Each day they grew larger; you could see this if you looked. Bob gave himself over to the joy he felt. When he and Lucy walked now, they both walked—Bob thought this—with more of a spring to their steps, and they were just—oh, they were just happy to be in each other's company.

Bob finally told Lucy all about the Matt Beach case: because he had to. She listened with great attentiveness. "Bob, my *God*," she said.

"Matt knows more than he's telling me. And he seems to be getting more and more depressed. Although he does love that cellphone, he plays games on it, he was telling me."

"Get the rifle out of his house," Lucy said, and Bob said, "I sort of tried. But he said he would just go to Walmart and get another one. So I let him keep it. I mean—" Here Bob stopped walking and gave a huge sigh.

"You mean it's his life," Lucy said.

"Well, yeah—" But Bob was uncertain, as he had been since the conversation had taken place with Matt. He looked at Lucy, and she said, "Yeah, that's a toughie. You need to speak to Diana one more time at least."

"Exactly. I'd rather see her in person than speak to her on the phone. I'll ask Matt when she's coming up here again."

THEY WERE HAPPY, these two—walking and talking—they were just *happy*.

BUT THEN LUCY told him this: She said, "Bob, it turns out I embarrass my daughters."

"What?" he said, stopping for a moment to look at her.

"Yeah. It makes me a little sick, but the last time I was in New York, Chrissy was having a little party—a dinner party at her house in New Haven for a few new moms, you know—and she didn't invite me, which was fine of course because it was for new mothers, but then I found out that one of the other grand-mothers was going—a woman I had met before. And that sur-prised me. So I asked Becka about it, and she hemmed and hawed and I suddenly said, 'Wait, do I *embarrass* Chrissy?' And Becka blushed, she *blushed*, and said, No, Mom, it's not that you embarrass her—"

Bob felt his phone vibrating in his pocket, but he ig-nored it.

"It's not that. Really, Becka finally said. And then Becka said, 'Oh Mom, you know Chrissy likes nice things, and—' And what? I asked her. Bob, it was so awkward! So I told Becka never mind, not to worry about it. But it was clear to me, Bob, something about me embarrasses my daughters, and when I think of what *I* came from and what *they* came from, oh it just makes my head spin—"

———

AND THEN BOB'S phone vibrated again. "Hold on," he said to Lucy. He took it from his pocket and glanced at it. "It's Margaret," he said. He looked quizzically at Lucy and said, "I better take this."

"Take it, take it," she said, with a flurry of her hand.

Bob stopped walking—Lucy walked a bit ahead and waited for him, he understood that this was to give him his privacy—and he answered the phone and said, "Margaret, are you okay?"

He realized that he had never heard her sobbing before. She said, "Bob, I might be losing my job! Right after I gave that fucking sermon in Boston! Oh Bob, Bob . . ." And she began to sob again.

He saw Lucy ahead of him, sunlight was on her, and she stood looking away. *Wrapped in goldenness* went through his head.

"Margaret, what are you talking about?" He turned away from Lucy.

And she said, through her sobbing, "A woman on the ministerial committee told me that Avery Mason is trying to get me out. *Bob!*"

"I'll be home as soon as I can. Hang on for fifteen minutes," he said.

"Okay," she said, crying.

BOB WALKED SLOWLY over to Lucy and said, "Margaret might be losing her job."

"Oh *Bob*."

They walked back to their cars in silence, and Lucy's presence never left him. He said as he got into his car, "I'll let you know about this as soon as I can," and Lucy said, "Don't worry, Bob. Oh God, I am so sorry."

He added, "And I don't believe your girls are embarrassed by you. I bet it's something else."

"Who cares, don't worry about that," Lucy said. "Just worry about Margaret."

                                   *

WHEN HE STEPPED inside his home Bob saw Margaret on the couch; she was still sobbing—oh she was sobbing!—and her dress, a deep blue cotton dress that, when she was standing, went far below her knees, was now twisted up, and he saw her white leg and it broke his heart; it had the look of something disembodied, as though it belonged to someone who had been murdered and dismembered. And Margaret herself looked terrible, her face splotched and puffy, the poor, poor thing.

And yet, as is often the case, those of us who need love so badly at a particular moment can be off-putting to those who want to love us, and to those who do love us. Bob, as he looked at her—she seemed like a beached sea animal to him with her eyes that had almost disappeared—he did love her, he did. And yet to go to her and hold her was a thing that was strangely difficult for him to do. And this was not because of Lucy, it was because she was Margaret and he had never seen her in such distress before, and it was—oh dear God—off-putting for him.

He sat down beside her, and she moved so that her head was in his lap, and she continued to weep. He touched her head, whispering, "Oh Margaret." And after a few moments, she sat up and said, "Avery Mason always falls *asleep!*"

*

THE HORROR OF Avery Mason's being on the board haunted Bob and Margaret in a way that was extremely dismal. But Bob noticed something soon after: that when he sat in his third-row pew now, he did not feel any sense of discomfort watching his wife. She spoke with a new tone, and it was interesting. She spoke one week with a quiet sincerity about forgiveness, and the next week about love. He even noticed that a few members of the congregation made a point of telling her after how moved they were by her sermons.

But she wept every night, and this broke Bob's heart.

*

BOB, ON HIS walks with Lucy, at first did not mention Margaret's nightly weeping, but then he did. And Lucy stopped walking and said, "Bob, that's so *awful*. Oh Jesus."

They kept walking and Lucy said, "How long will this take to get resolved?" And Bob said, "It could take months."

"God, I'm so sorry," Lucy said.

"Yeah. Me too. But here's a funny thing: She's better in the pulpit." And he told Lucy then about how when he used to watch Margaret he always felt the slightest sense of uneasiness, but now he didn't. "She's just talking straight to them."

"That's interesting. That's actually fascinating," Lucy said.

And they talked more about all that had happened to them since they had last seen each other. Mrs. Hasselbeck had finally figured out that her gin was watered down. "She *did?*" Lucy said.

"Two years later, and she finally said to me this week— I mean, she was nice about it, but she said, 'Robert, this is not full gin. You've watered it down, and don't tell me you haven't.' So I confessed to her, told her I was worried about her, and she said she would like to be treated like an adult and not a child. Which I thought was sort of a valid point."

"It is. So what are you going to do?"

Bob shrugged. "I guess give her the full bottle."

And then Lucy told Bob about the story that Olive had told her of Aunt Pauline and the fisherman she was in love with.

Bob felt a momentary pain in his stomach. "That's a terrible story. Why did you decide she shouldn't have married him?"

"Because he was already married."

"Okay."

"And also because Pauline liked nice things. And he probably wouldn't have been able to give them to her."

"Fishermen make a good living," Bob said.

"So you're on his side?" Lucy turned to look at him as she asked this.

"No."

"Why not?" Lucy persisted.

Bob waved a hand; he didn't want to talk about this. "Because he was married."

They had reached the spot for his cigarette, and because there was no wind today Bob had to keep moving as he smoked it. Lucy sat on the granite bench as he paced. "How are the girls?" he asked.

She said, "Oh, I wanted to tell you! Chrissy said the reason she's been a little cold is that she misses me!"

"And why does that make her cold to you?"

"She said because I moved to Maine, and even though I come to New York and go see her in New Haven, it's like she has lost me. Because I don't live in New York anymore. So we had a really long talk about it." Lucy shook her head. "I mean it's still breaking my heart," but Lucy looked at him and said this with a smile.

"But she knows *why* you moved to Maine," Bob said.

"Yeah, yeah. But people are people, Bob."

They could not help themselves, Bob thought. He and Lucy were just happy when they were together.

"Oh, and Bridget's going to come up for the weekend in a couple of weeks!"

"Hey, that's great," Bob said.

"I guess. I'm a little scared. I mean, she's William's daughter, not mine, but it should be okay."

"It will be good," Bob said.

"For some reason I think it's going to make me miss David. It already does. I mean, I guess because Bridget was never in my life with him." Lucy stared out at the river. "When William goes to New York he sees Bridget without me, I don't know her at all, really."

"Ah, Lucy. Good luck with it."

He finished his cigarette earlier than usual so that he could sit beside her on the granite bench. He held up the half butt. "Thanks, Lucy," he said, tucking it back into the pack.

"Of course," she said.

4

JIM WAS NOW back in Park Slope, in Brooklyn, and on one warm day in May as all the leaves moved high above him in the sunshine, he was walking back to his house from the grocery store when his phone vibrated in his back pocket, and he thought: Fuck it, I'll talk to whoever you are later. He hated going to the grocery store, hated eating, hated all of it.

After he let himself in, locking the grated door behind him and putting the few groceries away, he took out his phone and saw that it had been Larry's wife, Ariel, who had called him. He listened to her phone message.

Larry had been hit by a car as he was crossing Park Avenue. He was in a coma at the hospital.

AND THIS BEGAN a new odyssey in the life of Jim Burgess.

JIM WENT IMMEDIATELY to the hospital, was ushered into the intensive care unit, and there was his son, bloated-looking, with his eyes closed and a tube in his mouth and so many wires attached to him, so many blinking lights and sounds, a cast going up and over both his shoulders almost to his neck, he had badly smashed one shoulder and broken the other, and Jim sank down in the chair beside him and began to cry quietly and steadily as he looked at his son, who appeared to Jim to be the most innocent person who had ever lived in this world.

Ariel stepped into the room, and Jim was surprised by how kind she was to him. Looking exhausted, she said, quietly, "Talk to him, they say he may be able to hear." And she backed out of the room, with her finger raised in the air.

So Jim began to speak quietly to Larry. He put his face right up to Larry's ear, snot running down over his mouth as he spoke. "Larry, listen to me. This is your father and I love you with all my heart, Larry. Can you hear me? Larry, this is your father, and I love you and I have been an awful father to you." Jim repeated this again and again, as he continued to quietly weep.

The nurses were kind; they moved around him with agility.

IT WAS AS though Jim had been sliced wide open from top to bottom, and from this flowed his tears and his love and his guilt. *Flowed.* He wept steadily for two days, as Margot and Emily came and sat with him and with Larry. Ariel made Jim drink water; a couple of times she brought him a sandwich and begged him to eat it, and he did. But he did not stop crying. He slept fitfully in the chair, and only once did he go to the hospital lounge and lie on the long hard couch there and sleep for a few hours.

On the third day, as Jim was speaking quietly to Larry, repeating over and over that he had been the worst father a son could have, Larry spoke. "Dad?" he whispered. His eyes were still closed.

"*Larry*. Larry, you're there?" And Larry said no more.

In his entire life, Jim had never before experienced what he felt now sitting by his son. He bargained with God, although he had never believed in God. But he said, "God, make him be all right, and you can do anything you want with me. Anything. But make him be all right."

On the fourth day, as Ariel sat on one side of Larry and Jim sat on the other side, still weeping but with no sound, Larry opened his eyes and said, "Dad, is that you?"

"It's me," said Jim.

"What are you doing here, Dad?" Larry asked this with slight puzzlement in his voice.

"You were hit by a car and I've been sitting here with you."

And Ariel leaned over Larry and said, "Larry, do you know who I am?"

And Larry said, "Yeah, you're my wonderful wife."

"What's my name?" Ariel asked, and Larry said, "Ariel."

And Ariel began to weep as well.

Jim called Bob.

*

AND SO ONCE AGAIN Bob was at the airport in Portland about to fly to New York, but this time Lucy was with him; she was going to visit her daughters while Bob was with Jim. William had driven them to the airport in the morning, showing up at Bob's with his sunglasses on and his white hair sticking up from his head. "Get in the front, Bob!" William said in Bob's drive-way. "You're not small. Lucy will sit in the back." And Lucy did sit in the back, and William asked about Larry, and then talked about the University of Maine and the project he was working on, saving the potatoes from climate change. Bob felt a tenderness for this man. "You kids have fun now," William said as he drove away after dropping them off, waving from the window.

"Poor Jim," said Lucy now, meditatively. "But at least it looks like Larry will be okay."

"Oh, I know," Bob said. They were seated next to each other not far from the gate; they both had little rollie suitcases in front of them.

Bob was in a quiet state of bliss. He was going to New York with Lucy. And she had asked him if he would come to her little apartment once they got there—Jim was not expecting him until tomorrow, so Bob had a free night—and Bob had said yes. He pictured it as he had seen it in her photos: the white fluffy quilt, the white couch, the blue round tablecloth. He had no idea at all what would happen between them, if anything, but that morning he had stuck a pack of matches into his pocket in case—oh Jesus—he had to take a dump when he was there. But the possibilities filled his mind. Would he finally be able to *hold* her? Impossible—but maybe not.

Just as Bob started to say to Lucy that he was really looking forward to seeing her apartment later that day, the passageway to the plane opened and people were getting off, coming into the terminal, and a woman walked past them, carrying a large leather bag of bright orange, and just as Lucy said "Nice bag," Bob understood with a tiny jolt that the woman was Diana Beach. He had not recognized her immediately because she wore a scarf over her head and there was a slightly disheveled look about her. But something about the way she moved made him realize that it was Diana.

———

HE SAT FOR a moment and then said to Lucy, "That's Matt's sister." He rose and walked toward the woman, he was behind her, she was walking quickly. And then Diana turned around and saw him, she stopped walking and so did Bob, and Bob—for some reason—could not look away from her and could not smile either. They were caught in a look. And then—this was extraordinary—Bob watched as her face changed. It would be hard for him to describe this later, but her face quickly yet subtly became a different face. Her eyes seemed to recede and they had what appeared to be almost a film over them, they were *gone* in a way, and her skull appeared to become more apparent. Her mouth went down, but mainly it was her eyes; she had become a different person.

He said, "Diana! What are you doing here in town?"

Her voice was deep, almost croaky. "I've come to tend to business," she said. She turned and walked away, very quickly. She was wearing sneakers with a pair of jeans and a white blouse.

THROUGH A LOUDSPEAKER the gate agent was saying that passengers to New York could board in just a few minutes. Bob reached for the handle of his small bag and said, "Lucy, I can't go, I'm so sorry. I have a really bad feeling."

And she said, "I get it, go to Matt right now, Bob. Just *go*." And yet for a moment Bob hesitated. "Go!" Lucy said. "And be careful."

"Ah, Lucy—"

She placed her hand on his chest and said quietly, "Go."

———

DIANA WAS ALREADY out of sight as Bob hurried after her. He walked down to baggage claim and she was not there. She had not had a suitcase with her, he remembered, nothing but the large orange bag. He waited to see if she would show up as the bags became available, but there was no sign of her. He walked across the street to where the car rental place was, but she was not there either. Where had she gone? Was she in a restroom? He went back into the terminal and waited by the women's room downstairs for five minutes but she did not appear. Finally he went outside again to the taxi stand, and he asked the dispatcher there if a woman with a large bright orange leather bag had gotten into a cab, and the man said, "Yeah, I think so."

"How long ago?"

The man said, "Oh, not that long, twenty minutes maybe?"

Bob got into the backseat of a waiting cab and gave the address of Matt's house, and then he sat back. He fumbled for his phone, and he called Matt's number. "Pick up pick up pick up," he said softly, but Matt did not pick up. So Bob looked on his locator app and saw that Matt was in Shirley Falls driving over the bridge close to the hotel on the river.

IN JUST A few minutes Matt called back. "Hi, Bob," Matt said, sounding happy to have heard from him. Bob asked Matt if he was expecting his sister today. Matt said, "Yeah, she called me last night and told me to meet her at the hotel this morning. But I just got here, and they said she never checked in."

"Check her on your locator app," Bob said.

"Oh *yeah*! I'm so stupid, Bob. Hold on, hold on." And then after a few moments Matt said, "Bob? She's headed toward my house. I should—"

"Stay right where you are. Listen to me. Do not go back home. Stay where you are until you hear from me. Understand? Just stay where you are. Are you in the parking lot of the hotel?"

"Yeah, but what's happening?" said Matt.

"I'm not sure. But stay where you are, Matt. Stay right there until you hear from me. Okay?" And Matt said "Okay" in an uncertain-sounding voice.

BOB WAITED A few minutes, collecting his thoughts, and then he called the police. "No sirens. Probably best not to use any sirens at all," he said.

5

A WEEK LATER the new leaves shone in the early afternoon bright sunlight. Bob, sitting on the side steps of Matt's house, looked around and was struck by the beauty of the natural world, as though he had never really seen it before. A robin hopped across the side lawn, and white flowered bushes pressed against the windows of the house. Bob could even hear the faint burble of the stream that ran through the woods nearby. He was thinking about Lucy. He was thinking about how he was supposed to have seen her apartment a week ago; a shyness came to him as he imagined the two of them together in her small studio in New York. He thought of the packet of matches he had put in his pocket in case he'd had to use the bathroom while he was there. He had spoken to her once on the telephone. "Oh *Bob*," she had said. She was coming back to Crosby tomorrow.

But Bob had been staying with Matt. He had spent each night for the first five nights and had come over during each day just to be with him. Matt appeared now at the door and said, "Bob, I'm not doing so well."

"That means you're normal," Bob said, standing up and going back inside with Matt.

"I'm not normal," Matt said.

"Well, you're at least a lot more normal than you think you are," Bob told him.

*

FOR A WEEK the news of Diana Beach's suicide ran in the local
papers. Woman comes home to kill herself in childhood room,
one headline screeched. As it turned out, Diana had only recently become the number one suspect in the case: A red wig
had floated to the surface of the quarry pool—it was not red by
the time it was discovered, of course, it looked like a dead
brown animal—and the state police, having returned to the
quarry to look for fresh evidence, had found it. The police also
discovered that in a store an hour away from Saco, a red wig
had been bought, shortly before Gloria Beach's disappearance,
by a woman who matched Diana Beach's description and who
had paid for it in cash. Shown a photo by the police, the sales-
clerk still remembered her all these months later and said,
"This woman was acting strangely." The police had tracked
every car on the turnpike the night of the disappearance of
Gloria Beach—they had tracked this through E-ZPass—and
they found that a car with a Connecticut license plate registered
to Diana Beach had gone through a toll booth.

By the time the Connecticut state police were heading to
Diana's home with a warrant for her arrest, she was already on
her way to Maine to kill herself. The newspapers made refer-
ence to a suicide note, but its contents were not disclosed.

Matthew Beach was no longer a person of interest in the
case; the case was now closed.

BOB HAD TOLD Matt not to read any of the newspapers, and
Matt said, "I don't read newspapers anyway."

And now—mostly—Matt slept. He slept at night, waking in the early hours, crying out, and then he slept during the days, waking and saying, "Wait!"

THE FIRST EVENING after Diana had died upstairs on the third floor, Matt sat on the edge of his bed. He looked up at Bob and said, "I'm having some trouble."

"What kind of trouble?" Bob asked gently.

"I can't get any of this through my head."

"It's going to take time."

Matt asked, "How much time?"

And Bob said that he did not know.

Then Bob said, "Want to come stay at my house tonight?"

"No."

"Okay," Bob said. "Then I'm going to stay here."

Matt looked up at him. "You *are*?"

"Yeah." Bob turned partway toward the door. "I'll stay in your mother's room, if you don't mind." And when Matt didn't answer, Bob thought, Oh God, I have to stay.

AND SO HE DID.

He listened to Matt talking for over six hours. He listened as Matt spoke of the sexual abuse Diana had endured as a girl by her father since she was young. He listened as Matt described how their mother knew about this, and not only had she done nothing but she had seemed to resent Diana more as time went on.

"Did your brother abuse her too?" Bob asked.

"Oh man—I just don't know. Thomas left, and when Diana

was fifteen, I always, *always* remember this—Thomas had been gone for maybe two years—when Diana was fifteen, she said to my father one night, in this really deep weird voice, she said, 'If you ever touch me again, I will kill you. I will kill you, don't think I won't, because I will.'"

Matt looked exhausted. Finally he added, "I'll never forget her voice that night. And I think my father never did touch her again. He left maybe—I don't know? A few months later?—He just moved out, gone. My mother must have heard from him, because they eventually got a divorce, but I never heard a thing about him again until he died in North Carolina, where he was remarried and running an accounting office."

BOB LISTENED AS Matt told him that Diana had in fact been in the house a few days before their mother disappeared and that Ashley Munroe had been there on one of those days. Matt said, "Diana must've stolen the credit card and driver's license from Ashley's pocketbook. Ashley would leave her bag on the table by the side door, and Diana must have taken it out then."

And then Matt said, "But, Bob, when I heard my mother was found in the quarry, I *knew* Diana had done it. Because Diana was raped near that quarry when she was sixteen. By a friend of my father's who had always been nice to Diana, I mean, she respected him, and he was kind to her after my father left, and he took her to that quarry one Saturday, I think it was supposed to be some sort of fun outing, and when she got home she was hysterical and she said she had been raped, and my mother—my mother yelled at her and called her a whore." Matt paused, looking around the room. "This man—this man who knew our father, he was *kind* to her. And he raped her that day. So when I heard about the quarry I thought, Diana is getting her revenge. But I never told anyone, I couldn't turn my sister in. I couldn't *do* that, Bob."

"I get it," Bob said.

"But does that make me an accessory or something?"

"No, Matt."

Matt stood up and went to the corner of his bedroom, and when he turned back he handed Bob two notebooks. "My mother's journals," he said, and Bob took them. Matt also took a piece of paper from a drawer near his bed and handed that to Bob as well. It was Diana's suicide note. "I don't ever want to see this again," Matt said—and so Bob took that as well. Bob had read the note many times. In surprisingly good handwriting, rather girlish, it detailed Diana's confession to the crime of killing her mother and stated her intentions to kill herself. The killing of her mother had been "blocked as a memory," she had written. Not until she had found the dirt and twigs on her shoes after she had arrived home in Connecticut did what she had done come back to her in parts, like a dream. She wrote that her husband's desertion had undone her, and now she was a free woman. Free of her crime, free of her punishment, free of her pain. *But I did a good job with my life, for the most part,* she concluded. And then she added, *If Matt had been convicted of this, I would have confessed.*

*

AS BOB LAY DOWN that first night on Matt's mother's bed, he thought, Oh God, I can't believe I'm doing this. But he did.

He turned the light on and read through the two notebooks written by Gloria Beach. The woman had hated herself deeply.

She wrote of Matt's illness, "This is the only thing in my life that might redeem me, if I can keep him alive." And then Bob lay there for a very long time; he thought of Lucy—he had texted her that day, and she had texted back—and he thought of this woman, Bitch Ball, and all that she had gone through. He thought of Diana and the tragedies that she had suffered. And he felt that he—Bob Burgess—was one of the luckiest people alive.

Bob must have fallen asleep at some point because he heard, as though in a dream, the sound of a cat mewling and he thought, There are no cats here. And then he realized that it was Matt in the room next to him. Bob got up and went to the door of Matt's room, which was ajar. The mewling sound grew in intensity, and Bob walked in and sat on the bed and said, "Hey, Matt," and then Matt began to cry the gasping sobs of a child. He reached for Bob and clung to him and he cried and cried, the sounds becoming almost screeches at times. "It's okay, you go ahead and cry," Bob said. The crying grew more intense. It went on for almost an hour—Bob saw this on the clock that was near the bed—this man crying in Bob's arms. And then he finally slowed down, and he yawned. He yawned!

"Don't go," Matt said, and Bob said, "I'm staying right here."

And he waited a long time until Matt settled himself on the bed again, and still Bob did not leave him. He sat there in a chair by Matt's bed until dawn came through the tiny crevices of the shrubs by the window.

*

AND SO BOB stayed with him, as we have said, for five nights, returning to him again for much of each day. Margaret came over one of those days and brought them food; she showed up in a long flowery dress and told Matt that she was sorry about everything he had been through. After she left, Matt said to Bob, "How long have you guys been married?" "Almost fifteen years," Bob said. "She's nice," Matt said, and Bob said, Yes, she was. Then Matt said, "What's it like being married?"

Bob considered this, and he said, "It's good. What's interesting about it is that you get to know each other in new ways."

"What do you mean? What kind of new way have you gotten to know Margaret?" Matt asked.

And so Bob told him about how Margaret was in fear of losing her job at the church and how—paradoxically, he thought—it had made her a better minister.

"How?" Matt asked.

"I'm not sure how to put it, but she's just more sincere when she speaks to her congregation. She's just *talking* to them, she's more herself."

Matt watched Bob for a long time, and then he said, "Why?"

Bob nodded. "I've wondered, and I think it's because she was humbled. That's my thought."

Matt just watched Bob and didn't say anything.

*

ON THE THIRD DAY, as Matt slept in his room—he had been up most of the night—Bob drove into Shirley Falls and bought white paint, and he brought it back and painted the room in which Diana had shot herself; there were blood spatterings on the ceiling and the walls. He had already removed the mattress and pillow and quilt, putting them all out in a huge plastic bag that had been picked up by a special garbage truck. Matt walked up the stairs and watched. "Thanks," he finally said.

"No problem." Bob rolled the roller over the last part and turned to look at Matt.

"I CAN'T BELIEVE she used my gun," Matt said. He had said this before. Bob had gone over it with Matt many times. Razor blades were found in the room, and it was speculated that Diana had planned on cutting her wrists, but as the police drove up she must have panicked and gone to get the rifle in Matt's closet. The police officers had heard the shot.

"It's not your fault," Bob said. He placed the roller covered with white paint into a plastic bag. He had told this to Matt many times over these last few days.

Through the window the new leaves shone a bright green in the early afternoon sunshine. Matt turned and went back down the stairs, and after a few minutes Bob followed him; Matt was sitting at the dining room table. "I don't feel right," Matt said, and Bob said, "I keep telling you that means you're normal."

Matt's elbows were on the table, his hands holding his face as he gazed at Bob. "You look like shit," he told Bob, and Bob said, "So do you." There was a moment between them—not of humor exactly, but some sort of camaraderie, Bob thought.

"You called me son," Matt said after a few moments of silence. Bob raised his eyebrows. "When you called me that day while I was waiting in the hotel parking lot, you said, Come on home, son."

Bob stretched his legs out to one side. "I know I did." He added, "I've never called anyone son in my life."

"I liked it. But I'm way too old to be your son." Then Matt said—he had said this before—"Diana wanted me to go to the hotel to protect me, right?"

"That's right," Bob said. He understood that many things would have to be repeated.

"But she still knew I would find her."

"Well, you didn't find her," Bob said. "But she didn't want you around when she did it."

Matt's dog came into the room and slunk under the table. "Have you noticed he doesn't bark anymore?" Matt asked.

"I have," said Bob.

"I think he's either in shock or he's gotten used to you."

"Maybe both," Bob said.

*

ON THE FOURTH day Matt stood in his studio looking at his paintings and he said to Bob, "Stupid fucking things."

Oddly, Bob had been anticipating this. And Bob said now, "You're not going to be interested in painting for a while, but then you will be again. But, Matt, I'd like to get these out of the house for a time if you don't mind."

Matt turned to look at him. "You mean because you think I might destroy them?"

"It's gone through my mind." Bob added, "You're upset these days. That's natural."

Matt shook his head slowly. "Bob, are you a mind reader? Because I sort of was thinking of just slicing them up."

This alarmed Bob. "Okay, I'm taking them. Today. Okay?"

"Sure," said Matt.

So Bob called a friend who had a pickup truck, and he went to get the truck and drove it back to Matt's house, and Matt watched while Bob took the paintings—there were more than two dozen of them—and put them into the back of the truck. "Where're you taking them?" Matt asked, and Bob said, "To my house."

Bob put them in the upstairs spare room, leaning them carefully against one another, and then he drove back to Matt's house and found him lying on his bed. "Why are you being so good to me?" Matt asked. And Bob said, "Because I like you." He added, "I just like you."

Matt turned over on the bed. "I like you too," he said.

LATER, IN THE KITCHEN, as Bob was getting ready to leave, Matt's cellphone went off and he looked at it quizzically and showed it to Bob. "That's Margaret," Bob said. "Pick up."

So Matt said "Hello" with tentativeness, and Bob could hear Margaret's voice—but not the words—and she was talking to Matt with excitement. "Seriously?" Matt said. "Are you just saying that?" And Bob watched as Matt's face relaxed and then became almost happy. "Cool," Matt said. "Yeah, sure. You don't have to pay me." They spoke a while longer, and as Matt hung up he said to Bob, "She loves the paintings. She just got home and found them, and she said they were *brilliant*. That's the word she used. And she wants to buy one, of a woman who modeled for me about four years ago. Margaret said you guys have the wall for it. Is she just being nice?"

"She's not just being nice. They *are* brilliant, Matt. I keep telling you."

*

AS THE SUN was just leaving the sky that night, William called
Bob. "Bob! How are you? What a mess you've been through!"
And Bob said, Yeah, it was a mess. And William said, "I read
the papers and I kept thinking, That poor guy, that poor brother.
Jesus, Bob!"

This was moving to Bob. He spoke to William about it at
length; William seemed to want to know about Matt, he was
interested in the paintings. He was just *interested*. Not a word
about his parasites.

"Lucy comes home tomorrow. She'll be glad to see you,"
William said. He added, "And Bridget comes this weekend."
William's innocence killed Bob.

AFTER WILLIAM AND BOB hung up, Margaret said, "Come,
Bob. Look at where I think this painting should go." And she
brought him upstairs on the way to their bedroom and pointed
at a spot on the staircase landing. "Right there," she said. So the
two of them went to get the painting of the young woman in her
early stage of pregnancy, and Bob saw that Margaret was right.
It did, in fact, look brilliant. He texted Matt: In case you're
awake we've decided to hang your painting on the stair landing. It's beautiful. Bob sent a picture of it. And Matt texted
back: So cool—

6

AND THERE WAS Lucy Barton, standing by the fence. She stayed where she was while he parked; he felt a shyness coming from her, and he felt shy himself. He walked to her slowly. "Lucy," he said, stopping a few feet from her. "Bob," she said. And he saw her face turn pink. "Ah, Lucy. Man." And he shook his head, he could not speak. They stood there for a few moments, not looking at each other, and then Lucy finally looked at him and said, "I am so glad to see you."

The day was sunny, and Bob put his sunglasses on. And then off they went for their walk. Lucy said, "Tell me everything. Tell me every single thing. And don't leave anything out."

Bob said, "I feel like I haven't seen you in months," and she said, "I know."

"First tell me how the visit with Bridget went," Bob said, and Lucy waved a hand. "Bob, she drove me a little bit crazy. She's just—oh I don't know, she's just an ordinary—I mean she seems so ordinary—teenage girl, and she was a little bit snotty to me. It was fine. But it *exhausted* me. Now tell me what you've been going through!"

And so Bob told her about the day of Diana Beach's death, and about how after he'd left Lucy at the airport he'd taken a cab to Matt Beach's house, pulling into the long driveway at the end of the road. Bob had seen the four police cars and an ambulance. He paid the cabdriver, who said "What's going on?" and Bob asked him to please just leave. He told Lucy how he had gotten out of the cab just as two policemen were coming through the side door of the house; they had moved slowly, so Bob knew.

"SUICIDE ON THE third floor," the policeman had said, nodding toward the house, as Bob approached him. "Classic signs. Note left, door locked from the inside. They'll be moving her out in a bit. The medical examiner is on her way." He added, "We heard the shot as we were getting out of the car."

Bob asked, "She's gone, though, right?" and the fellow said, "Oh yeah. She's gone."

One of the state troopers nodded his head, indicating that Bob should follow him, and Bob had gone into the house with him, careful not to touch anything, and the cop said, "She left this." On the kitchen table—nothing else was on the table— was a piece of paper, and on it was a handwritten message in quite good handwriting, signed Diana Beach. Bob brought out his glasses and read the note. He memorized it, and now he told Lucy what it said.

"OH GOD." Lucy whispered this. Then she said, "Keep going."

So Bob continued on with the story. He told her this:

A TROOPER HAD looked at Bob with seriousness, asking, "Where is Matthew Beach?" And Bob told him that Diana had sent Matt to the hotel on the river. The trooper nodded and then said, "We'll need to see him. He's next of kin."

"But he's no longer under suspicion," Bob said.

The trooper was a tall man, as tall as Bob, and he looked at Bob and said, "Right."

Bob had sat down then. The weariness he had felt increased, and he thought for a moment that he could go to sleep if they would let him.

The tall trooper said to Bob, "Bring him home, we'll get her out of here as soon as the medical examiner shows up and does what she has to do."

BOB HAD GONE outside to wait. It was sunny and warm, what a glorious day it had been out there by the Beaches' home on that day in May. All the shrubs by the windows were green or had white flowers now, a very slight breeze moved through them. There was the sound of birds. He had sat on the front steps, dazed. And then he had texted Jim, who had been expecting him the next day. Jim texted right back: Fuck.

As Bob sat there his legs started to tremble slightly, and he understood it was from a sense of vast relief. His legs trembled more and then they finally stopped. He called Margaret and told her, and her voice was soft as she said, "Oh *Bob.*" He said, "I'm not sure when I'll be back, Margaret, I have to stay here with him for a while."

"Stay for the night, if he needs you," Margaret said.

Bob just sat there, hearing the birds. A strange calmness had come to him. He called Matt and said, "Come on home, son."

A slight breeze had blown the bright green leaves up a little bit and then back down; he remembered this now.

———

LUCY SAID QUIETLY, "You called him son."

"I did." They had reached their granite bench, and Bob pulled out a cigarette.

Lucy stayed quiet, as though absorbing all he had said. Then she said, "Her husband going off with her best friend—I think that's what finally did her in."

And Bob nodded. He turned his face to her and said, "How are the girls, and Aiden?"

"Oh, they're all fine. Just fine." Lucy waved her hand. She said, "Tell me more."

"Turns out the Connecticut police were supposed to be watching her house, but she'd left early in the morning. Apparently, no one saw her go."

Lucy glanced at him and shook her head slightly.

"I feel—" Bob hesitated. "I feel awful. I mean physically awful as well. I feel like I've been put into a washing machine, and I'm sort of on the spin cycle."

"Yeah, of course." Lucy said this quietly. Then she said, "I keep thinking of that story Olive told me about Janice Tucker, and how I thought Janice was a sin-eater. Like you are. Oh Bob. Please take care of yourself."

"Matt said I look like shit." He gave a small smile to Lucy, who said, "You don't. But you do look exhausted."

They spoke more, in quiet tones, there was an intimacy to the way they spoke to each other, this is what Bob thought. The leaves on the birch trees were out, all the bright green leaves were there, and they could not see the river as clearly as they could in the winter. When they stood up they bumped into each other—Bob had turned, and Lucy had turned—and they stepped away from each other quickly.

As they walked back, Lucy said little. And Bob said, "You're right, I am exhausted. Talk to me, tell me anything."

So Lucy told him about an elderly couple she had seen by the elevator in the lobby of her building in New York. "They were old, Bob. Like maybe ninety, and she had a cane and was shorter than he was. He was a big man, I don't mean fat, but he was big and tall, and he was leaning toward her and laughing, I mean he was really laughing, his chest shook with laughter— and *then*—" Lucy turned toward Bob. "And then he reached over and touched her face. Her *hair*. He smoothed her hair back behind her ear. Bob! It was the sweetest thing I've seen in ages." She added, "And then they sort of hobbled off, slowly."

"Nice," Bob said.

"It was so nice."

After they parted, Bob felt a surge of deep sadness. He did not know why.

BUT LATER THAT night as he got ready for bed, he had this thought: Make it go away, please make the whole thing go away. He meant his feelings for Lucy.

7

"COME IN!" yelled Olive, and Lucy Barton walked in. It was the very end of May now and the weather was *hot* today, right out of the blue, and Lucy was wearing a dress with small flowers on it, and also green sneakers on her feet.

"Okay, I'm ready," Lucy said, placing her bag near her feet and sitting down on the couch.

Olive said, "Now, I happen to know the point to this story. Is it an unrecorded life? It is. But it is more than that. So, see if you can guess the point by the time I'm done." Olive straightened the thin jacket she had on; this jacket, which was new, tended to fall slightly off her right shoulder, which bothered her.

"I hope I can," said Lucy, and Olive said, "Hope you can too. It came to me a few days ago. Now listen."

Lucy leaned back on the uncomfortable couch, then rearranged herself, sitting back up, crossing her legs. "Go."

"Okay. Now, years ago—a million years ago—I taught with a man named Muddy."

"Muddy." Lucy said this.

"That's right. Always known as Muddy. Muddy Wilson. Ever since he was a kid his name was Muddy, somehow short for Martin. I cared a great deal for that man. A very great deal. Turns out I knew him way back at the university, and he was

Muddy back then too. So. Muddy taught history at the high school here in town. I taught junior high, but for several years we were in the same building, and I was always glad to walk into the teachers room and see him there."

Lucy was watching her with expectancy on her face, Olive thought.

Olive continued. "Muddy was a wonderful teacher. Oh, did he *love* history. And he got the kids to care for it too. You'd see him walking around town with a bunch of his students pointing to this statue and that, he adored the local history—but all history, as far as I could tell. And his students looked up to him, which was no small thing. He had *enthusiasm*.

"He also had a very pretty wife named Sally. I can't remember where he picked her up. But they got married young—as people did back then—and had two daughters, one very pretty, the other sort of pretty, but they were both nice girls. Oh."

Olive held up her finger. "Here's a detail that matters, cannot believe I almost forgot this. But Muddy's mother had died when he was young, just a small kid, and he and his father lived alone together. Never heard much about the father, but once in a blue moon Muddy would recall some memory of his mother. Of which—apparently—he had only a few."

"Good memories?" asked Lucy.

"Oh yes." Olive paused, nodding her head. "Yes. Always had the feeling that Muddy had loved his mother. Don't know what she died of, but she did. He was just a small kid, as I said. All right, so Muddy and Sally and the two girls, can't remember their names, they'll come to me—"

"Did Sally work?" Lucy asked, tucking her hair behind her ear.

"No. Well, yes. Because in the summer they had a farm."

Olive pointed over her head. "Out past the Larkindale fields is where they lived. It was a small farm, but they lived there, and they farmed it in the summer, and Sally would be out at the vegetable stand selling corn. Did I already say Sally was beautiful? There was something about her." Olive looked out the window; there were daffodils there, yellow trumpets in the air; one of them had just opened earlier this morning. "How can I put this? Sally had a glow. And the glow made her more than pretty."

"You mean she looked beatific?" Lucy asked.

Olive turned to look at her. "Explain what you mean by that," she said.

Lucy uncrossed her legs and then crossed them again—her legs were bare, Olive noticed—the other way and said, "Oh, sometimes a person, it doesn't have to be a woman, but they just have some sort of natural glow. I met a man years ago who just glowed, he beamed a certain glow, and right after I met him, he got on his motorcycle and was hit by a car. He died. But he had that look. Like he was already on his way to heaven."

THIS IRRITATED OLIVE.

She thought the heaven part was stupid, and also—Lucy was spoiling her story. She blew out breath from her mouth. "Anyway, the woman did indeed have a glow. Every *second* she looked like that. That I ever saw her anyway. She just had that certain thing about her." Olive paused, swinging her foot up and down. "And then one day Henry and I stopped by the vegetable stand, and we bought some corn, and she was out there working and—"

"She didn't have the glow?" Lucy asked.

"Different than that." Olive was squinting, remembering this. "She looked kind of yellow. She'd always had dyed blond hair, and she still did that day, but as we drove away I said to Henry, She looked wrong, she looked yellow."

"Did Henry see this too?"

"Can't remember, to be honest. Anyway." Olive looked out the window again and then back at Lucy. "Within six months she was dead. Liver cancer."

"Oh God," Lucy said. "How old was she?"

"Probably early forties. The oldest girl had just gone off to college. So Sally died. And—"—Olive held up her finger, pointing it to the ceiling—"—the point is this: Muddy fell apart. Became a different person."

"Tell me how," Lucy said, and Olive said, "Hold on, I'm going to."

Olive swung her foot again, rather vigorously, and then she put both her feet together on the floor. "Muddy grew a beard, he grew his hair long, he wore floppy leather sandals even in the winter. Back then the hippie movement was starting, and he looked like that. Like a hippie. Only he was too old to be a hippie."

"Oh God, this is going to be an awful story," Lucy said.

"Gets worse." Olive gave a nod toward Lucy. "So Muddy starts to look like hell. And there was a girl in the school, her name was Marion Tiltingham. I'd had her a few years earlier and she was crazy. Just a nut. She also had a glow, but hers was a nutty glow. Went through a phase of thinking she was a witch, that sort of thing. I remember hearing that she and a boy at school locked themselves in a dark closet one day to see which one would go crazy faster."

"Which one did?" Lucy asked.

"Who knows. So, this Marion Tiltingham graduated from high school that year that Sally died, she was eighteen years old, and the next thing we knew she had moved in with Muddy as his housekeeper." Olive raised her hands and made little quote marks with her fingers as she said the word housekeeper. "That's what they both said for a while, that she was his house-keeper, but of course she wasn't. She was sleeping with him."

"How do you know that?"

"Oh—everyone figured it out after a while, but one day Henry and I stopped by Muddy's house and she walked right out of the bedroom, which was downstairs, and she looked all sleepy and we saw it immediately. Anyway, so Muddy had fallen very much in love with her. She was about the age of his oldest daughter, and of course the girls naturally hated her, but I don't remember either of them acting out or anything. I think they very much loved their father. But how hellish for them. So the nut Marion—well, after three years, when Marion was twenty-one, she ran off with some young man she met who worked at the small grocery store that was in town back then. Out there near the Larkindale fields. And Muddy was devas-tated. As he'd been with Sally's death. He stopped bathing, never smiled, looked like absolute hell, and within a year he had married a woman who had four little kids of her own, and they all moved in with Muddy, and that lasted about a year. No idea what happened. She was a very unpleasant person, that woman, I had known her years earlier when she was quite young, and she was just cold. Meanwhile, Muddy's teaching was going downhill, he didn't care about it anymore. Horrible thing to watch. Flopping around in those leather sandals with long dirty toenails, awful.

"Then he married *another* woman, she was slightly more age-appropriate, and that lasted about three years. At this point the high school had been built and so I didn't see Muddy as much, but we'd have him over to dinner, and so strangely this wife never came with him, and he'd just sit there, and talk about nothing, you know—"

Olive seemed to be losing steam. "Finally, we heard that they were divorced, and he went off to California to get some kind of doctorate or something, both his girls were long out of the house by then, and while he was in California, he married yet another woman. I met her. He brought her back to Crosby and they showed up at the house, and this poor woman was so dumpy, his age—finally—

"The point is that Muddy," Olive said, with a huge sigh, "the point is that Muddy was a mess. Still a mess. And then he died."

"How?" Lucy asked. She leaned forward slightly as she asked this.

"He got some kind of cancer and he refused to be treated for it. He wrote me a letter about that, and he said, 'I always loved you.'"

Olive blinked her eyes. This was painful for her. She had really liked Muddy.

THE TWO WOMEN sat in silence as though absorbing all that had just been said. Finally, Lucy spoke. "So what's interesting about this is that Muddy was completely dependent on Sally. She made him who he was. And for five minutes he transferred that onto that Marion girl, but it couldn't last."

Olive nodded. "That's right. And I think—I could be wrong—that because he had lost his mother so young, he loved Sally with all the love not just of a husband but of a son as well, and when he lost her he got thrown back to that bad thing that happened to him as a little boy, and he could not cope. Could not do it."

"I think you're right about that, I agree," Lucy said.

Another silence stayed in the room, and then Olive said, "She was his linchpin. He used that word once, as she was dying. Said Sally was his linchpin."

"You know," Lucy said slowly, raising her hand and sort of drawing a small circle with her finger, "this is what I wonder. I wonder how many people out there are able to be strong—or strong enough—because of the person they're married to."

"Ay-yuh, I've been wondering that too." Olive crossed her legs and swung a foot again. "I've been thinking about Henry. One could say he was my linchpin, because he was. And yet—" Olive shook her head slowly. "And yet I was able to get remarried and live a fairly okay life with my second husband, Jack. He was never Henry, but my life went on."

"Because you're you," Lucy said.

Olive looked at her. Lucy looked slightly different, though Olive could not have said why. And then Olive thought that every time she saw Lucy, Lucy looked just slightly different. "Tell me what you mean," Olive said.

"Well," Lucy said, looking at the ceiling for a while and then back to Olive. "You are you. And Muddy was Muddy. And even though I know you had a difficult background, you still knew who you were. Or are."

Olive considered this. "Go on," she said.

Lucy sat forward, and then she sat up straight. "You know that Bob Burgess took the Matthew Beach case, right?"

"Oh yes. I even told him some things that were helpful," Olive said.

"Right. Well, he told me some details, and honestly, I hope—now that the case is closed—they're not confidential details—" Olive waved a hand to dismiss such a thought, and Lucy nodded and kept on. "My point is, we all know that the sister, Diana, came home to kill herself and she confessed to the murder of her mother. But my question to Bob is, *Why* at the age of sixty-five does this woman decide to kill her mother? That's not young, Olive."

And Olive said, "No, it is not." Olive had wondered the exact same thing.

"And it turns out, this poor woman who had been abused for the first many years of her life—Olive, she had a *really* sad story—" Olive nodded. "The point is, this woman who had been abused so much in her youth suddenly decides at the age of sixty-five to kill her mother. Why?"

"And what is your theory?" Olive said.

"My theory is this: That in spite of everything in her life going wrong she was able to keep it together. She kept it together, Olive, until her second husband came home and said, I am having an affair with your best friend. And I want to leave you."

Olive did not know that about the affair with the best friend. She waited.

And Lucy continued. "People are mysteries. We all are such mysteries. Diana Beach had so many problems, but she lived a life. She did. She left her first husband for this second one, and she was—apparently—a successful high school guidance counselor for years. And yet when that second husband leaves her for her best friend—" Here Lucy sighed and shook her head in a tiny way. "Well, the sense of betrayal that Diana had experienced, really since her earliest memories, must have just been too much."

Olive thought about this. "Ay-yuh. I suspect you might be right."

"Most of us have a few more reserves, though in truth probably not that many, but enough to get us through things. But Muddy and Diana just didn't."

Olive gave a big sigh. She was tired now. "Well," she said. "That was the story of Muddy Wilson."

*

AFTER LUCY LEFT, Olive realized she had forgotten to tell her that Charlene Bibber had a boyfriend.

*

MATT CALLED BOB one day—this was a few weeks after his sister had died—and said, "Bob, I want to paint you."

"*Paint* me?"

"Yeah. You know. Paint. I want to paint a picture of you."

"In the nude?" Bob asked; he was alarmed. "No, I'm not doing that."

And Matt laughed. He really laughed, and said, "No, Bob. The idea of you sitting in the nude is not attractive to me. But just come sit. Wear your awful jeans and that rumpled shirt you always wear."

And so Bob sat for over an hour in Matt's studio; no paintings had been returned to it, and it had an empty feel as Matt
worked. Through the open window came the smell of two huge
lilac bushes that grew below. It was strange to watch Matt; his
face became different as he worked; he was inside somewhere
else. "Need to do some sketches first," he said, working with a
stick of charcoal, and then he added, "I don't want you looking
at this."

"No problem," Bob said, holding up a hand.

"Put your hand back down."

MATT WANTED TO paint the picture for Margaret—and this
sort of killed Bob. "I like her a lot," Matt said.

8

THREE WEEKS AFTER Larry had been hit by the car—during which time Bob, up in Crosby, Maine, was suffering over his love for Lucy and sitting for his portrait with Matt—Larry left the hospital in an ambulance and was driven back to the apartment he shared with Ariel; it was decided he would recuperate there, and Ariel said that Jim could stay in their spare room. The spare room was filled with books from Larry's time in college, stacked from the floor to halfway up the wall, and there was a single bed that tucked itself beneath a sloping ceiling. Larry's sisters showed up and sat by the hospital bed that had been set up in the living room, not unlike—except the place was smaller—where Helen's bed had been when she was dying. The living room looked out over the East River; barges could be seen going back and forth.

Jim still wept quietly on occasion, though he tried hard to control his weeping now. But what he could not believe was this: Larry was kind to him! Larry was good to him!

Larry would say, "Oh Dad, you're killing me, buddy. Man, you're killing me, Dad. We're okay now, do you hear?"

WHAT JIM WAS experiencing was not unlike what a person who has fallen in love experiences—he was exalted. All his grief for

Helen—and for his entire life, it seemed to him—came pouring forth in this new state for his son.

And he once more would apologize for everything he could think of—and there were many things—that he had done wrong with Larry. "I never should have sent you to summer camp," he said, and he felt the truth of this go through him, the anguish that Larry had experienced at those stupid summer camps, because Larry had not been athletic, had been homesick, had never fit in.

But now Larry just watched his father and said, "It's okay. You know why it's okay? 'Cause you mean it." One day he said, jokingly, "Dad, I should have almost died sooner," and Jim just shook his head, he could not speak with the constriction in his throat.

AND SO, in this way, with Larry in a hospital bed as Helen had been only a few months before, Jim felt the multitude of gifts being given to him in a manner that previously would have seemed unimaginable.

In short, he felt transported into another world, a world where all he felt was love and sorrow, and yet the love was stronger than the sorrow. It was *strong*, and when his girls came to visit, he felt as though the country he had been living in had shifted abruptly, and for whatever reasons—was it a gift from *God*?—he was now in an altogether different country, and it was a country of purity.

THIS IS WHAT Jim felt for two weeks in Larry's apartment.

———

AFTER TWO WEEKS of Larry being home—the physical therapist came in every day, and the occupational therapist came as
well, and nurses were there around the clock—after two weeks
of his son being home, Jim asked the nurse if he and Larry
could have some privacy and she said, Sure, and went into the
kitchen.

And Larry, who looked puzzled, watched as his father pulled
the chair closer to the hospital bed. "Larry, listen to me. You
really should know exactly the kind of shit I've been. You're
too forgiving, and so I need to tell you something, because you
should know."

A look of slight fear passed over Larry's face.

"You know how you always thought it was Uncle Bob who
killed our father by playing with the gearshift?"

Larry looked really frightened now.

Jim said, "Well, it was me. I was eight years old, and Bobby
was four years old, and I remember it, and he doesn't. But that
day Dad had said to me, Okay, you can be in the front, the
twins in the back. And so they were in the back of the car, and
I—I was the one—who was playing with that gearshift, and as
soon as the car rolled over Dad, you know what I did? I shoved
Bob in the front seat of the car. I blamed it on him. I did that."

Larry stared at him with his mouth slightly parted. "You
did?" He asked this quietly.

"I did."

Jim sat back. What had he expected? He did not expect what
was about to happen.

Larry finally spoke. "That's unbelievable. That's a really
unbelievable thing."

Jim said, "I told Bob about fifteen years ago, and he said it fucked him up a lot. Because he had lived his whole life thinking he had done it. He said I had taken away his identity, or his fate—something like that."

Larry said nothing.

"And your mother knew too. Bob told her."

Larry kept staring at him. "What did she say?"

"She wasn't happy with me at that time. She thought it just showed that I'd always been a piece of shit." What had Jim been thinking as he told his son this?

Because Larry's lips had lost their color now, and he finally said, "Dad, that's evil. I'm sorry, but that's just fucking evil. You've been evil your whole life. Dad, please go away now. Because I really have to think about this." He turned his face away from Jim. "Go away. Please go away now," he said.

*

AND THE DESPAIR that Jim felt after that was—literally— *almost* unendurable as he moved through his brownstone in Park Slope, waiting for Larry to call. And Larry did not call. When Jim called Larry, Ariel always answered and said, "He doesn't want to talk to you, I'm sorry."

Oh Jim. Jim.

HE CALLED BOB.

9

BOB WALKED UP the steps of the office building where Katherine Caskey had her social work practice. Her office was in a large old wooden building a few blocks away from Bob's office, it also held within it an accountant's office and a small law practice, and then the office of Katherine Caskey.

"Hello, Bob," Katherine said as she hugged him, and she looked the same as she always had, this is what Bob thought. A small woman who had a litheness to her, with her auburn hair and black slacks and green top. "It's *so* good to see you, come in, come in."

"How's Elton?" Bob asked.

"Fine." She smiled warmly at him. "You indicated this is business."

"Personal business. Doesn't mean I can't ask about your husband," Bob said.

"Honestly, Bob? I think he's better. So: Phew."

BOB SAT DOWN in the chair across from Katherine's desk, and she sat down in a chair not far from his; she did not sit behind her desk. Her walls held framed posters: pictures of the ocean and an old house covered with rosebushes. She said, "Now tell me why you're here." On her desk was a begonia plant, and as

Bob looked at it, a blossom fell off. He had a small, strange feeling that something he had done caused it to fall. He looked at Katherine with a quizzical look. "What?" she asked, and he nodded toward the plant. "You just lost a blossom," he said.

"Oh, that happens all the time." She waved a hand.

And so Bob told her once again about the accident that had killed his father, about how he had always thought he'd done it and that Jim had told him years ago that *he,* Jim, had done it. Bob settled back in his chair. "So my question is, just because I was four and Jim was eight, does that make his memory more real? Honestly, Katherine, we've never *talked* about this, except for Jim's confession to me ages ago."

Katherine sat forward with her legs crossed and asked him many questions about his memory of the accident. Bob had very few memories of it, only that he was positive that he and Susie had been in the front seat, and he also had a memory of bright sunshine. "Even now, a glaring sun causes me to feel sort of sick."

Katherine asked Bob what Jim's relationship with their father had been, and Bob did not have an answer for that. She spoke about a variety of studies done on memory and traumatic events, and then she said, "What does Jim think the weather was that day?"

Bob just looked at her. "No idea."

"Ask him."

"Hold on." And Bob took out his cellphone and called Jim. Jim picked up the phone right away and said, "When are you getting here, Bobby?" And Bob said, "Tomorrow. But I want to ask you. Do you remember what the weather was when our father died?"

"The weather? Yeah, it was pouring. Absolutely pouring

rain." Then Jim added, "And it was windy. All the foliage was coming off the trees because of the wind and rain. Bright orange leaves falling to the ground, wet, wet, wet."

Bob waited a moment and then he said quietly, "But, Jimmy, our father died in February."

Jim was silent for a long time. And then he said very quietly and slowly, "Holy fuck. You're right. There couldn't have been any foliage."

Bob hung up and reported this to Katherine, and she said, "Well, there we are. Bob, no one will ever know what happened."

"Hold on again," Bob said, and he called Susan, who also picked up right away. "Susie, do you remember the weather on the day our father died?"

"Really sunny," she said.

BOB LEFT KATHERINE'S office believing that no one would ever know who was responsible for his father's death.

*

WHEN BOB ARRIVED home and walked in the door, eager to tell this to Margaret, she said, "Bob! Avery Mason died. He's *dead*." And then she said, "Three people on the board all called me today to tell me they were sorry about how he was trying to get me fired, and they want me to stay at my job. Plus, Avery's wife wants me to do his funeral! Which I will, of course."

*

SO BOB FLEW to New York the next day, and he took a taxi directly to Larry's place; he had told Jim he was going there first. It turned out to be a very hot day in the city, and as he rode in the taxi past buses and cars and people walking along the sidewalks, a sense of enormous weariness came to him. He was not aware of how much had been taken out of him by his concern for Matt Beach, for his brother, for Margaret, for the many people who depended on him. Nor was he aware of just how much his feelings for Lucy were taking from him. His weekly walks with her recently had left him simultaneously exhilarated and despondent. It was not Bob's nature to think in a reflective manner, and so he simply felt an exhaustion that seemed almost dangerous to him. In fact, these words went through his head as he paid the driver, then stepped from the cab. *Dangerously exhausted.*

It was a gorgeous apartment—Bob had never seen it—it had five rooms and looked out at the East River. It seemed very grown up for a couple like Larry and Ariel, this thought went through Bob's head. He did not care for their artwork on the walls; it was popular-type junk, he thought, having been deeply influenced by Matt's stuff, which seemed so *authentic.* As he stepped into the living room and saw the sudden wash of golden color that is sent—bizarrely—back over the East River for a few moments each evening, he thought, How strange it is that these kids—he thought that word—live in such a place.

There was a leather sofa and a big television screen, and chairs that were yellowish and a coffee table that was very long and thin.

And there was Larry, sitting in a large easy-chair-type thing; his hair had grown out a bit, and he looked good. He still had a cast on one shoulder, the other shoulder was now in a sling contraption. Ariel had let Bob in; she knew of course that he was coming, but she had not told Larry. It was to be "a surprise."

And Larry did seem surprised. "Uncle Bob! What are you doing here?" But his face held gladness. "Have a seat," he said, nodding toward one of the yellowish chairs.

Ariel said, "I'll leave you guys alone." And off she went into another room; Bob heard a door close.

SO BOB SAT. He was, as we have indicated, completely worn out.

And he said this: "Larry. You can think whatever you want to about your father. But I'm going to tell you he is not evil. And you can listen or not."

Larry looked at him, and Bob saw his face become hard.

"Are you going to listen? Because I'm not going to waste my time if you're not listening."

"I'm listening," Larry said.

"I want to tell you about this case I just had in Maine. A guy takes care of his mother, she disappears, it turns out that his older sister took her in a car one night and drove the car into a quarry. You know why?"

Larry, watching him, gave a tiny shake of his head.

"Because that sister had been sexually abused by her father for years as a young person, and her mother knew it. And then her father leaves, and one day one of her father's friends takes her for an outing. He takes her out to this quarry, and he rapes her. When she gets home her mother calls her a whore. Now think about that for a moment, Larry."

Larry said quietly, "Jesus."

Bob continued. "And just before you get all ready to judge her *mother,* her mother's story was this: She had also been sexually abused for years as a kid, got pregnant by her uncle, her parents kick her out of the house, and she and her baby live at a hotel while she works the front desk, and the hotel owner abuses her as well. You know why I'm telling you this, Larry?"

"Because that's evil?" Larry asked.

"No. That's not evil, Larry. These are *broken* people. Big difference between being a broken person and being evil. In case you don't know. And if you don't think everyone is broken in some way, you're wrong. I'm telling you this because you have been so fortunate in your life, you probably don't even know such broken people exist."

Larry only watched him.

"What do you have to say to this?" Bob asked.

After a moment Larry said, "Well, I feel sorry for those people. But they're not my father. My father never went through any of that stuff, and he came out evil. What he did to you was evil, Uncle Bob."

BOB SAT FORWARD, he was really not feeling well, and he was getting angry now. "What you had, Larry, was a father who was fucked up. That's all. And you know why he was fucked up? Because he thought he'd killed his father. And you know something else? *No one in this world* knows who killed our father. Your father thought the leaves were falling off the trees and it was raining that day. Well, the man died in February and there were no leaves falling. And Susie and I remember there being bright sunshine. No one knows, Larry. No one will *ever* know.

"And what you had was just a fucked-up father, and, yeah, he sent you to summer camp. Because he thought that's what kids should do. And you hated it. And he made you stay there. Terrible. But you know what, Larry? What you had was just a normal fucked-up *super*-wealthy background. Nothing more."

Bob stood up. He was furious now.

"That's all I have to say to you, Larry. Go ahead and hate him. And then someday—not that long from now—he will die. And you might, or you might not, remember that he sat next to you in that hospital room as you were struggling to live, and wept, you might not remember that, but ask your wife, she'll remember, and that he felt just awful in a way that an evil person cannot feel—are you listening to me? And then when he is dead, and your child is fifteen and may not be the child you thought he—or she—ought to be, then maybe you can have some sympathy for your father.

"But right now, you have no sympathy from me. You are still too young. And you have had my sympathy your whole life, but when you say your father is evil, well, your father is not evil. Is he broken? Yes, we're all broken. Frankly."

And then Bob had to sit down. His chest was hurting. When he looked at Larry, Larry was pouting; this went through Bob's mind. The kid—who should have been a grown man—was sitting there pouting, and this was unattractive to Bob.

*

LATER, IN PARK SLOPE, Jim listened to Bob in his study and then said quietly, "Thanks, Bob. You're a good brother."

"Well, your son is really pissing me off right now."

Jim waved a hand listlessly. "Let him go. Let him be."

Then Jim looked at Bob and said, "Are you all right? You look kind of awful."

"I'm tired." It came out as a murmur.

"Ah, Bobby. You shouldn't have had to come here for me. For this crap with my son." Jim sat back in his chair, putting one leg across the other. "Also, you need a haircut."

Bob said, "I promised Helen when she was dying that I'd help out between you and Larry, but I just fucked it up more because I was so pissed off at him."

"Bob, really, I'm telling you, you tried, and I appreciate that. Don't take it so personally."

Bob held a hand up for a moment. He waited a while and then he said almost in a whisper, "I've fallen in love, Jim. I'm in love with Lucy Barton." Tears began to roll down his face. He could not stop them. His big chest shook as he wept.

Jim leaned forward, watching him carefully. Then Jim sat back and said quietly, "Oh you poor fuck." Jim shook his head slowly and said, "You poor, poor fuck."

They sat in silence while Bob continued to weep, wiping at his nose and eyes with the backs of his hands, and then Jim said, "Is she in love with you?"

"No idea."

Jim shook his head slowly. "Oh Jesus, Bob. You are the only person in the world who doesn't know if someone is in love with him." Jim sat forward again. "Of course she's in love with you. You two take walks all the time, and you talk, right?"

Bob nodded.

"I always remember reading—it was years ago now—an article in which a famous director said: There is nothing sexier than talking. I always remember that. And that's what you and Lucy do—you *talk*. All right, now listen, Bobby. Don't tell her you're in love with her. Do not have that conversation with her. Because once you do, once you start confessing this stuff to each other, you're going to be screwing like rabbits, and your whole *world* will fall apart. Margaret will probably die as a result, even William might die, so don't do it, Bobby. It's not worth it. Do not do that."

"I know. But I *want* her, Jimmy. Oh God."

"You're going to have to get over that. Seriously. Take it from me, I've been there, and I know you, and you will not be able to live with yourself. You can live with being in love with her, hard as it is, but you will *not* be able to live with yourself if you touch her. You're Bob Burgess. I know you."

IO

AND SO LIFE continued in Crosby, Maine. Margaret was now firmly once again in her job after the death of the previously-often-sleeping congregant Avery Mason—her homilies stayed sincere and good, Bob noticed—and Mrs. Hasselbeck asked Bob to once again water down the gin he brought her every other week, she said she had almost had a bad fall, and so Bob watered it down even more than half, and the locksmith who was a heroin addict took off for Florida, or so it was said, and also it was June, which is a glorious month in Maine, although it rained a lot and was chilly. The rhododendron screeched out their color against many houses in town. Tourists began to appear once again, people grumbled about them, but for Bob they brought a sense of openness to the place. Matt Beach had received two letters from women who wrote to say that they were very sorry about all they had read in the newspapers. Matt asked Bob what he should do, and Bob said, "If they sound like nice people, you should answer them."

*

AND CHARLENE BIBBER did in fact now have a man in her life. She had found him online at a political site she frequented, and it turned out that he lived two towns away and had been divorced for years. His name was Carl Dyer, and he was tall and lanky and had pale hair and was two months older than Charlene. Charlene's life had changed completely, as these things will do. He wanted to know everything about her—everything! As they lay together on her bed, she told him about her friendship with Lucy, and he wanted to know more, and so Charlene told him, as she stroked his long, gentle arm, about Lucy's sister not liking Lucy and how Lucy was now living with her ex-husband at that house way out on the point. Carl pulled the sheet down and gazed at Charlene, who blushed at this sudden exposure. "What a beauty you are," Carl said.

She touched her stomach and said, "Oh right, this flab is beautiful, that's for sure," and Carl said, "All the more for me to nibble," and he began to do just that as Charlene shrieked with laughter.

The week before, Louise from upstairs had called Charlene to complain about all the noisy sex she and Jerry had to listen to. "Jerry's *sick*," she had said. So now Charlene was staying mostly at Carl's house. Carl owned a roofing business, but he'd had an accident, and so now his employees worked without him. He asked her why she worked in the food pantry, and she told him about how when she was a kid there was sometimes not enough food in the house. Carl turned on his back and said he knew some people who didn't really need the food and who had stolen from the food pantry in his town, people who just drove up and took it, and when he got done with the story, Charlene felt an uncertainty.

"But it's up to you if you want to keep working there," he said, looking over at her.

As time went by, Charlene stopped volunteering at the food

pantry in Crosby, and she gradually stopped taking Lucy's phone calls.

AND IN THIS way the situation in the country divided itself further.

*

THEN THERE WERE Bob's walks with Lucy.

He craved them in a way that almost sickened him, and oddly it made him think of Pam, and how she had given up booze, because he felt addicted to Lucy, felt he would have done anything to see her, and maybe that was what it had been like for Pam with her drinking. So he called Pam, and she was cheerful. "Bob, I'm *good*. I have so much more energy, I can't believe it, and I'm going to suggest—next week, in fact—to Ted that we separate, except that scares me, and so I don't want to do it quite yet, but I'm getting ready. How are *you*?" she asked.

And Bob said he was all right.

"What's the matter, Bobby? I can hear in your voice, something's wrong. What's wrong?"

"Nothing at all," he said, and this was a lie, and Bob did not like to lie, so he asked more about her, about the boys, and then they hung up.

When he saw Lucy standing by the fence the next day, he almost did not like her. She was causing him too much pain, and so he walked to her slowly. "Are you okay?" she asked; he could sense her looking at him, but he did not look back.

"I'm okay," he said.

As they started to walk, Lucy talked about a woman she had known in college. Her name was Addie Beal, and Lucy was thinking about telling Olive the story she had just finished telling Bob about this Addie Beal. It had been quite a long story.

"Yeah, tell her. Great story. But super sad," Bob said.

He asked about her girls, and she said that they were both being lovely to her. He told her about Larry, and she listened. "Oh, wow, poor Jim," she said.

But when their walk was done, Bob felt that he had not quite seen her distinctly. And he realized that he had been feeling that way for a while, even when he had been happy to see her—in his memory he could not remember their talks all that well either, and he could not picture her, except for fleetingly.

AND SO BOB was a mess. He could not sleep, he had to use every bit of energy to get through his evenings with Margaret. He could not eat, and he started to lose weight.

*

BACK IN New York City, Pam was watching with horror as the sky outside her window changed. It began as a strange look of dawn, although it was eleven o'clock in the morning. Two hours later the sky was an eerie orange, and to Pam it looked like space aliens were about to invade. She did not go outside for three days; a forest fire in Canada was sending over its debris, and people were warned to avoid going outside. A strange smell wafted into her place, although all the windows were closed tight.

A few times Pam closed her eyes as she thought: Oh, this poor earth!

On the second day of this otherworldly-looking occurrence, Pam heard her door unlock and she sprang up from her couch to hear her husband call out, "Pam?"

"Ted!" Pam walked to him quickly; he looked unwell. His clothes appeared to fit him badly and his hair had not been combed. But he also had deep pockets beneath his eyes, and Pam said, "Come, sit down, what's happened? Are you okay? How did you get here, did you drive?"

"I drove." He nodded, then went and sat in a chair beside a glass table in the corner by the window.

"Oh my God, I hope you had the windows rolled up." She lowered herself onto the couch.

"I did." He looked at her, then took his glasses off, rubbing his hand over his face.

Pam felt a quickening in her stomach. She said nothing as she watched him.

He sat forward with his arms on the glass table, and he said, "Pam." The look he gave her was one of a dismal desperation; she had never seen him like this before. "Pam, I miss you," he said.

Still Pam remained silent.

"Did you hear me? I said I miss you, Pam. I miss my wife." He gave her a sad, wry, and small smile.

"Oh God." Pam said this so quietly, she was not sure that he heard.

He stood up then but did not walk toward her. "Are you having an affair?" He asked this gently.

It took her a moment, but she said, "Am *I* having an affair?

Am I having an *affair*? *You're* the one having an affair, Ted, with that fucking idiot Lydia Robbins! Jesus Christ, Ted!"

He stood there, and she had never seen his face so sad. He said, "I can't stand Lydia Robbins, Pam. I honestly cannot stand that woman."

"Well, that's not what I heard!" She was ready to have it out with him.

But he sat down at the table and cried.

I I

OLIVE KITTERIDGE SAT waiting for Lucy to show up. Olive's son, Christopher, had just called from New York City, where he lived, and he had been uncharacteristically talkative, and Olive kept glancing at the clock because Lucy was to arrive at ten, and as her son went on talking she became anxious—to tell him she had to go would be an awful thing because whenever she spoke to him again he would probably not be this talkative—but he finally wound down and she said, "Okay, Chris, nice talking to you," and he said, "You too, Mom"— which was a pleasant thing for Olive to hear.

And now she sat waiting. Lucy always showed up early, but today she was five minutes late and Olive was rolling her eyes when there was finally a knock on her door.

"Come in!" yelled Olive, and Lucy came in, wearing a striped blue-and-white dress, the material reminding Olive of a seersucker suit Henry used to have years ago, and Lucy looked nice in the dress. It went almost to her ankles with a slight tuck at the waist, and she wore her green sneakers, which was too bad, because they didn't go with the blue. "I like that," Olive said, putting her hand down in front of herself to indicate Lucy's dress.

"You do? Really? We went to Rockland last week and I

bought this. I spent a lot of money on it," Lucy said, as she sat down on the small couch.

"I bet you did," Olive said.

"And now I'm thinking it wasn't worth it."

Olive said, "It looks fine, I told you I liked it. Now let's hear your story."

"Okay." Lucy placed a new bag—at least Olive hadn't seen it before—on the couch next to her. The bag was blue canvas with two long leather straps. Olive almost said that she liked the bag too, but Olive didn't think overcomplimenting someone was anything she cared to do. So she kept quiet.

Lucy folded her sunglasses and put them into the blue bag, and then she sat back and said, "Okay. Here is my story. I don't know what to make of it. I'm going to tell you that right up front. It *is* one more story of an unrecorded life, but beyond that—I don't know."

Olive waved her hand to indicate that Lucy should just begin.

"So." Lucy folded her hands on her lap. Then she crossed her legs and bent forward just slightly and said, "There was a girl—well, a woman, but back then we were girls—I went to college with. Her name was Addie Beal and she was two years behind me. Addie was an only child. Her mother had been sixteen years old when she had her. And they were almost more like sisters, I mean they just adored each other. The mother especially, her name was Lindsay, and she was just *crazy* about Addie." Lucy wiped back some strands of hair that had fallen in her face.

Lucy continued, raising her eyebrows at Olive. "So, as awful people say, Addie didn't come from much."

"Meaning what?" Olive asked.

"Meaning money, but also, her mother was not educated, I mean she never finished high school because she gave birth to Addie, and so she did secretarial work, and they really had no money, Addie was at school on a full scholarship like I was. So we had a little bit of an immediate connection because of that. Even though most of my friends—I think, anyway, I'm not sure now, looking back—did not realize the extreme situation I had come from myself.

"But Addie was a pretty girl, sort of sparkly in her face, and she was in the theater department, and of course she got all the ingenue parts."

"Where did she come from?" Olive wanted to know.

And Lucy put one hand up and said, "Exactly. She came from Maine."

"Maine? Beal is a Maine name. Where in Maine?" Olive asked.

Lucy looked slightly bewildered. "Oh, I don't really know."

Olive was irritated by that, as though all of Maine was just one big place to Lucy, and what part of it you came from didn't matter. Well, Lucy wouldn't know the different parts, but it still irritated Olive. "Go on," Olive said.

"But when she got that scholarship, her mother moved out to Illinois and rented a little apartment a few towns away from our school; the town was sad, not unlike Amgash, where I had grown up. But Addie would go see her mother every couple of weeks, and sometimes I went with her."

"How would you two get there, did the mother have a car?"

Lucy looked appreciatively at Olive. "No, we'd take a bus. A Greyhound bus. Up and back. And because I didn't like to go home myself at *all*, I remember one time I went and spent New

Year's Eve with them. It was strange, because of course my parents never drank and never celebrated New Year's Eve—"

"Stupid holiday," Olive interjected, and Lucy said, Yeah,
it was.

And then Lucy went on. "So Lindsay and Addie drank beer
out of champagne glasses, oh they had a wonderful time. It was
a really little apartment, tiny, but they seemed to love it." Lucy
gazed off to the side, out the window, but she did not seem to be
looking out the window, she seemed to be far away. "It was just
interesting to me, I think now, because they had very little, but
they had each *other,* and that sort of seemed enough for them."
She looked back at Olive. "The apartment was dark. And Lindsay slept on the couch and Addie had a little bedroom."

"Was Lindsay pretty like Addie?" Olive crossed her ankles
and sank back in her chair.

"Lindsay was attractive, I'd say. Perfectly attractive, big
brown eyes. But not pretty the way Addie was." Lucy sort of
shrugged and then said, "But here's the thing. So one time I
was there, one of the first times, maybe it *was* the first time, and
Addie went into her tiny bedroom and brought back a stack—
and I mean a really *huge* stack—of scrapbooks. And inside
these scrapbooks were newspaper articles about Addie since
she was barely two years old. She had been Miss Maple Tree,
Miss June Bug, Miss Moxie, oh she'd been everything you
could be, and as the photos progressed there she was with her
baton and little boots, she'd been a mascot at some college in
Maine—maybe it was the university, because they had a band,
I don't know—but this whole huge stack of scrapbooks contained everything she'd ever done, and Lindsay watched with
such happiness as I looked at each clipping, and Addie herself
was so excited to show me."

Lucy stopped. Then she said, "So there was that."

"And what else?" asked Olive. She thought this was a far better story than the one about Lucy meeting that man on the train.

"Oh, one time Addie read to me a quiz from a women's magazine. She and her mother had these magazines, I'd never really seen them, I mean my mother had never had them, but some women's magazine had a quiz, and Addie said, all excited, sitting with her legs up on the couch, 'Lucy, I want you to take this quiz.' "

Lucy held up her hand. "Hold on. I left out a detail."

"Tell me the detail." Olive tugged her cotton vest together.

"It must have been near my birthday or something, because Addie had given me a present not long before this quiz. I mean at the apartment the same day. And the present was a knit thing, I can't even remember, but she had knit a circle or something, with a design to it, and it sort of confused me, but she was very happy as she watched me unwrap it, so I made a big deal out of it and said, Oh, I love this, I just *love* this. That sort of thing."

"Ay-yuh. Go on," Olive said.

"So then she made me take this quiz. She read me the questions and I would answer them. I can't even remember the point of the quiz. I only remember this: that one of the questions was: A friend gives you a gift and you don't care for it. You (a) say thank you, but this is not really me, or you (b) say oh this is nice, but I'm going to give it to my sister, or you (c) say I love this so much, oh thank you.

"Which of course is what I had just done. So I said: c. And Addie just continued on, I don't think she even knew that I had just done that, and then she added up my score, and I can't remember the rest of it, except Addie was so happy and excited."

Lucy stopped talking, and after a moment Olive said, "That's it?"

Lucy looked at her quickly. "*No*. Oh no, there's more."

"Well, let's hear it."

"Okay." Lucy plucked at the center of her dress, looking down at it as she did. "You sure this dress works?"

Olive said, "I already told you that. It reminds me of a seersucker suit Henry had years ago."

Lucy said, "So Addie had a father."

"You didn't mention a father in the picture."

"Well, he wasn't in the picture. Not by the time I knew her. But she had a father who was an alcoholic, and the mother—Lindsay—oh, she'd divorced him years ago, but back when Addie was little, she'd go and spend weekends at her father's house. She never said much about it. But he still wrote her letters, even when I knew her. Because she read me a letter from him one time and it said, 'I would kill myself except I lack the intestinal fortitude.'" Lucy bit the inside of her lip and then said, "That was the first time I'd heard that. The intestinal fortitude thing."

Olive just watched her.

"Anyway." Lucy raised a hand and dropped it back onto her lap. "Two more things. No, three more things."

"All right," said Olive. She found this interesting.

"So the first thing is that Addie, it became clear to me by the time I graduated, she was an alcoholic too. She'd get really drunk at parties, and very slowly I thought: She drinks a lot. Only later did I realize that she was probably already an alcoholic. And then there was this: She slept with *everybody*. One time I saw her come out of this guy's room—"

Olive interrupted her. "Lucy, I don't need to hear about this girl's promiscuity. I don't care to."

Lucy looked surprised. "Okay, but she got syphilis once, she had these sores on her mouth and—"

Olive held up her hand. "I get the point. Now, you said there were three things, and so far that's only two, what is the third thing?"

"Right." Lucy nodded vehemently. "*This*. Near the college, down one of the side streets, was a woman who read fortunes, and Addie went to her, sophomore year, she goes to this woman, and she came to see me after, and her eyes were just *shining* with excitement. The woman had told Addie that she was going to die young. And somehow—in her youthful way—Addie found this romantic, I suppose. She really was excited about that, and she kept saying 'Lucy, you should go to her!' And I said Absolutely not."

"So she died young?"

"She did." Lucy nodded her head slowly and looked out the window. "I think when she was in college, she felt she was really someone. You know, people liked her, and as I said she starred in every show the theater department did, and she was just so excited—and drunk, I think—about her life. *Full* of life."

Olive rearranged herself on her chair. "So when did she die?"

"About the age of thirty. After she left college, her life went nowhere. She took a job at the local mall selling clothes and she married the maintenance man there, but that ended within a few years, and then she lived with her mother. Still in Illinois in that tiny apartment."

"What did she die of?"

"Some kind of cancer. I wasn't in touch with her at that point. She did not want a funeral, but in the newspaper her mother wrote a really long and loving obituary of her. And she said in that obituary that Addie had not wanted a funeral. So I guess Addie must have been mad. I mean, who wouldn't be. But Lindsay had written about how all the doctors just loved Addie. It was really so awful."

"Ay-yuh, I guess it was," Olive said.

Lucy pointed her finger and shook it slowly. Lucy said, "Only years later did I realize that she might have been sexually abused by that father. Because one night when she was drunk, she said something—I can't remember exactly—about her father putting lipstick on her when she was a little girl."

The two were silent for a while, and then Olive said, "Just like Diana Beach."

"Right." Then Lucy added, "We don't know if Diana was promiscuous. But we do know that it got her all screwed up."

"Of course it did."

Lucy sat forward. "But, Olive, here is my question to you. Okay, so Addie's life was one more unrecorded life, but what was the point of it? What was the *point* of her life, Olive?"

Olive sat back and watched Lucy. Lucy seemed quite distressed. "Lucy Barton, are you asking me what the point was of this young woman's life? What is the point of *anyone's* life?"

Lucy looked at her. "Well. Yeah. What *is* the point of anyone's life?"

"I thought you believed in God," Olive said.

Lucy shook her head slowly. "I never said I believe in God. You're mistaking me for that guy who said 'God bless you' to me in the taxi. I don't *not* believe in God, by the way. But I don't believe in some father figure sitting up there in the clouds. I sort of believe—no, I do believe—that there's something larger than us. But that doesn't help me with the question: What is the point of anyone's life?"

Olive thought about this. "Well, Henry and I believed that the point to our lives was to work hard and help people. So we did." Olive started to rock her foot up and down and she looked out the window.

Lucy said, "Diana Beach was apparently a very good guidance counselor, she helped a lot of kids. So she had a point to her life, I guess. But what was the point of Addie's life?"

Olive squinted across at Lucy. "Lucy. Are you *depressed*?" This had only now occurred to Olive.

Lucy looked surprised, and then she said, "Yeah. Sort of."

"Why?"

Lucy shrugged.

"How's your friend Bob?" Olive asked her, and she saw Lucy's face become pink; this is what Olive thought she saw.

"I haven't seen him much lately. I think he's really busy."

"Busy doing what?" Olive asked.

"Not sure. Helping Matt Beach, maybe."

"Ay-yuh" was all Olive said.

*

BUT BOB HAD had a haircut ten days earlier, the day after he had last seen Lucy.

MATT HAD TOLD him to get his hair cut, Jim had told him, and Margaret had told him the same thing. So Bob went to his local barber—it was a brilliantly sunny day—and on that particular day the man who usually cut Bob's hair was not in. So a young woman with long dark hair that Bob had never met before swept a little apron over his shoulders, and she worked with her lips pressed together in great concentration; she wore a scent that smelled to Bob like bug spray. "Not the chatty type?" she asked him at one point, and he said, No, he was sorry, that he was tired. "Oh, that's okay," she said cheerfully, swinging her long hair back and then snipping his hair with the scissors. Bob closed his eyes. It was taking forever.

When he opened his eyes, he wanted to die, he did *almost* want to die. His hair was so short: He looked like a fat twelve-year-old kid with an old man's face. He was really horrified. He couldn't get out of there fast enough, paying her, tipping her, thanking her; he was panicking.

He got into his car and drove home and went straight to the bedroom mirror and he could not believe what he saw.

When Margaret came home, she said, "*Bob*, what happened?" So it was real. He looked like an idiot.

AND HE COULD not see Lucy looking like this. Again and again, he saw the face of a twelve-year-old kid in his (sort of fat) old man's head. He could not tell Lucy why he was too embarrassed to see her, and when she texted to ask him to go for a walk, he texted back that he was too busy.

"Try wearing a hat," Margaret suggested. Bob never wore a hat except for a woolen one in the winter, but when he went to buy a baseball cap and tried it on, he thought he looked even stupider. Margaret said, "It will grow out soon, Bob. Don't worry."

*

MATT ASKED BOB to come back to sit for the painting Matt was doing of him. But Bob told him, "I got my hair cut and I look like a dickwad."

"Come over anyway," Matt said.

When Bob showed up, Matt looked at him and said, "Ouch." Then Matt said, "Come on upstairs, I'll work on your body."

So Bob went and sat for Matt. "Just so you know, it's not as bad as you think it is." Matt said this as he took the charcoal stick in his hand.

"Yeah, it is," Bob said.

"It's not, though." Matt glanced up, his hand working. "You know why? Because you're still Bob Burgess. Nothing can take that away."

Bob sat there for an hour, and he thought about what Matt had just said.

AS HE WAS LEAVING, Bob walked through the dining room, and Matt came with him. Matt sat down, and so Bob sat down across from him. "How're you doing?" Bob asked him.

"So-so." Matt held out a hand and rocked it slightly to indicate this. "One of those women who wrote me, turns out she's pretty nice. We've talked on the phone a few times and she sent me a pic of herself. But she wants to have dinner."

"So have dinner." Bob shrugged one shoulder.

"Bob. Have you been paying attention at *all* to who I am? I don't know *how* to have dinner with a woman." Matt's face looked pained.

And then Bob had a thought. "Listen," he said. He held both hands together before him on the table. "Tell her you need just a little more time, that you're still going through stuff, and meanwhile go see Katherine Caskey. She's a social worker in town, and I swear she could help you."

Matt looked alarmed. "You're sending me to a *shrink*?"

"Hold on, and listen to the story of Katherine Caskey," Bob said. And sitting there he told Matt the whole thing, about his father's death, his mother going to Reverend Caskey's house with him in the backseat of the car, how he stared and stared at this little girl who was standing on the porch with her father. "She's a lovely woman," Bob concluded. "I swear to God she could help you."

But Matt's mouth was partly open as he gazed at Bob. "So— you thought you killed your father?" He asked this very quietly.

"Yeah, but that's not the point."

"Bob, that's pretty hardcore." Matt turned his gaze to the window, and then finally back to Bob. "Is that why you took my case? Because you thought maybe I had killed my mother and you'd spent almost your whole life thinking you had killed your father?"

Bob's face broke into delight. "Matthew Beach. You are so smart. You're smart and you're a brilliant painter. Matt, Matt, Matt." He pointed a finger at him. "Go see Katherine Caskey."

"Only if you'll come with me."

"I'll walk you into her office. That's all."

AND SO, three days later, Bob—having made the initial phone call to Katherine Caskey—walked up the steps to her office with Matt, who had put on a shirt with a collar and washed his jeans, which were still wrinkled from the dryer. He was killing Bob. Katherine opened her office door, and she did not hug Bob (as he knew she would not), but her smile was lovely as she greeted both men. "Come in, Matt. Oh, do come in. I'm so happy to meet you."

And Bob left them, Matt stepping into her office like a guilty schoolchild.

AN HOUR LATER Bob got a call from Matt. "She's wonderful!" Matt said. "God, she's great! I'm going back next week for *two* sessions!"

*

SOMETHING ABOUT GETTING Matt to go see Katherine made Bob miss Lucy in a more clearheaded way. And so he texted her—Bob was standing out by the old inn that had the vines all over it, smoking a cigarette—and said, Call me when you can. It was midafternoon.

She called him right away.

"Bob, have you been *mad* at me?" Lucy asked this immediately.

"Oh Jesus, no." He paused and then said, "This is really embarrassing, Lucy. But, ah, I got this haircut—" Bob ran the hand with the cigarette over his face and his head. "And I look like an idiot. No, I really do. And it made me too embarrassed to see you, and I'm even embarrassed to tell you because it makes me seem vain and I guess I am because I just couldn't stand you seeing me with this, Lucy, it's *bad*."

"Oh Bob." Lucy said this—he thought—with quiet under-standing. And then she broke out into laughter. "I'm sorry to laugh, but I'm just so *relieved*. I really thought you didn't like me anymore."

"It's just my haircut, Lucy. It's embarrassing."

"Listen to me. I don't care what you look like. They could cut your head *off* and you'd still be—you'd still be Bob."

This surprised Bob. It was what Matt had told him.

But as we have said earlier, Bob had very little sense of who he was. Which is true for many of us, but this was especially true for Bob.

AND THEN TWO days later, Bob got a zit on his forehead. "Margaret, I can't believe this." She squinted at him as they got ready for bed, and she said, "I think it's because you keep rubbing your hand up over your face and head to see if you have any hair. Just go pop it," she said, getting into bed, she was wearing her summer nightgown, it was white and sleeveless and cotton.

And so Bob went into the bathroom and put a very hot face-cloth to his head and the zit popped. But in the morning, it looked like what it was: a popped pimple.

12

WHEN LUCY SAW him by the fence she laughed, and Bob could feel his face becoming hot. "Bob!" Lucy looked at him and said, "Oh Bob, you're blushing."

"I look awful," Bob said.

They began to walk, and Lucy said, "You kind of look like a kid, except you don't."

"I know, I look like a twelve-year-old with an old man's face," Bob said.

She looked over at him again and said, "Who *cares*, Bob."

And gradually his face cooled down. But later, in the after-image in his mind, she had not looked at him with the kindness he had expected. And also, as they walked, it seemed to him later, she did not look at him much at all.

IT SHOULD BE NOTED: Bob had read the memoir that Lucy had written a few years earlier about her ex-husband, William. We have mentioned this before, how Bob—when Lucy had been talking about doing childhood cartwheels—remembered from that book that William had told Lucy he married her because she was filled with joy, and how could that be, coming from what she had come from?

What Bob did *not* remember was how toward the end of that same book, when William had shown up with his white hair cut very short and his huge mustache shaved off, Lucy felt that William had lost his authority with her. Many of us forget things we read in books, but had Bob remembered this, perhaps he would not have agreed to see Lucy. But he did not remember it, and so here they were.

IT WAS THE middle of June now, but the day was oddly cold, and the wind was furious, it seemed to bite at them as they walked. It was very much like an autumn day even though they passed trees with their bright green leaves swirling in the wind. Lucy had worn her spring coat, and she kept saying "I'm freezing, I'm so cold!"

"You want to go back?" Bob asked, and she shook her head.

Lucy listened while he told her about Matt going to see Katherine Caskey, and she nodded and said, "Good." He told her that Matt was painting a portrait of him, and Lucy did glance at him then and said, "Oh nice."

Then she told him about seeing Olive Kitteridge and telling her the story of Addie Beal.

Lucy sat beside him on the granite bench, she took her sunglasses off and then she poked his leg as he was lighting his cigarette, and he looked at her, and he was surprised to see her eyes were rimmed with red, and she said slowly, "So, Bob, here's the thing. Olive and I have been telling each other all these stories of unrecorded lives, but what do they mean? At least Diana Beach got to be a good guidance counselor. And yet still—I don't know. I keep thinking these days about all these people, and people we don't even know, and their lives are un-recorded. But what does anyone's life *mean*?" She added, "Please don't laugh."

THE SMOKE HE inhaled got stuck and he coughed—hard. He stood up. He turned toward her as he coughed and coughed. When he was done coughing, he said, "Did you just ask me what anyone's life means?"

She nodded.

"Lucy."

"What?" She squinted up at him.

"Are you ten years old?" He said it without thinking (why did he say that?), and he saw her receive this as a blow.

"Probably." She looked down, then back up at him. "I've always thought I was about five." She added, not nicely, "You're the one who looks twelve."

It took a moment for that to sink in, but he found her remark gratuitously mean, even though he was aware that he had of-fended her first.

He looked above her and then at her. "What about love? Isn't that what life might be about?" He smoked for a moment and then he added, "And for all your worry about Addie, she had a mother who loved her. Maybe the rest of her life sucked, but she had that. I wouldn't be so quick to say that her life meant nothing."

Lucy stood up and put her sunglasses back on. She was shiv-ering in the wind. "Solzhenitsyn said the point of life is the ma-turity of the soul. Jesus, Addie didn't have *time* for her soul to mature. Oh, never mind. Can we go back now?"

He dropped his cigarette onto the ground and stepped on it and left it there—he had never done this before. "Of course," he said, and they walked. "What about all the people getting blown up in the Ukraine right now? What do *their* lives mean?" He asked this with belligerence.

She said, without looking at him, "It's Ukraine, Bob. Jesus. Not *the* Ukraine," and Bob felt his face becoming hot once again.

"All right, what about the people in Ukraine getting blown up as we speak? What do their lives mean? And what about those people I saw near Portland when I came back from New York? Living in tents right there by the highway? What about the homeless here in town who live in the woods out behind Walmart? What about them?"

Lucy said, "I said never mind!"

He understood that he had insulted her. And she had insulted him back. He wanted to apologize, but he did not apologize. Without his being fully aware of it a crack of anger had begun in him, rising inside himself as he stood there. They walked back to their cars in silence. But right before they reached the parking lot Bob stopped walking, and so did she. "Lucy," he said. He said it kindly, quietly.

"What?" Lucy did not say it kindly or quietly. "*What?*" she demanded when he did not answer. She took her sunglasses off once more, and he saw that her eyes were not red-rimmed, as he had somehow thought they might be.

He raised both arms and brought them down slowly. "Nothing," he said.

They walked again, Lucy hugging herself against the wind, and when they reached the parking lot, she kept walking to her car and just said, "See you later, Bob."

———

WHAT HAD just happened?

DRIVING BACK TO his house, he went over what he could remember of the conversation. He had been unkind about her—
to his mind—immature question. And then she had been
unkind to him. He thought of her telling him weeks ago that
there was an arrogance to her, and he had the thought now
that her response to Addie was somewhat arrogant, even as he
understood that this made little sense. And yet the crack of
anger inside him did not go away. And with it there was some
odd sense of relief, as though he had been carrying a large
burden for a long time, and perhaps did not have to carry it
anymore.

*

BY THE TIME he got home, the anger had grown slightly, become larger within him. Why did she ask such a stupid question, about the meaning of life? She wasn't a kid—except she
was, as Margaret had said—and who in the world knew the
meaning of life?

IF BOB HAD had children, he might have recognized the incident as a kind of pulling away that an adolescent does to be
free of their parent, but he had not had children and—as we
know—he had always been good to his mother during his
own adolescence. Also, Lucy was not his parent, nor was he

hers. But the sense of strain that their relationship had put Bob under seemed unsustainable to him, although this was mostly unconscious on his part; as we have said, Bob was not a reflective fellow.

THAT NIGHT HE lay in bed with Margaret's head on his chest, her leg across his. He said, "Lucy wanted to know the meaning of anybody's life today."

Margaret moved her head to look at him, then put it back on his chest. "Well, that's not a small question."

"It's a stupid question."

"No, it isn't, Bob. My heavens."

"It seemed stupid to me, it seemed—immature."

"Oh well—she's just Lucy."

"She ended up quoting someone, some Russian guy, I think, about life's meaning being the maturity of the soul."

"Oh, right. What's-his-name said that."

Bob gave a huge sigh and said, "Who in the world knows the meaning of life unless you're a Buddhist monk or some deeply religious person who's been handed a plate of these answers?"

Margaret said lightly, "Bob, that's offensive."

"Well, anyway. Tell me more about your day."

"I already did," Margaret said, turning to give him a smile. Then Margaret said, "I was thinking of having Lucy and William over for your birthday, but how about we just have a quiet day, the two of us?"

"That sounds great," Bob said. His birthday was in three weeks.

———

HE BENT HIS head and kissed his wife.

*

MATT CALLED HIM the next day and said, "Bob, I cried in front of Katherine Caskey. I could die."

Bob told him, "No, that sounds healthy to me."

"That's what she said. I brought in my mother's journals, and we went through them together, and I started to cry."

"Cry your head off. That's exactly what she's there for. Trust me, she's seen everything, and I'm sure she likes you. Don't worry, Matt," Bob said.

"I love her," Matt said.

And Bob told him that was healthy too. "That happens with a therapist all the time."

"It does?" Matt asked.

"Yeah. Perfectly normal. I keep telling you, Matt. You're a lot more normal than you think you are."

13

FOR THE NEXT three weeks there was no contact between Bob and Lucy. He was amazed by this, and yet he did not reach out to her. As people do in such situations, he occasionally listed to himself her faults: She was a child. She could be petulant. She was a hovering mother, why didn't she just let her girls be? She blew off Arlene Cleary in the grocery store. She had not been kind about William's daughter Bridget. And so on. Back and forth his feelings went, and yet he could not deny to himself feeling a sense of relief. And he could not deny either that he was slowly beginning to enjoy Margaret's company more than he had in a long while. He and Margaret—now that it was light late in the evenings—would go for a drive sometimes after their dinner, and they spoke with the intimacy of people who have been married for years. One time she packed a picnic, the weather had turned warm again, and they sat at a public table a few towns away by an inlet of water and he felt an unhurried gladness move through him.

ONE OTHER EVENING—when the sun was streaming through the trees—Margaret suggested that they drive to a town half an hour away where they could buy ice cream at a stand they both remembered. As they got into the car Bob said, "Oh, I forgot my wallet," and Margaret said it didn't matter, she had money. Driving through the narrow roads with fields on one side and small inlets on the other, the sun slashing through the trees, everything so green and glorious, Bob felt a sense of open happiness. And yet when they got to the ice cream place a sign outside it said CASH ONLY, and it turned out that Margaret had no cash. They drove further to a gas station where there was a machine for Margaret to get cash, but when she returned to the car she said gaily, "I couldn't remember my PIN number."

Bob's happiness left him.

And as they were driving back home the clouds had come in and the town seemed dreary and stark.

*

THE DAY BEFORE Bob's birthday, William called Bob. "I need your advice. I'm going to go take one of those electric cars for a test run tomorrow, and I'd love to have you come with me. There's no one else I know I can talk to about getting an electric car."

"Sure," Bob said. He knew nothing about electric cars.

When he checked with Margaret later, she said, "Oh, that's fine, just be home by five o'clock." She added, "Wear a nice shirt, though, you don't want to look dumpy for William," and Bob found that a little strange.

So the next afternoon, William pulled into their driveway and Bob went with him three towns away where these electric cars were being sold. William seemed laconic about the whole car business; Bob had thought he would be telling Bob the whole way over why electric cars were so great. As they drove over the large bridge the water twinkled below them, and then they were near all the car dealerships.

As they turned into the electric car area, William pulled into a parking spot and said this: "I asked Lucy to marry me again, and she said yes."

Bob looked over at him. With William's sunglasses on, Bob could not see the man's eyes, but his tone had sounded serious and glad.

"You did? She did?"

Through the open car window, the wind made William's hair stick up on the side as he turned his face briefly toward Bob's. "Yes to both your questions. I mean, we're getting older, what's wrong with us getting married again? It would make me feel better. But for a while she kept saying no, she said she didn't see any reason for that." He added, "She said something about screwing up the girls again—you know they had a hard time when we got together again during the pandemic—but that was then, and this is now." William pushed his hand through his white hair. "It's not like I'm going to cheat on her again at this age. And then two nights ago she said, Let's do it, William." William turned the engine off.

Bob looked out his car window. He felt an odd tingling in his chin.

"But that's great, William. That's really good," Bob said, turning to look at him again.

William said, "I have to tell you, Bob, it makes me so happy. I'm crazy about Lucy. Now tell me how you are? By the way, I know I talk about my parasites too much. Lucy told me that, and I'm sorry."

"I think they're interesting," Bob said.

The whole time that William was talking to the car people, the whole time he was taking a test drive in the car, Bob's mind was fuzzy. Lucy was going to marry William. On the drive back, Bob had trouble concentrating on what William was saying, something about his half sister, how great she'd turned out to be. "Life is *good*, Bob," William said.

THEY PULLED INTO Crosby at almost five-thirty, and as William drove down Main Street to Bob's home, Bob saw more cars than usual parked along the road. And then he saw two congregants of Margaret's hurrying into his house. "Oh fuck," he said quietly.

William pulled into the driveway and said, taking his sunglasses off, "What?"

Bob said, "Is this a surprise party for me?"

William sighed. "It is. Now you go in there and act surprised."

"I have to go in there and act surprised?"

William tapped him on the arm. "You do and you can. *Pretend*. Just pretend."

*

BOB FELT LUCY'S presence as soon as he stepped inside the room—and then he saw her, far off, standing on the first step of the staircase in the living room, and they looked at each other for a moment. To Bob, for the rest of his life, it was one of the most intimate moments he had ever experienced, because in the glance he was saying to her pained face: You're here, and that is all that matters, and her glance said, Bob, I'm right here, do not ever worry about that. And there was a finality in their glance as well, he saw that in her. That whatever they had shared was not over but would be different from now on.

Turning to the room filled with people, Bob said, "Whoa! What's going on here?" He hugged Margaret, who said, "Were you surprised?" "Was I ever," he said, and he waved to all those who had come into his home, he was deeply moved by all the people who had come to celebrate his birthday, Jim and Susie and—oh sweet God—Gerry O'Hare (he and Susie were holding hands!) and many other people he knew, including Katherine Caskey and her husband. He walked through the group greeting them all, a few men putting their hands on his shoulders as he said hello.

And Pam! She walked out of the bathroom—without a mask on—and said, "Bobby!"

He was so glad to see her; he thought she looked wonderful and he told her so. Then he said, "What's happening with you? Did you leave Ted?"

"Bob." Pam looked at him with her eyes wide. (He saw that on one eye the eyeliner was a little above where it should have been, the way he had seen on old women in New York at times.) She leaned her head in toward him and spoke quietly, confidentially, "Bob, he *cried* when I told him we should separate. He sat there and wept like a baby. Bob!" She pulled back and looked at him.

"Jesus," Bob said.

"I *guess* to hell Jesus," Pam answered; he saw that she was drinking sparkling water.

"So what are you going to do?" Bob asked.

Pam shook her head. "I have no idea. No idea at all. But honestly? I think I might stay. We just started couples therapy—after all these years."

Bob felt his phone vibrate in his pocket, and pulling it out he saw that it was Matt. He said to Pam, "Hold on, so sorry—"

"*That* Matt?" Pam asked, having glanced at Bob's phone. "Take it, Bob."

So Bob stepped out into the hallway and he said, "Matt?"

"Yeah. Something happened today I wanted to tell you about. But I know you're having your birthday party, Margaret invited me, except I didn't want to come."

"That's okay, tell me what happened today," Bob said, just as a woman he didn't recognize approached him and said, "Where's the bathroom?" Bob pointed back to where she had come from, and she went back inside.

"Were you surprised?" Matt asked, and Bob said, "No, but I pretended I was."

"Awkward," said Matt.

"Tell me what happened to you today," Bob said.

What had happened to Matt was that he had asked this woman he had mentioned before, who had written to him kindly, he had asked her out to dinner. For tomorrow.

"I don't think you have anything to lose if she sounded nice. Did you google her?"

"No, good thinking. Okay, go back to your party now, Bob. I'll talk to you soon."

*

MARGARET TOOK A knife and clanked it against her glass, and in a moment the room quieted down. She looked around at the people gathered there and she thanked them all for coming. Then she said, "I would like to toast my husband, the one and only Bob Burgess. There is no one in the world like Bob." She turned to Bob and said, "Happy birthday, Bob, I love you!" And she kissed him, putting her arms around him. People said, "Hear, hear," and Bob said, "Thank you *all* for coming," holding up his own glass.

But then half an hour later, William clanked his glass, and when people stopped talking, he said, "Lucy and I have an announcement. We're getting married again!" He held her hand and raised it in the air. People said things like "Oh, that's nice," and yet there was a slight awkwardness to it all, so Bob raised his glass and said, "To William and Lucy!" And a few people clapped then.

JIM MOTIONED FOR Bob to step into the hallway, and Bob did. "So what's the story with you guys?" He nodded his head back to where Lucy stood in the living room.

"No story anymore."

Jim looked at him, Bob saw his brother look at his whole head. "Maybe it was your haircut," Jim said. And Bob said, "The truth is, I'm relieved. Sad. Super sad sometimes. But relieved."

"As long as you're all right."

"I'm okay," Bob said.

"I can see why you liked her. She looks like a scared rabbit, but when she talks to you, she's *really* listening." After a moment Jim added, "But it's not you, Bobby, to have an affair. It would have killed you. I'm glad you're okay."

"I'm okay *enough*," Bob said. And Jim said, "Well—yeah. She just announced her marriage. How okay could you be?"

Then Jim pulled an envelope from his pocket. "Look what I received in the mail the other day." He unfolded the letter that was inside the envelope, and Bob put on his glasses and read "Dear Dad," and then the page was empty except for at the bottom where it was signed, "Love, Larry."

"That's about as good as it gets," Bob said.

"That's what I thought." And Jim returned the letter to his pocket.

OLIVE KITTERIDGE SAT in a chair in the corner and watched. She watched as Margaret gave her toast to Bob, she watched as William made his announcement about Lucy. Olive watched and watched, and every so often a person might lean down and say "Hello," and Olive would say, "Hello, who are you?" And it was usually a congregant of Margaret's. Another woman came and spoke to her. "I'm Bob's first wife, Pam," she said, smiling down at Olive.

"Where do you live?" Olive asked, and the woman said, "New York City."

"What do you do?"

And the woman laughed and said, "I do nothing. I'm just a rich woman who lives in New York. It sounds pretty ghastly, and it kind of is, but that's what I do."

"I see," Olive said, turning her head, and so the woman walked away.

BUT OLIVE WATCHED EVERYONE. For two hours she sat there and studied everybody in the room. Margaret brought her over a piece of birthday cake, and Olive said "Thank you" and ate the cake. It was not bad; she would have liked another slice, but Margaret didn't return, and so she put the paper plate down on the floor beside her. A man approached her and said, "Hi, I'm Jim Burgess, Bob's brother." He stuck his hand out, and Olive shook it with no enthusiasm. "How are you?" she said to him, and he laughed slightly and said, "I'm miserable. My wife died a few months ago and my son doesn't like me." Olive looked up into this man's face. "Ay-yuh," she said. "Well, join the club." She liked his face; she thought it had character in it. But then the Pam woman tapped Jim on his shoulder, and they walked away together.

As soon as Bob was within hearing distance Olive called to him, and he turned, his face bright, and he came to her and said, "Yes, what is it, Olive?" Olive told him she wanted to go home. "I know it's your party, but I want you to drive me home. It will take a while to get me down the front steps but then it shouldn't be long, and you can get back to your festivities."

"Of course." Bob helped her up, found the light coat she had been wearing, got her cane, took her arm, and said to Margaret, "I'll be back, Olive wants to go home."

"Goodbye, Olive!" people called to her, and this surprised Olive. She waved a hand over her head, and she allowed Bob to help her down the front steps and then into his car. He had a firm grip on her, which pleased her.

As they drove out of the driveway, she was quiet, but when they got onto Main Street, Olive said, "You know, Bob, the first story I told to Lucy was about people living with ghosts in their marriage. Did she tell you?"

"She did."

"We also discussed that day a crush without consequences

that a person can have in a marriage and how that's very different from living with a ghost in the marriage. Now, I have
thought all along that you and Lucy lived each with the ghost of
the other, but I saw tonight that I was wrong. What you had
was a crush."

Bob turned his head to look at her. He did not say anything.

"And I also saw tonight that Margaret is your linchpin. The
story of Muddy Wilson and his wife being his linchpin."

"I don't remember that story so well."

Olive flapped her hand. "To tell you the truth, I never
thought much of Margaret before tonight, but she came across,
did a good job. And she *is* your linchpin, meaning you are lucky
to have her."

"I am," Bob agreed. He said nothing about Margaret forgetting her PIN and the quiet worries he had had as a result.

"William is a snot-wot, but that's Lucy's business, not mine.
I couldn't believe he announced their upcoming marriage at
your birthday party." Olive held up a hand as though to ward
off any objection Bob might give to this. "I'm just saying I
thought that was *very* poor manners."

"What about the Addie story? What was that about?" Bob
asked Olive, looking over at her.

"That was about the same thing that every story Lucy and I
have shared is about. People suffer. They live, they have hope,
they even have love, and they still suffer. Everyone does. Those
who think they've not suffered are lying to themselves.

"Say," Olive said, in a lighter tone. "I was interested in
meeting your brother Jim tonight. What a tortured man! But
oh, I liked him. He was *real*. Not easy to find someone who is
real. Your first wife, what was her name?"

"Pam Carlson." He had turned in to the parking lot of the Maple Tree Apartments. He pulled into a parking place near the back door of Olive's apartment and turned off the car.

"She seemed a little nitwitty to me."

"I love her," Bob said.

"Yuh, I know you do. I could see that."

"And your sister Susan," Olive continued. "Pleasant. With her old fatty boyfriend."

"Is he fat?" Bob asked this sincerely.

Olive looked at him. "Well, he's not a skinny-pinny. Where'd she find him?"

"High school. They had three dates and he dumped her. But he was the chief of police during the time that Susan's son got into all that trouble with the pig's head in the mosque."

"*That* was Susan's *son* who did that? Oh my word, I remember that. That whole thing was awful."

"Yup. Yeah, it was. He was a kid. He's straightened out now."

Olive was silent for a long moment. Then she said, meditatively, "It's quite a world we live in, isn't it. For years I thought: I will miss all this when I die. But the way the world is these days, I sometimes think I'll be damned glad to be dead." She sat quietly looking ahead through the windshield. "I'll still miss it, though," she said.

Bob was watching her. He said, "I like you, Olive."

"Phooey. Now help me get out of this car," Olive replied.

14

THE HEART WANTS what the heart wants. This is true, and Bob's heart still wanted Lucy. But there is another thing to consider, which is that the heart is only one part of an organism, and the organism's job is to survive. This desire to survive was already in ascendance with Bob, and this desire grew, and the desire of his heart— It did not shrink, but it did not continue to grow. And there was discomfort, of course, as there is in such things, but Bob held on to the new sense of hope he felt in living his life with Margaret. He watched her for forgetfulness, but he noticed nothing new.

There were moments, though, when he endured a keen sickness of loss, and then it would pass. And so back and forth he went in these swings of emotion. But he did not contact Lucy between his birthday party and her wedding, which took place two weeks after Bob's party. And she did not contact him.

*

MARGARET HAD BEEN asked by William to perform the nuptials, and so on an evening in the middle of July, Margaret and Bob drove up the steep driveway to the house that William and Lucy lived in by the sea. As they walked to the door, Margaret repeated to Bob what she had told him before, that it was sad the girls had not been able to come up after all, that Aiden had gotten sick, he was fine, but then Becka got sick, and they had all decided at the last minute not to travel.

Lucy answered the door in a blue-and-white pinstriped dress, and she said, "Come in, come in." Stepping through the door, Bob saw William approaching them, and William was wearing a red tie against a white shirt, and the sight of that tie somehow killed Bob. It just killed him. William had dressed up for his wedding.

Bob was not wearing a tie, but he had showered, and his hair was drying now, it lay across his head in a few waves, it was finally growing out. Margaret wore her long flowery dress. And she was very happy, she hugged both William and Lucy and said, "What a wonderful day this is."

The sun was setting, and it was glorious as the pinkened glow fell over the porch and into the living room. There was a huge bouquet of peonies and delphiniums on the living room table, and Lucy said, "The girls sent these. Wasn't that *nice?*"

And Bob thought: Oh Lucy. He thought this with great compassion, as though she was a child he had known in his youth who had still retained her innocence.

A cake with white frosting sat on the kitchen counter.

"Oh, here—" Bob handed Lucy a card. On the front of it was a dandelion, and inside it said Happy Birthday. Bob had crossed out Birthday and written Wedding. He signed it Love from Margaret and Bob.

Lucy said as she looked at it, "Oh *Bob*, thank you!"

BUT AS THEY stood in the living room, Little Annie and her big sister the no-name plant off to the side of them, Bob standing slightly off to the left of William, Bob felt as though five panes of glass were between him and the scene. Lucy's face got pink as she said her vows, and then it was done, and William gave her a tight hug. After William released her, Bob went to Lucy and took both her hands in his—and he was appalled at how ice-cold her small hands were. He lifted them slightly and said, "Lucy, congratulations." She looked up at him and said, so softly he almost could not hear her, "Thank you, Bob."

THE NEWLYWEDS WERE off to Italy the next day for two weeks.

*

LIFE CONTINUED IN the town of Crosby.

One of Mrs. Hasselbeck's sons came to visit her for three days. She told this to Bob with her eyes shining. "Robert, please sit down." And so Bob sat. And Mrs. Hasselbeck told him about her youngest son, who had come to see her that week. His wife had had an affair, but now the fellow she'd had the affair with was done with her and she wanted to return to Mrs. Hasselbeck's son. For over thirty minutes Bob listened to this, heard about the kids of this couple, who were teenagers, he listened to it all. Finally, Mrs. Hasselbeck said to Bob, "What do you think of all this?" And Bob said slowly as he stood up, "It's life, Mrs. Hasselbeck, it's just called life."

And Mrs. Hasselbeck said, "I had an affair once."

Bob thought: I am not going to sit down again. So he stood there as Mrs. Hasselbeck looked up at him and told him how she had had an affair for almost a year when her boys were in high school, and they had found out. And Bob stood listening and then he turned away, saying once again: "It's just life, Mrs. Hasselbeck, that's all it is. Life."

She thanked him for coming, and he said, "Sure."

*

MATT FINISHED THE painting of Bob, and Margaret hung it in the living room, though Bob objected, not because he didn't like the painting—he did—but because he thought the placement was too prominent. "Nope, it's staying right there, I *love* it," Margaret said. And it was a wonderful likeness of Bob, it caught—in its abstract way—the essence of Bob, the thatch of gray hair on top of his head.

Margaret continued to preach her sermons in her sincere voice. And Bob and Lucy—eventually—continued their walks, though not with the frequency they had done in the past. As they walked, there was still a very slight frisson between them, as though long ago they had been lovers but were now just old friends. But here was something interesting: Each time they parted now, Lucy would say, "Take care, Bob," and she would reach out and hold his arm, and Bob would say, holding her arm for a few moments as well, "You take care too." It was gentle, that touch of the other's arm.

William did not talk nearly as much about potatoes and parasites when the four of them got together.

IT WAS NOT always easy for Bob. Although he somehow understood—and this turned out to be true—that it would get easier with time. And we are talking about his feelings for Lucy.

His sense of loss ebbed and flowed but remained manageable. He often walked alone on the river where they walked together, and when he did sometimes a strange calmness came to him. He never sat in the spot where they sat for him to have his cigarette, he walked past that and went all the way to where the river turned slightly, and then he would walk back. Often, he did not have a cigarette at all. He would be deep in thought, but he could not remember later what it was he had been thinking. Except for this: As he was walking back to the parking lot one day, he had a sensation of the air around him being not just air but something full and wonderful. And that's when he wondered about God, and whether there was a personal God who cared about every living thing on Earth or a much more generalized God who had created the universe, and he thought: It doesn't matter, it is the same. He understood that this would not make sense to people, and so he did not even tell Margaret about it. But this understanding came to him with great clarity one day. And he remembered it.

*

ON A LATE summer day, when more than one tree had started its turn to red, Bob went to his office in Shirley Falls to clean it out. He brought cardboard boxes into which he put many old files with their bent yellow folders, and in another box he placed his books. He took his desk lamp and bent down to put it into a box that was on the floor. Standing up, he happened to glance out the window, and he saw a man and a woman walking on the sidewalk together. They were both younger than he was (almost everyone was these days), but they were not kids. And the woman was laughing, and once or twice she bumped her hip against the man she was with, and then Bob realized that the man was Matt Beach.

Bob stood at the window and watched them; it was extraordinary. Their faces were happy as they walked side by side, and then Matt reached and held the woman's hand. Bob watched until they were out of view.

LEANING AGAINST HIS DESK, Bob thought then of Little Annie, the plant that Lucy had. How Lucy was afraid that the plant had died, but it had not. Every leaf had fallen off, but then it broke through, a tiny little new green leaf at the top of it.

WHAT A THING this life force was, Bob thought.

HE CALLED MARGARET and told her what he had just seen. "Margaret, it makes me so *glad*."

"It should, Bob." Margaret's voice was warm. "And now listen to me, are you listening? You did this, Bob Burgess."

"I didn't have a thing to do with it."

"Bob, listen to me carefully. You. Did. This. You cared for that man after all he had gone through, you encouraged his painting, you got him a cellphone, and you got him to see Katherine Caskey." She paused. "And that's because you are Bob Burgess."

"Okay."

After they hung up, Bob sat at his desk. What did she mean,

he was Bob Burgess? In fact, for Bob it did not mean anything at all.

BOB LEANED OVER and picked up a box, which he then took down in the elevator to his car parked on the street right outside the building. It was a Sunday, so he could park there, and not another person was around now that Matt Beach and his girl-friend had passed by. As he slammed the car door shut before heading back upstairs for another load, Bob caught a glimpse of himself in the store window that was right there. He was star-tled. Who was that tall older man? Was that him? A sense of bewilderment came to him. He turned away, then turned back to the window once again.

AND HE SAW that it was him. It was not an unacceptable image. Bob stood for a moment, and then he gave himself a very slight nod and headed into the building again.

*

OLIVE KITTERIDGE was sad.

She was now ninety-one years old, and her friend Isabelle Goodrow was sleeping more and more; she had even fallen asleep as Olive read her the paper just the other day. So Olive was glad when Lucy called and said, "I have a story for you, Olive."

And Olive said to come on over anytime.

So—not long after Bob cleaned out his office—Lucy arrived at Olive's apartment, and she looked—to Olive's eyes—to be radiant. She was wearing a pair of jeans with her green sneakers and a simple yellow top. Lucy sat down on the couch and said, "Okay, Olive—here is a story. It is not the saddest story ever told, that would be a false sentence to say that, but it has sadness in it and *beauty*. Tell me if you think this story isn't one of real beauty." Lucy's eyes were shining as she said this, and Olive said, "Okay. Go."

Lucy began.

And for two hours Olive sat there and listened; she was transfixed. Only once did she get up to use the bathroom, her bowels making horrible sounds as she emptied them, but she didn't care; it was Lucy out there.

Returning, Olive said, "Keep going."

Lucy told the story, sometimes weeping (Olive wept too and snapped her fingers at Lucy to give her a tissue, which Lucy did, returning to her seat still talking). And then at other times Lucy's face glowed with a happiness, and Olive felt this too.

When Lucy was done, they sat in a long silence together.

Olive finally said, "That's one hell of a story, Lucy. You should write that down, you've written personal things before."

"Never going to write it. You are the receptacle." Lucy opened her hands in a gesture of giving.

"But I'm going to die, and this should be out there."

"It's in you, I gave it to you." Lucy said this open-faced and calmly.

And after a long silence, Olive said quietly, "Thank you."

Lucy looked at her and said, "You're welcome, Olive Kitteridge. Thank *you*."

After a few moments the tree by Olive's window sent down one leaf. And then one more followed. "Why are the green leaves falling?" Lucy asked, and Olive, glancing out the window, said, "Who knows."

"Exactly. Who knows anything," Lucy said.

WHEN LUCY LEFT, Olive sat for a long while.

The story that Lucy had told her was this: Lucy's love affair with Bob Burgess, which had never happened. The part that made Lucy and Olive cry was when Lucy told of meeting Bob after his haircut, and how Lucy had loved him *even more* as soon as she had seen him. "He looked so innocent, Olive, he looked like a child, and it just slayed me. I wanted to take him in my arms and say: Bob! You are *you*! But at that very moment I somehow realized: We will never run away together, because you are Bob. And I got so mad at him for that, Olive, I was just so mad at him, because I loved him more than anyone except my daughters and David, but Bob was not available. Something about that moment, when I could have taken him in my arms, with that sad, adorable haircut he had—

"And we kind of broke up that day. Because Bob, being Bob, saved us both from getting together in that way, which would have been a terrible mistake. And I understood after a while that—I told you I thought Bob was a sin-eater—that he was eating my sin of wanting him, oh that poor man! And then later I agreed to marry William. Which was right. I met William when I was practically a child, and we've gone through so much together, I love him, and also— It's odd, but he makes me feel safe. And Bob is with Margaret, which is right too. So it's not the saddest story ever told. Love is love, Olive."

"What do you mean?"

"I'll tell you what I mean. *Years* ago I read an article and the title was 'Love Is Love,' and in it the writer said that when she was in college and had her first boyfriend and was desperately in love with him, her great-aunt, recently widowed, came to stay at her parents' house, and the writer remembered standing in the bedroom with this tiny old woman who was frightened and had terrible breath and realizing: I love her the same way that I love my boyfriend! She didn't want to go to *bed* with this old woman, but the love she felt for her was distinctly related, of the very same cloth. And I've *always* remembered that. Because I understood it. Love comes in so many different forms, but it is always love. If it is love, then it is love."

OLIVE ROUSED HERSELF now, and she got her cane and made her way across the bridge to tell Isabelle. But Isabelle was asleep. And so Olive sat there and waited. She watched the small rising and falling of Isabelle's thin chest, the purple veins that ran across her aged hands, twisted with arthritis. Love is love. Olive kept thinking about that as she waited.

ACKNOWLEDGMENTS

I WOULD LIKE to acknowledge the following people for their help in my writing this book:

Ellen Crosby, Jeannie Crocker, Jeff McCarthy, Marcus Hinchey, my editor Andy Ward, my agents Molly Friedrich and Lucy Carson, Maria Braeckel (the best publicist in the world), and last but never, ever least, Benjamin Dreyer.

ABOUT THE AUTHOR

ELIZABETH STROUT is the #1 *New York Times* best-selling author of *Lucy by the Sea; Oh William!*, which was shortlisted for the Booker Prize; *Olive, Again; Anything Is Possible*, winner of the Story Prize; *My Name Is Lucy Barton; The Burgess Boys; Olive Kitteridge*, winner of the Pulitzer Prize; *Abide with Me;* and *Amy and Isabelle*, winner of the *Los Angeles Times* Art Seidenbaum Award for First Fiction and the *Chicago Tribune* Heartland Prize. She has also been a finalist for the PEN/Faulkner Award and the Orange Prize in London. She lives in Maine.

This book was set in Fournier, a typeface named for Pierre-Simon Fournier (1712–68), the youngest son of a French printing family. He started out engraving woodblocks and large capitals, then moved on to fonts of type. In 1736 he began his own foundry and made several important contributions in the field of type design; he is said to have cut 147 alphabets of his own creation. Fournier is probably best remembered as the designer of St. Augustine Ordinaire, a face that served as the model for the Monotype Corporation's Fournier, which was released in 1925.